JORDAN POINT

JORDAN POINT

A BAY TANNER MYSTERY

KATHRYN R. WALL

JORDAN POINT

ISBN 978-1-62268-077-1

Library of Congress Control Number: 2015940963

Printed in the United States of America on acid-free paper.

Also available as e-book: ISBN 978-1-62268-078-8.

Cover artwork courtesy of James Hartley Smith.

Book design by Bella Rosa Books.

BellaRosaBooks and logo are trademarks of Bella Rosa Books

10   9   8   7   6   5   4   3   2   1

In loving memory of my husband, Norman
Always in my heart

CHAPTER ONE

I didn't recognize the name that had appeared overnight in the *2PM* slot in Monday's electronic calendar: *Sylvie Reynaud*. Exotic. Obviously French, I thought. My late mother's roots could be traced back to the early Huguenot migration to the South Carolina coast, and our antebellum home on St. Helena Island just off Beaufort is named Presqu'isle, so I had some background.

Later, I felt a little embarrassed that I hadn't made the connection immediately.

At the time, however, the appointment simply seemed an annoyance, another example of the Universe piling on. I guess I should have expected it since my life had been purring along quite well of late, thank you very much. My husband's ex-wife had successfully completed her round of chemo with very hopeful results, so things were sort of back to normal for his two kids. Their weekend visits had resumed, with a lot of the tension having eased over the past couple of months.

After the defection of Stephanie Wyler the previous fall, Simpson & Tanner, Inquiry Agents had been prospering, relatively speaking, on a number of fronts. Our clients had been mostly white-collar or institutional, a little boring sometimes, but also devoid of anything resembling danger. I figured that would make my partner Erik Whiteside very happy, not to mention my husband and somewhat reluctant employee. As a former sheriff's officer, Red had had his fill of drug deals, Saturday night bar brawls, and the general mayhem created by the annual influx of over two million tourists to our home base, Hilton Head Island.

On that particular Monday morning, Red and I had arrived together as we usually did, although in separate cars. It often fell to my husband to do the legwork if a case required it, so we tried to make sure we were both mobile at any given moment.

Sharese Thomason, our new receptionist, greeted us with her

customary pleasant smile and steaming cups of caffeine. When Stephanie had suddenly bolted to Arizona, Sharese's had been the first name that popped into my head. I'd encountered her working at a bank that employed a teller who had come under scrutiny in the disappearance of one of our clients. I'd been impressed with her appearance and demeanor, and it hadn't taken much to woo her away from a job that, at least on the surface, had appeared both boring and unchallenging.

I smiled back and picked up my chai tea latte. "Good morning." I took a sip, realized it was still terrifically hot, and headed for my office.

"Good morning, Mrs. Tanner. Sergeant."

Sharese felt Red's former title a suitable one for his position in the firm, I guessed, and she used it unfailingly.

"How was your weekend?" My husband always stopped to chat, inquiring about our new employee's boyfriend, an earnest young man we'd met on a couple of occasions. He was just finishing his business degree at the USC campus at New River, out on the highway between Hilton Head and Beaufort, and a summer wedding had been hinted at. Providing he found a job after graduation, a dicey proposition in these challenging times.

"Fine. Byron needed to work on a paper, so we just hung around his condo. At least it was warm enough for me to get in a nice long walk on the beach."

"Good for you. It's been a nasty winter."

Red followed me into the office and settled on one of the client chairs. A few seconds later, Erik wandered in and took up residence on the other.

"How're you doing?" I always asked, although I could tell that Stephanie's desertion still weighed heavily on him. Lanky and thin by nature, Erik had lost some weight he couldn't afford along with the ready smile that had always seemed a large part of his boyish charm.

He shrugged. "Okay, I guess. Played tennis most of the weekend. A couple of guys I knew in Charlotte were down visiting, so we batted it around a little. Nothing special."

Besides being our receptionist and part-time operative—not to mention the daughter of my late partner Ben Wyler—Stephanie had also been Erik's fiancée. Even after all these months, he still hadn't recovered. I'd counseled him to give her time, but as far as

I could tell, she had yet to be in touch. Other than to return the ring, an act of honesty that gave me hope.

I mentally shook myself and turned on my iPad, a Christmas gift from Red. Being a confirmed technophobe, I had at first resisted. It had taken me only a couple of days to fall madly in love with the little gadget in a way I never had with my laptop or smart phone. That's when I noticed the appointment that had been added to my calendar app. It for sure hadn't been there on Friday, the last time I'd allowed business to intrude.

I buzzed the front desk.

"Yes, ma'am?"

"Who's this Sylvie Reynaud, my two o'clock?"

"Oh, sorry, I meant to tell you about that the moment you walked in. She left a message with the service, and I picked it up first thing this morning. She sounded pretty upset, and you didn't have anything scheduled, so I just slotted her in." A pause. "I hope that was okay."

I sighed. I'd planned to put in an appearance and then head up to Presqu'isle. I'd had a very unsatisfactory conversation with Lavinia Smalls, my caregiver since childhood and now the old mansion's sole resident. Except of course for Julia, but that was another story entirely. Our weekly Sunday chat had been strained, and the lump of anxiety that never wandered far from the center of my chest had slipped easily back into place the moment I hung up the phone.

Still, business was business, as my late father the Judge had often reminded me. We had founded the agency together, more as a lark than as a serious endeavor, but it had quickly become a source of livelihood for both Erik and Stephanie. And now Red and Sharese. Our reputation for integrity had been hard-won, and we gave every case we accepted our full effort and commitment. Even the ones I secretly wanted to slither out from under.

"She couldn't come in any earlier? I had plans to be out of the office this afternoon."

"I can call and ask. She left her cell number."

I glanced at my watch. "Yes, do that, would you please? If she could make it before noon that would be great."

"I'll call her now."

"Thanks." I turned to the men waiting patiently in front of my desk. "How about you two? Anything shaking?"

Erik forced a tentative smile. "I'm still working on collating the information for the women's shelter's attorneys. Roy Don Rymer's trial starts next week."

The wife beater, abuser of his own children. I'd been so pleased when Erik's computer skills had enabled him to backtrack the threatening emails to this moron's home computer. Almost simultaneously, Rymer had confronted the shelter's founder, demanding to know where she had hidden his family. Having 911 on speed dial had probably saved the woman from a beating of her own, and prompt response from the Beaufort police had put the slimeball behind bars. Erik's testimony would cement the case against him, and he'd at least go down for menacing and some as yet unspecified computer crimes. Certainly not anywhere near what he deserved, but maybe it would give his wife and children some breathing space, a chance to relocate while Rymer cooled his heels in jail.

"If you need help, you know you can call on Sharese. She certainly isn't in your league when it comes to the cyber stuff, but she's a whiz on the keyboard." I cut off what I knew would be some reference to his vanished fiancée. "I know she's not as good as Stephanie, but you need to give her a chance, Erik. We're paying her good money. You might as well make use of the skills she brings to the table."

"You're right," he mumbled. "Anything else?"

"I guess not."

With a nod, he rose and moved back toward the screen that provided him some privacy from the comings and goings in the main reception area. One of these days, I thought, watching his bent shoulders, he's going to have to get over her. I voiced as much to my husband once Erik was out of earshot.

"Give him time."

"He's had time. That was November, and it's nearly St. Patrick's Day. I don't think she's coming back." Red didn't respond. "Do you?"

"Probably not. But hope dies hard." He smiled up at me. "As it should."

I knew his reference was to his own dogged pursuit of me after his brother—my first husband—was murdered by the drug cartel he'd been investigating for the state attorney general's office. Sometimes the vivid nightmare of his plane exploding on takeoff, showering me with hot metal and anguish, seemed as real as the day it happened.

"I suppose. But I miss the old Erik. He has to force himself to smile. It makes me sad."

Red reached across the desk and took my hand. I squeezed back, glad of his understanding.

"I'm going to head out in a few minutes," he said. "I'm meeting Malik for coffee when he takes his break, see if he's come up with anything on that guy we're trying to run down for Mrs. Tennyson."

"The gardener? I was hoping she'd decided to let it go. I told her she's going to end up spending more on our fees than he supposedly took out of her wallet."

"You're not convinced it was even him, are you?" My husband ran a hand through his thick brown hair in an unconscious gesture that always reminded me of his dead brother.

"Nope. You haven't met her son. Or his friends."

"Well, you could be right, but there's no way she's going to accuse Junior. Much easier to try and nail the Hispanic laborer than her snotty kid."

"Let's just drop the case. I don't much like her."

My husband laughed. "Really? I'd never have guessed."

I returned his smile. "I get that we don't have to like the client. *My* rule, if you recall. There's just . . . something sort of smarmy about her, know what I mean? She's perfectly willing to lay the blame on some poor working guy when the problem is almost certainly closer to home. You said the kid's been in trouble before."

"According to Malik. That's one of the reasons the sheriff has been dragging his feet a little about trying to locate the gardener. But you know what they say: Money talks and bull—"

Red bit off the rest at Sharese's sudden appearance.

"Sorry to interrupt, but I have Ms. Reynaud on the line. She wants to know if she can come right now."

I checked my watch. Even if it took an hour, I could still get to Presqu'isle by early afternoon. Maybe I could even mooch lunch from Lavinia.

"Fine. Tell her to come on in."

"Yes, ma'am."

Red and I exchanged a grin as Sharese returned to her desk.

"I hate being called *ma'am*. It makes me feel about a hundred years old."

"What can you do? Her mama raised her right." He rose. "Anyway, I'll see you later on. If we don't make connections, I'll be home probably before you are. What's happening for dinner?"

"Your call," I said, stacking the file folders on my desk into a couple of neat piles. "Surprise me."

"Be careful what you wish for," he said and waved on his way out.

At least that part of my life was back on track. I spared a moment to think about what I might find at Presqu'isle, then shoved that into one of my convenient mental compartments when the front door opened. I caught a glimpse of a tall, willowy woman in baggy cotton trousers, a brightly jeweled T-shirt, and sparkling gold flip-flops. A mane of startling red hair cascaded down her back as she turned to close the door behind her.

She must have been lurking in the parking lot, I thought, and leaned back in my chair.

"Sylvie Reynaud for Mrs. Tanner."

"Of . . . of course," Sharese replied shakily.

Who was this woman that the voice of my usually imperturbable receptionist should be quivering in . . . fear? Awe? I craned my head a little, trying to see without being seen, when Sharese stepped into my line of vision.

"Mrs. Tanner, your appointment is here. Shall—?"

The tall redhead expertly inched her way past and displaced Sharese in the doorway. I opened my mouth to protest her rudeness when she stopped me in my tracks.

"Hey, Bay Rum, what's shakin'?"

A hearty laugh followed, one that took me back a few decades. To middle school. To three or four gawky preteens huddled in the girls' bathroom, sharing a forbidden cigarette.

For a moment, I refused to believe this exotic creature filling my doorway could be—

"Pudge?" I almost couldn't get the word out, it seemed so impossible.

"In the flesh. And a lot less of it than the last time I saw you, *n'est-ce pas?*"

And Sylvia Reynolds, aka Pudge, apparently also aka Sylvie Reynaud, pirouetted once, then plopped into the client chair.

CHAPTER TWO

"I can't believe it."

It was probably the third or fourth time I'd uttered the inane sentence, but it kept swirling around in my head and popping out of my mouth.

"Sorry," I mumbled.

"Don't be. It's actually very flattering. If you'd recognized me straight off, I'd probably have to fire a lot of people who work their asses off to keep me looking like this."

Pudge. The nickname had been appropriate if a tad cruel. Sylvia Reynolds had potential, we'd all agreed on that, but she just couldn't seem to shed the extra thirty pounds that mostly bunched around her middle and puffed up her face. But she'd been one of us, and we'd threatened dire consequences to anyone outside the group who dared call her that in our hearing. The smoking aside, we'd been good students and rarely in serious trouble. Our bond was being outside the norm in an era when lip service had been paid to non-conformity, but the fact of it had been systematically crushed by the adults in our world. We had been the cool girls, at least in the eyes of our peers. And, to be truthful, mostly ourselves. My own claim to fame was being a head taller than all the other girls and most of the guys. And having a wealthy, aristocratic drunk for a mother.

"You're a model. In New York. I've seen you on the cover of those magazines, but I swear to God I never recognized you."

"Neither did anyone else. At least not from down here. I even had a hard time convincing my parents that is was really me." She laughed, that same unladylike guffaw that used to send the rest of us off in a fit of giggles just from hearing it.

"I'll bet your mother had a cow."

"Believe it. At least in the beginning. Now she brags on me to the ladies in the home, even though I've been out of the modeling end of the business for a lot of years." She leaned back in the chair and crossed one long leg over the other. "Most of us don't last much past thirty. And that milestone has been a long time in the rearview mirror, eh?"

"Well, you still look fabulous." I was pretty certain Sylvia/Sylvie hadn't made an appointment with me at the office to hash over old times and discuss the vagaries of the fashion industry. "What can I do for you?" I asked. "Are you in some kind of trouble?"

The dazzling smile faded. "No. Not me." She squirmed and resettled herself. "Let me give you some background."

I held up my hand. "If you're thinking about hiring me, I need to record this. Any problem?"

She shook her head, and the amazing mane of red hair gleamed in the sunlight streaming in through the window behind me. *Pudge.* She had turned into one of the most beautiful women I'd ever encountered.

I fiddled with getting the tape set up and running, stated the date, time, and those present, and leaned back in my father's old leather desk chair. "Okay. The beginning."

It took nearly an hour, and I was forced to admit I had a hard time keeping track of the cast of Pudge's narrative. I sat for a long time after she'd left, the contract and a hefty retainer check staring at me from the middle of my desk. Of course I'd accepted her as a client, even without consulting Erik and Red. She was my friend. At least she had been. I couldn't quite figure out why I felt this tug from a relationship that had effectively been terminated—or at least suspended—a quarter century before, why it had never once crossed my mind to refuse her plea for my help. I suppose it didn't matter *why*, not in the long run. The commitment had been made.

The guys wouldn't like it. I had kept my word for the past few months, rejecting any case that smacked of even the potential for violence. And I got their point. Looking back over the few years Simpson & Tanner had been in existence, I had to admit that we'd all found ourselves in danger way too many times. We'd taken on causes—mostly at my insistence—that had exposed us to enough heartbreak to last a dozen people a lifetime. We'd all agreed that we needed a respite, a break from chasing down bad guys, from looking over our shoulders. From being afraid. We'd lost people—friends, family, lovers. It was good to step back and regroup.

And boring as hell.

I smiled at the admission just as Sharese stepped into the doorway.

"I'm going out to lunch now, if that's okay. Can I bring you anything?"

"No thanks, I'm good. I'll be heading out myself in just a few minutes. Anything I need to know about?"

"No, ma'am. Erik has some things he wants me to do this afternoon. Unless you have something?"

I slipped the tiny tape from the recorder. "If you have time, you can transcribe this and open a file."

She reached for the cassette. "Is Miss Reynaud going to be a client?"

Again I marveled at the note of awe in her voice. "Yes, but let's keep that just between us for now."

She frowned but nodded. We didn't usually have secrets when it came to the operations of the agency.

"How do you know her?" I asked to deflect any complicating questions.

"Oh, I don't *know* her. I've just seen her on a lot of magazine covers. I didn't recognize her name right off, but I knew it was her the minute she walked in the door. She's done commercials on TV for the kind of perfume I like." Her warm brown skin flushed a little. "Not that I can afford it, but Byron likes to buy it for me on special occasions."

"We went to school together," I said, gathering my bag.

"Here?"

"Yes. We ran in the same crowd in high school."

"But isn't she French?"

I chuckled. "Not when I knew her. She had a Southern drawl you could slice. She's lost that somewhere along the way, too."

"I've heard her. In the commercials. She sure sounded foreign."

I moved around to the front of the desk. "I suppose she just reinvented herself. I think a lot of people would like to do that, but they just don't have the nerve. Or the talent."

Sharese stepped back away from the door. "I guess."

"If you get a chance to work on that tape, print me out a separate list of the names and contact info she mentions. The five women."

"Yes, ma'am. Have a good afternoon."

"You, too. Call if you need me. I'll be at Presqu'isle."

"Yes, ma'am. Give my best to Miss Lavinia."

I nodded, called goodbye to Erik, and slipped out into the warm sunshine of spring in the Lowcountry. I pushed aside the unsettling feeling Pudge's revelations had lodged in my chest. At least for the hour it took to drive to my old family home.

That personal set of problems would require all my attention and a whole lot more patience than I could normally muster. I settled into the soft leather of the big Jaguar and plotted how to pry Lavinia out of the clutches of my half sister.

"Julia!"

I knew she could hear me, even through the solid pine door to my old bedroom in the antebellum mansion which had stood for nearly two centuries against the onslaught of flood and hurricane and the wrath of General William Tecumseh Sherman. We weren't about to be defeated by some interloper with the mind of a ten-year-old.

I swallowed my anger and frustration and lowered my voice. "Julia, it's Bay. Please open the door." I paused. "I'm not mad at you." A blatant lie because I would cheerfully have throttled her with my bare hands. Maybe not literally, but then again . . .

I turned at the sound of measured footsteps behind me on the graceful staircase. A moment later a bent head clustered with tight, white curls was followed by the creased brown face of Lavinia Smalls, longtime housekeeper at Presqu'isle as well as my surrogate mother and the last link to my vanished childhood.

I tried not to cringe at the small strip of bandage over her left eye and the darkening of the leathery skin on her cheekbone. "I asked you to let me handle this."

"And I told you to let it be. It was an accident."

"Like hell it was."

"Language," she said automatically, and suddenly we smiled at each other, the old relationship still intact in spite of the passage of forty-plus years.

Just like with Pudge, I thought and pushed the unsettling intrusion aside.

It was an argument I knew from experience that I'd never win, so I leaned into the door and rattled the knob for the second or third time.

"Come on, Julia. I have to go home soon, and you promised to show me Rasputin's new collar." As if on cue, her giant, lumbering beast of a dog sent up a howl from his pen in the narrow strip of yard bordering St. Helena Sound. "See? He needs you." I almost hated how good it made me feel to utter the next few words. *Almost.* "Hear that? Maybe he's hurt."

"Lydia Baynard Simpson Tanner! That's just cruel." Lavinia planted her hands firmly on her narrow hips and glared up at me.

I shrugged. "Tough. I've had enough of this game, and she needs to explain herself." I felt the fear rising in my throat. "How am I supposed to get a decent night's sleep if I have to be constantly worrying that she's going to haul off and belt you again?"

"I told you—"

"I know. It was an accident. She just accidentally shoved you so hard you bashed your face into the cupboard, accidentally making you bleed." The time for pulling punches was long past. "She's dangerous. I've been trying to tell you and Neddie that for the past few months, and both of you just stick your heads in the sand. She's gotten sly and secretive, and I think she has a plan. She wants Presqu'isle, and you're standing in the way."

"Oh, Bay." Lavinia dragged herself up the last three steps and collapsed into the small padded chair set beside a demi-lune table with a vase of fresh flowers from my late mother's winter garden. "You're being so unfair."

I could have fired back. I could have marshaled a hundred arguments, cited dozens of examples to bolster my claim, but it would have fallen on deaf ears. Ever since I'd discovered the existence of my bastard half sister just a short time before our mutual father's death, I'd done my best to overcome my initial distrust. Everyone seemed to forget that Julia had attacked me with a knife in our first encounter at Covenant Hall, the old rice plantation just off the Charleston road in Jacksonboro. Yes, she'd been seeing my former college roommate and renowned child psychologist, Dr. Nedra Halloran, for the past few months. Neddie swore they were making progress, but I just couldn't see it. And she and Lavinia refused to give any credence to my fears. Even after Julia's former caretaker had tumbled to her death down these very stairs . . . even after our strange encounter in the attics on the floor above . . . And now she'd attacked Lavinia. It was time for her—and Neddie—to take off the blinders, to quit ascribing all Julia's strange and erratic behavior to her childhood post-traumatic stress disorder. She may have had the mind of a child, but my half sister carried the body of a middle-aged woman. She could do damage, as she'd already proved.

And at this stage of the game, I didn't give a damn *why* she'd become a danger to those I loved. I just knew I had to put a stop to it. Right then. Right there.

CHAPTER THREE

In the end, I retreated. Not *surrendered*. A strategic retreat.

At least that's what I told myself as I followed Lavinia down the stairs and into the kitchen. I flopped onto the chair that had been mine since I'd been old enough to sit up straight and rested my elbows on the scarred oak table. Lavinia fussed with something on the stove that smelled fishy and wonderful, and my stomach rumbled.

"What are you making?" I asked to break the uncomfortable silence.

"Nothing special."

Okay, I thought, *it's going to be like that.*

"It smells heavenly. Frogmore stew?"

"No."

I stared at her back, ramrod straight as usual, but I couldn't help noticing that her shoulders sloped a little. Lavinia Smalls had been the rock of my existence, shielding me from my alcoholic mother's alternating bouts of rage and depression, for as long as I could remember. Alienating her was the last thing I wanted to do, but I couldn't ignore the knot of fear that took up residence in my gut every time the subject of Julia came up between us.

I knew Lavinia missed my father. His death had been as devastating a blow to her as it had been to me. Their relationship had been a strange mix of employer/employee, friendship, and a deep, mutual respect that somewhere over the years had blossomed into love. I'd never probed for details, happy in my ignorance, and grateful for her tender care of a man who had been confined to a wheelchair for most of his final years.

All of us owed her an enormous debt that could never adequately be repaid.

Which is why I was determined to keep her safe. At any cost.

"It's very annoying to have to keep speaking to your back," I said with more than a little asperity. "You'd accuse *me* of being rude."

I saw the tension in her relax a little as she turned to face me.

"Of course you're right. I'm sorry."

I resisted the urge to leap up and hold her close to my heart. We'd never been a *touching* household, and I knew she'd squirm and fuss at such a display of emotion. Still, I hoped she could read in my eyes how much I cared for her. And how afraid I was.

She set down the spoon she'd been using to stir the bubbling pot, crossed the short space to the table, and took her accustomed seat. "Okay, honey, have your say. I'm listening."

Again I detected that hint of weariness in her eyes, the way she slumped a little in the chair, and my heart turned over. There had been so many losses already. I couldn't bear it if . . . I gathered my thoughts and ordered myself to speak calmly.

"I'm worried about your safety." I hurried on before she could contradict me. "Tell me exactly what happened between you and Julia, and maybe you can put some of my fears to rest. My only concern is for you. I know she's my blood relation, and that counts for a lot in your book, but you and I have been together, one way or another, my entire life. Given a choice, I'm going to come down on your side every time. And it's not that I'm trying to find some excuse to get rid of her. I agree that this is where she probably belongs. At least for now. But even you can't deny that her behavior has become . . . erratic at best over the past few months. I believe I have a right to be concerned."

I finished on a long breath and settled back in my chair, my gaze never leaving the face of my dear friend.

Lavinia looked me squarely in the eyes. "It was an accident, Bay. If you need me to swear on the Bible, I will."

You didn't get a much stronger commitment than that from the very Baptist Lavinia, but I still felt a niggling doubt.

"So tell me."

"We were cleaning up after dinner last night. I told Julia she could take the table scraps out to Rasputin, but instead she brought him in here. I spoke sharply to her about the dog tracking in who knows what from his pen out there, and he became . . . excited. It was my tone of voice, I'm sure, and you know he's very protective of her. Anyway, we were both trying to get him calmed down and out the door, and in the process I got knocked into the handle of the cupboard. I honestly can't say whether it was the dog, Julia, or my own clumsiness." She sighed and rested her elbows on the table, another breach of etiquette that was so uncharacteristic. "That's what happened."

"Then why did Julia go racing up the stairs and lock herself in her bedroom almost the moment I walked in the door?"

Lavinia straightened, and this time her eyes danced with the old familiar fire. "Because you began yelling at the poor child before I even had a chance to get two words of explanation out of my mouth." Her steely gaze relented, just a little. "She worships you, honey, don't you know that? It devastates her when she thinks you're upset or disappointed with her."

I had serious doubts about that statement, but I let it ride. Instead, I voiced the one indisputable fact that was the primary cause of all my fears. "Are you forgetting about Miss Lizzie?"

Julia's longtime caretaker, who had moved with my half sister to Presqu'isle due to her failing health and some serious financial worries, had fallen to her death down the grand staircase. Lavinia had found Julia standing near her body. No one could say for certain how Elizabeth Shelley met her fate. I had my suspicions, based on Julia's behavior and demeanor, and that creepy encounter in the attic a few days later. And yes, on some entirely unsubstantiated gut feeling I couldn't even adequately explain to myself.

"You are the only one who believes the child was the cause of that terrible tragedy. Dr. Halloran—"

"Quit calling Julia 'the child', will you please? She's older than I am."

I watched Lavinia struggle not to lash back at me. "As I was saying, Dr. Halloran believes *Julia* was traumatized by that whole incident, and she's been working very hard to bring *Julia* back to some state of normalcy. We need to give *Julia* all the love and support we can right now, not jump down her throat for imaginary transgressions. And that's all I have to say on the matter."

She threw herself out of the chair and back to the stove, snatching up the wooden spoon and attacking whatever it was she had simmering on the front burner.

I rested my own elbows on the table, dropped my head into my hands, and mentally raised the white flag.

• • •

Eventually, my half sister ventured out of her room—*my* room, in the old days—and crept silently into the kitchen.

I forced myself to accept her mumbled apology, which brought an answering smile from Lavinia. We chatted about nothing for a few more minutes before I pled an urgent business obligation and fled. As I pulled away from Presqu'isle, I glanced reflexively into the rearview mirror, half expecting Julia to be standing on the front verandah, gloating as she watched me disappear down the rutted Avenue of Oaks.

I had lost the battle, but the war was far from over.

I stopped off at the office to pick up the file Sharese had compiled for me.

"I don't have a lot of information yet on the women you asked me to check out. I verified the addresses and contact information Ms. Reynaud . . . I mean Reynolds gave you earlier. I think maybe Erik should do the deep background checking. I don't feel real confident with those databases yet."

I admired the fact that our newest employee felt comfortable asking for help and told her so.

"Thank you. I'd love to learn all that so I don't have to keep bothering Erik."

I smiled, thinking to myself that she had no trouble referring to my partner by his first name, but I was always *Mrs. Tanner* or *ma'am.* And Red was *Sergeant.* Funny how an age difference of just a few years—okay, maybe more than a few—could move you from a contemporary into the venerated category of respected elder.

I hated it.

"That's fine. I'll take this home and glance over it this evening. Anything else?"

"No, ma'am. Erik had a dentist appointment, so he left a little early. And the sergeant said to tell you he's working on dinner." She smiled at that thought. "You go on home. I'll lock up."

"Thanks. You have a good evening," I said on my way out the door.

"You, too. Let me know how dinner goes tonight."

I laughed at the impish grin on her face, happy that Stephanie's replacement was working out so well. Sometimes things just

went the way you planned.
Or not.

CHAPTER
FOUR

Red's solution to being assigned the hunter-gatherer role usually had one of two outcomes: steak on the grill or a burger at Jump & Phil's, our favorite watering hole on the south end of the island.

The smell wafting down from the back deck that hit me the moment I stepped out of the Jaguar told me the former option had won the day. I climbed the steps from the garage into the house, dropped my bag on the console table just inside the door, and made my way across the great room to the French doors. I found my husband hovering over his newest acquisition, a hulking chrome behemoth that did everything but cut the meat for you. I'd glanced at the instruction manual while Red had been assembling his latest toy and decided I'd stick to the oven and the microwave.

"Hey, honey," he said as I flopped onto one of the chaises on the wide deck that surrounded the house on three sides. "I haven't put yours on yet, since you like it just the other side of bloody."

"Yours smells good. What else is on your menu tonight, chef? Anything I need to do?"

"Nope. I stopped at Publix and picked up a salad, and there's garlic bread in the oven. Good enough?"

"Perfect," I said. "How long?"

"Ten minutes?"

I heaved myself back up. "I'll go change. Are we eating out here or inside?"

"Your call." My husband looked out toward the ocean, just a short distance away across the sheltering dunes. "The wind's picked up some, and it's looking a little iffy out over the water. Could be a storm brewing."

I watched the sea oats swaying rhythmically and heard the soughing in the tops of the towering loblolly pines. "Inside it is. I'll be ready in ten."

I stopped off to retrieve the Reynolds file from my bag and drop it onto the desk set up in one corner of our bedroom. Ever since Elinor and Scotty had gotten old enough to need their own rooms on their weekend visits, I'd lost my home office. It now sported pale pink walls, posters of ballerinas and rock bands I'd never heard of, and a ruffled bedspread that made me smile every time I looked at it.

I had been an unapologetic tomboy, the bane of my mother's existence. While she'd done her level best to turn me into a young lady worthy of being presented to old Beaufort society, I'd sneaked out at every opportunity to join the Judge on his hunting and fishing expeditions. Whenever the subject of dancing class came up, I would usually flee to the safety of the higher branches of one of the many live oaks that draped our property.

I didn't even want to think about what she'd make of my current profession.

I slipped into old comfortable jeans and a Salty Dog T-shirt, then walked barefoot into the kitchen. I had just divvied up the salad and pulled the garlic bread from the oven when Red carried the platter of steaks up the three steps and deposited it on the small table by the bay window.

"All set?" he asked, sliding mine onto the plate.

"You'd make somebody a really good wife, you know that?" I said with a grin, and he made a half-hearted attempt to swat me on his way by.

"Women cook. Men grill. They're two completely different skill sets."

"So you say." I took my seat and waited for my husband to fill his mouth with New York strip and salad before I added, "I took on a new client today."

The unspoken agreement had been, especially over the past few months, that none of us would make a commitment until we'd discussed the job and all been in accord about accepting it. As I had planned, it took him a while to answer, allowing him time to swallow both his food and any sharp retorts that might have leaped into his head.

He took an extra breath. "You get a retainer?"

I nodded. "A pretty darn good one, actually. And a contract."

I sliced into the rare steak and bent my head to my dinner.

"What's the job?"

"Do you remember my talking about the gang of girls I used to run with? In high school, I mean."

Red stared at me for a long moment. "I only know about Bitsy Elliott. And not all that much, since you haven't been speaking to her for nearly a year."

I sighed and laid down my fork. "It hasn't been that long. And she deserved it." All of a sudden I could feel tears pooling behind my eyes. "She broke my trust. And the results were disastrous, especially for—"

I broke off, unable to say the name that lurked in the back of my conscience every time my mind stilled. I wondered if I'd ever be able to shake the guilt.

"It wasn't her fault, Bay. Or yours. Blame the son of a bitch that killed that poor girl. And take some comfort from the fact that he's going to be paying for it with the rest of his life."

I wasn't so sure about that last statement. Appeals had been going on for some time, and I'd heard around town that the remaining occupant of Canaan's Gate had been financing them, something that both shocked and saddened me. The old man had been as much a victim as anyone else, and it boggled my mind that he'd contribute even a penny to the defense of the author of all that misery.

I stabbed my fork into the crisp romaine leaves. "Anyway, it's the woman who made the appointment for this afternoon. She came in almost as soon as you'd walked out the door."

"The one with the weird name?"

I sniffled and offered a weak smile. "It's not weird. It's French."

"Whatever. So what does she have to do with your misspent youth?"

I resisted the temptation to fling a hunk of bread in his direction. "She used to be Sylvia Reynolds, but we called her Pudge. She ran with our crowd."

"And she was French?"

"It's a long story. Let's just finish eating, and you can take a look at the file. I brought it home with me."

"At least give me a hint."

"It can wait," I said, suddenly certain my husband and my partner would both balk at what Pudge wanted us—*me*, actually—to do. "Want another beer?"

Red gave me the look, the one that said he knew exactly what I was up to and wasn't fooled for a second. "Sure," he said, after a long pause, and I let out a small sigh of relief as I rose and crossed to the refrigerator.

The storm was short, but nasty, and we gave up our usual post-dinner stretch on the chaises on the deck, settling instead on the sofa in the great room. I'd handed Red the transcript of my conversation with Pudge and kept the list of names for myself. With the reading lamps on, we sat side by side, the only sounds the intermittent drip of rainwater from the trailing branches of the live oaks through the open French doors and a soft rumble of retreating thunder as the weather moved inland toward Bluffton.

The five women were all pretty much of an age—*mine*, in fact—and two of them I'd recognized the moment Pudge had mentioned them. Mary Alice Pierce and Beatrice Ballantyne had been part of our group, although *Bebe* only tangentially. She'd been a little too *girly* for our loose confederation of nonconformists, her hair always perfectly brushed into soft blond waves and her clothes a little too preppy for our taste. Still, we'd tried to include her in our escapades, even though she generally declined, either from fear of getting caught or creasing her perfectly tailored slacks.

I chuckled, and Red lifted his head from his reading. "What's so funny?"

"Just remembering. When I think back on the kinds of trouble we could have gotten into—you know, drugs or gangs or whatever—our misdemeanors seem pretty tame. Although, we thought of ourselves as very daring."

"You recognize the names?"

"A couple of them. Not their married names, but how I knew them back then. And we had nicknames for just about everybody." I tapped the paper I'd rested on my lap. "Beatrice Ballantyne was Bebe, of course. Mary Alice was Scarlett. We voted her most likely to end up in a house like Tara."

I chuckled again. Based on her address—the exclusive Buckhead section of Atlanta—it's possible we had been right on target about Scarlett's future.

Red scooted over and draped an arm around me. "And what

about you? What'd they call you?"

I felt the pain and embarrassment of my nickname wash over me as I recalled how carelessly Pudge had tossed it out earlier in the day. You'd think the passage of nearly three decades might have dulled the shame a little. Or maybe I'd never adequately communicated how much distress it had caused the teenaged me. I was—and *am*—a firm believer in the old adage about never letting them see you sweat. Or cry.

"Bay Rum. Like the old hair tonic, you know?" I swallowed and forced a smile for my husband. "And, of course, because of my mother."

"That was cruel," he said, drawing my head down onto his shoulder.

I shrugged and burrowed my face into the familiar smell of his skin. "So was calling Sylvia *Pudge*. Teenagers can be vicious. But you know, I have a hard time thinking of her any other way. And we all cared about each other, as much as you can when you're that age and so completely self-involved." I wriggled around and brought my feet up onto the cushions. "What about you and Rob?"

Red ran his hand absently over my tangle of hair. "Oh, I didn't have one, not officially. Rob used to call me *Junior*, but only to piss me off. No one else used it."

"What did you call him?"

"Mostly things Mom would have been shocked to hear. You know how boys are."

"No, actually, I don't. None in my immediate vicinity when I was growing up at Presqu'isle. Except for Lavinia's son Thad, but he kept out of the way most of the time."

"Your mother's doing?"

"Not really. I think Lavinia realized how much of a blessing it was that she was allowed to have her child with her at Presqu'isle, and she made him almost invisible." I paused, remembering how curious I'd been about him, and how swiftly my questions had been quashed by both my mother and her housekeeper. The Judge, on the other hand, had given the inquisitive young man the run of his considerable library, only I'm not sure how much Thad availed himself of the opportunity. He'd ended up marrying a local woman and going to work for the post office.

"And he's black," Red added, and I bristled.

"I don't think that had anything to do with it. My mother may have been an unrepentant snob, but I never thought of her as a racist."

My husband ruffled my hair. "Sorry."

I relaxed my shoulders and snuggled back in. "Anyway, what was Rob's nickname? He must have had one."

"*The Senator.*" I could feel Red's smile. "He was always such a damned straight arrow. I don't think anyone who knew him was surprised when he opted for law school."

I allowed a moment of intense grief to wash over me, before I pulled myself up and retrieved the list from the coffee table where I'd tossed it.

"Anyway, what do you think?"

"About?"

"The case. I can't see any real down side to it, can you?"

I felt him stiffen beside me.

"Of course not! Getting tangled up with a bunch of women, some of them from your distant past, who think someone's beating the crap out of one of their friends? Wanting you to go undercover and nose around in their lives, with the strong possibility that somewhere along the line you're going to run into a man who enjoys using his fists on women?" He shook his head and closed the file. "Nah, honey, no down side. For you it'll be a piece of cake."

Stunned by his sudden change of demeanor, I watched him push himself off the sofa, turn his back, and stalk off toward the bedroom.

"Well, at least he didn't say no," I muttered to myself and stared at his retreating back.

CHAPTER FIVE

By Tuesday morning and his second cup of coffee, Red had cooled down. He hadn't really been angry with me, not in any meaningful way. He worried. I understood that. There had been plenty of times when he needed to.

With both men seated in front of my desk, I laid out the plan of attack.

"Pudge says they're all convinced Mary Alice is getting the hell beaten out of her on a regular basis. She always has some story, and she's even missed a couple of the get-togethers because they suspect she's been too banged up to show her face. Her excuses are lame, at least according to Pudge, and they're worried to death about her. They want me to meet with them—actually just Pudge and Bebe to start with—and then join them for one of their long weekends. They've been meeting at Pudge's new place on Jordan Point, so I'll be close to home."

"Where's that?" Erik asked. "I've never heard of it."

"Neither have most other people. I had to do some checking on Google Maps to find it exactly."

"Listen to you," my partner said with a grin that made me glad inside. "*Google Maps*. We may drag you kicking and screaming into the twenty-first century yet."

In a completely adult and professional response, I stuck out my tongue. "It's on a small spit of land that looks out over Skull Creek across to Pinckney Island. It's the only house out there, although it seems as if there were plans at one time to put a development in that area. There are some roads to nowhere starting to branch off the main one, and some curbs, but they just peter out after a few yards. It's pretty isolated, but I guess that's the way Pudge wants it."

"Far from the maddening crowd?"

"Actually, it's *Far from the* Madding *Crowd*, not maddening.

Thomas Hardy." I smiled. "A lot of people make that mistake."

Erik stuck *his* tongue out at *me*, and I laughed.

"Leave it to you to know that. Have any famous or pithy quotes you'd like to throw at us while you're at it?"

I shook my head, loving that the huge smile on his face actually reached his eyes.

"And what exactly is it that you're supposed to be doing?" he asked.

Red snorted. "Use her superpowers to make this Mary woman come clean, then scare the crap out of the husband, I suppose."

"You're starting to tick me off," I said in a suddenly sober but reasonable tone. "Seriously." I sighed and directed my attention exclusively to Erik. "Her husband, James—never Jim—Madison Stuart the Third—grew up around here. Old family, as you might have guessed from the name. DAR, related to Madison the president somehow a million years back, yadda, yadda, yadda. Anyway, they knew each other forever. I remember him, although he was a couple of years ahead of us in school. Four-point average, good looking, captain of the debate team, destined for greatness. The rest of us couldn't stand him, but Mary Alice never looked at anyone else." I paused and risked a glance at Red. "He must have changed a lot over the years if he's degenerated into a wife-beater."

"Assuming it's him," Red interjected. "And assuming it's even a question of someone hitting her."

"Are you being argumentative just for the hell of it?" I snapped. "That's the whole point of the exercise. To find out."

"You know, not all of them are scumbags like Roy Don Rymer," Erik offered in an obvious attempt to broker peace.

"I know that. But somehow it's easier to think of him as capable of it. I guess that makes me as much of a snob as my mother."

Red finally smiled. "You've got a long way to go before you can claim that title."

I felt my shoulders relax. "Thanks. I think. So anyway I don't see any downside to spending a few hours doing some research and a couple of more hanging out with Pudge and Bebe. Maybe when I get all the details, I'll decide it's a non-starter. But I feel as if I owe it to them to at least hear what they have to say." I looked at each of them in turn. "Problem?"

"I don't see one," Erik said promptly. "I can start a preliminary background check on the husband, see if anything shows up. You have their address, right?"

"Sharese has it in the file. They live in Atlanta, but they keep a boat down here. So maybe start local and move to Georgia if nothing pops. Red, can you check with the sheriff's office to see if he's ever been arrested or if they've ever been called out on a domestic while the Stuarts are on the island?"

"Sure," he said with just a tad more enthusiasm than he'd been showing of late. "Malik should be able to access that info pretty quick."

I slapped both hands lightly on the desk. "Okay, so let's get on it. I'll call Pudge and let her know I can meet with her tomorrow night. Bebe's driving down from Charleston, so I'll do my best to get as many details as possible. In the meantime, I'll go over what you've gotten on the others in the group, just to cover all our bases. Especially the ones I don't know."

Erik headed for his computer, and I laid a hand on Red's arm as he started to rise. "Hang on a sec, okay?"

He settled back in the chair and waited expectantly.

"I'm sorry if you don't like this case. It really isn't dangerous, and I think you know that. So what's up with all the sarcasm?"

Red glanced over his shoulder toward the open door, then leaned his elbows on the desk. "I don't know, exactly. I read the file, and all these women sound as if they're seriously screwed up. And why didn't they ever ask you or your friend Bitsy Elliott to be one of these pajama party girls?"

I laughed, and his face relaxed.

"What?"

"Pajama party girls? You sound like something out of one of those beach blanket movies from the fifties. Or *Grease*."

"Well, I don't know what to call them. It just sounds a little flaky to me, grown women getting together all the time to sleep over and gossip or whatever it is they do."

"But if a bunch of good old boys hang out every Thursday to drink whiskey and play poker, that makes more sense?"

My late father had been a member of just such a group, old-timers from Beaufort who shared a status and a history. I'd been honored to be invited into a couple of those games, but that was a rarity.

"Point taken," my husband said, rising. "Just don't decide you want to join this sorority, okay?"

"Don't worry. You should know by now that I'm not a joiner by nature. And that I much prefer the company of men."

"That's reassuring," he said with a genuine smile. "I'll carry that thought around in my head for a while."

"I'll let you know when you have to start worrying."

"No problem. That's pretty much my natural state anyway."

He tossed a wave over his shoulder, stopped to tell Sharese he'd be gone for an hour or so, and headed for the door.

Sometimes I wondered just how much truth there was at the heart of all our bantering. Or maybe I didn't really want to know.

I propped my feet up on an open desk drawer and leaned back in the Judge's old chair, the printout of the preliminary background on the five women who made up Pudge's little circle resting on my knees when a thought struck me. I hit the intercom button.

"Yes, ma'am?"

"Sharese, will you add Pudge . . . Ms. Reynolds to that list you gave Erik? I'd like some more digging done on her as well."

"Yes, ma'am. Right away."

I smiled as I set the receiver back in its cradle. One of the things I'd taken a long time to learn after setting out to become a legitimate detective was not to take things at face value. People you'd known, people you'd grown up with, people you just took for granted because they'd been in your life so long. I'd been surprised a few times, genuinely shocked in a couple of instances, and stunned at one or two outright betrayals. It wasn't a good idea to trust any of your assumptions, no matter how benign. People lied. They cheated. That's just the way it was. Of course, I told myself, they could also amaze you with their generosity and bravery. I picked up the file again. Time would tell on which end of the spectrum these six women fell. Or if, like most of us, they hovered somewhere in the middle.

Mary Alice Pierce Stuart, the supposed victim, had lived the life her parents and her heritage had pretty much mapped out for her from the time she drew her first squalling breath. She and James had married in a ceremony that was apparently still talked about in the social circles I avoided like the plague. Thankfully I'd been away at college and able to escape the hideous bridesmaid dress routine. Three children, all grown, one granddaughter.

That gave me pause.

Rob and I had talked about kids, had planned on eventually starting a family, but we never made it. After that, I'd done my best to put the idea out of my head, arranging my life in such a way that I'd never notice that particular blank spot. But sometimes, especially now when I saw Red chasing his two along the beach, their shrieks of laughter echoing across the water, I had to admit to a little tug. I wasn't overwhelmed with maternal instinct —or longing—but every once in a while . . .

I shrugged off the feelings. My biological clock had already pretty much struck midnight.

I forced my focus back to the business at hand.

James had followed his father into his law practice, then branched out to become a highly successful attorney for one of the large corporations headquartered in Atlanta. The boat they kept docked at Skull Creek drew them to the island on a regular basis. I was surprised they hadn't opted for the more prestigious mooring at Harbour Town in Sea Pines or even closer to Mary Alice's parents across the sound in Beaufort.

They belonged to all the right clubs and organizations, and my old friend seemed to keep herself occupied with boards and charity work. Not much of a life, at least not from where I was sitting, but she might have been thrilled to have attained the social and economic status she'd been destined for. Would have bored me silly, but hey, that's just me.

I moved on to the other member of the group with whom I had some history. Beatrice Ballantyne had also followed her destiny, such as it was, although why on earth she ever married someone whose last name began with a B escaped me. Ralph Bedford also came with a pedigree, although not nearly as impressive as James's, and it appeared that his fortunes had not been quite as dazzling. I made a note to have Erik check out their finances. Their address in an exclusive area of Charleston had recently been exchanged for what sounded like a modest condo in Mount Pleasant. It probably didn't have a thing to do with the case, but it intrigued me. It also seemed surprising that, like me, she'd never had children.

Gillian McDonald, Jenny Carson, and Anne Elizabeth Gilchrist were strangers to me. All of them had backgrounds that didn't originate in the Lowcountry. Gillian had had a short stint as a model, which probably explained her friendship with Pudge. Divorced and childless, she lived in a town I'd never heard of in New Jersey. Anne was a New York socialite, divorced as well, one daughter. Her address sounded as if it could be one of those fabulous Manhattan apartments with tons of light and a view of Central Park. Or maybe a brownstone. I shrugged. What I knew about New York City, outside of *Law & Order* reruns, would fit in a thimble.

Jenny Carson presented something of a conundrum. She was a school teacher, third grade, in northern Virginia. I retrieved my iPad from my bag and tapped on the Google Maps icon. The town was small, at the foothills of the Blue Ridge Mountains, and very rural. Her husband Ted taught high school American history and served as the head football coach. Why was someone like that hanging out with the high rollers from uptown? *Interesting.* I scratched another note to have Erik dig a little deeper into Jenny's background.

And that left Pudge. Because she hadn't been included in the initial list I'd given Sharese, I had nothing concrete except what little she herself had told me. And my own recollections. If my mother had been alive, I was certain she could have supplied me with all the gossip about Sylvia. And her parents. I remembered then that she'd mentioned her mother's bragging about her to the ladies at the home. So she was institutionalized? Where? And what for? And what about her father? I vaguely remembered that he'd been some sort of mucky-muck with one of the local banks. The Judge would have had the scoop on him. I sighed, the sadness of his death never very far from my mind. He had been overbearing, interfering, larger than life. I missed him. A lot.

It flashed briefly into my head that Bitsy Elliott could have been another source of information about the doings of those who flew in the higher strata of local society, but I immediately squelched that idea. I knew that sooner or later I would have to make peace with my oldest friend, but I wasn't ready. Not yet. She had made a couple of overtures in the months since our last conversation, but I'd let her calls go to voice mail. The last time she hadn't bothered to leave a message.

So many losses, of one kind or another.

But, as that great sage Paul McCartney wrote, "Ob-la-di, Ob-la-da, life goes on."

I smiled and awarded myself two points.

CHAPTER
SIX

By Wednesday morning, Erik had managed to ferret out a lot
more information about all the players in the current drama,
although I wasn't sure just how much help it was going to be. Red
had returned the previous afternoon without much to report regarding the Stuarts during their frequent sojourns on the island.
He'd slumped into the chair in front of my desk a little before
three looking tired and frustrated.

"Bad day at Black Rock?" I'd asked, forcing a reluctant smile
from him.

"Nah, not really. There's nothing on the record about your
friend and her husband, other than they reported an attempted
burglary a year or so ago."

"The boat?"

"No, their car." He consulted the small notebook he had
tucked into the pocket of his shirt, reminiscent of Ben Wyler. I
shooed that thought away.

"Lexus. They came out from a party somewhere and found it
broken into."

"Anything stolen?"

"Just vandalism. They both had their phones on them. I
suppose the goal was to steal it, but most cars are pretty much impossible to hotwire these days."

"Suspects?"

"Nope. There had been a rash of those kinds of break-ins
around that time, but nobody ever got nailed for it. Drove us all
crazy. Probably kids who got scared off or decided they'd had
enough walks on the wild side."

"Just cars?"

"Mostly. A few boats that aren't kept somewhere they have
security. No houses. Too many chances to get nailed by home-

owners or alarm systems or plantation patrols. They managed to make off with a few laptops, tablets, and phones, but nothing ever turned up at the pawn shops. Just one of those cases you have to toss on the cold pile and move on."

"But there was nothing about any domestic calls?"

"No, not even a hint." Red had straightened up at that point, regarding me seriously across the expanse of desk. "You might want to rethink this whole case, honey."

I understood where he was coming from, but it was early times yet. "Let me get together with Pudge and Bebe, see what they have to say." I raised a hand. "I know, but it won't hurt."

"There are people's lives and reputations at stake here, you know. It's not just some intellectual exercise."

"Got it. I'll tread lightly." I had tried then to change the subject. "Anything more about old lady Tennyson and her missing hundred-dollar bills?"

Red had held my gaze for a moment longer before relaxing back into the chair. "Malik says she still calls them just about every day. I wonder why she hasn't been beating down our door, too. She hired us to find the gardener, and so far we've been spectacularly unsuccessful."

I had to laugh at that. "Yeah, well, I haven't exactly been giving it the full-court press. Besides, she penny-pinched me about the retainer, and Erik has used that up doing searches and backgrounds. If she wants more, she's going to have to part with a few more of those hundreds."

Red had laughed, too, and we'd moved on to other topics . . .

Now I sat at my desk with six file folders spread out in front of me, wondering if all this information-gathering would turn out to be a waste of time. Red had come up empty with the local sheriff's office, and it would take Erik a lot longer to access records in Georgia, if he was even able to do so. Not that I should have any reason to doubt that he'd pull it off. When it came to his cyber sleuthing—a phrase he preferred to *hacking*—we operated under the don't-ask-don't-tell policy. So far, even though I had a strong feeling he often skated pretty close to the legal edge, he'd escaped detection.

I opened the file on Sylvia Augusta Reynolds, alias Sylvie Reynaud, world-class model and national TV spokeswoman. I skimmed over her early curriculum vita, primarily because I'd lived through most of it with her. One thing I'd forgotten was that she had an older sister—much older, to judge by her birth date. I guess in some dusty corner of my mind I'd known that, and I wondered why she'd played such a minor role in Pudge's life. I did some quick math and realized Carrie would have been college age when we were just stumbling out of elementary school, so maybe that explained it.

Pudge had kicked the dust of Beaufort County, South Carolina, off her Birkenstocks and made a beeline for New York City almost before the ink had dried on her high school diploma. I remember being afraid for her, striking out for that unknown metropolis where she didn't know a soul. But I had been in the throes of preparing to head off to Columbia and the absolutely terrifying—and thrilling—prospect of living on my own for the first time in my life. The Judge would have loved it if I could have followed his career path at the Citadel, but in those darker ages, women were not yet being admitted. As it turned out, I left USC for the frozen pathways of Northwestern after declaring myself unwilling to study law. And after that bold declaration had angered the Judge enough to cut off my support.

"Got a minute?"

Erik's soft voice and sudden appearance in the doorway startled me out of my meander down memory lane. If I wasn't careful, I'd get so bogged down in the past I wouldn't be fit to deal with present.

"Sure. Come on in."

He planted himself in one of the client chairs and crossed one long leg over the other knee.

I waited, but now that he was seated, he seemed distinctly ill at ease.

"What's up?" I prompted.

"Well . . ." He stopped and cleared his throat. "It's kind of slow right now, don't you think? I mean, other than this thing with your friend."

I did not like where this might be leading. "You have your work for the Rymer trial. Is that all set to go?"

"Just finished and sent everything over to the county solicitor's office. They said they'd let me know if I needed to testify, but right now they don't have any plans to call me in person. I signed an affidavit laying it all out."

"Backgrounds up to date?"

We did a lot of business with local public and charitable organizations making certain their employees and volunteers had clean records on a number of fronts. In fact, that constituted the bulk of our income since we'd decided to back off anything criminal or dangerous. While that had been a gut reaction to the havoc of the past couple of years, I had always feared that it might not have been the best business decision. My family trust fund along with a reviving stock market provided me with more than a cushion, but I knew Erik—and Sharese—depended on the agency for their livelihoods. Red drew a salary, and I knew it was important to him to bring home some bacon so that he didn't feel as if he were living on my dime. I'd do whatever it took to make certain he felt needed and appreciated.

"Where's this going?" I asked, forcing myself to smile. "If you need a vacation, all you have to do is say so. We're partners, which means you don't need to ask permission from me or anyone else."

"It's not that."

I felt like a dentist trying to draw a particularly tenacious molar.

"Then what is it?"

He fidgeted a little more, and his eyes swiveled away from mine. "I guess I'm feeling kind of restless. I'm wondering if it isn't time for me to move on."

I felt the bottom drop out of my stomach, but I kept my voice even. "Move on to where?"

"I don't know."

I had a sudden flash of insight, and I had to work hard to maintain my appearance of calm. "Out west, maybe? Somewhere like, oh, I don't know, Arizona?"

His head snapped up. "What if it is? You don't have to sound so damned sarcastic about it!"

Erik rarely used profanity. And he almost never stared at me with such intensity. Involuntarily, I leaned back in my chair, away from his cold glare.

"Oh, Erik. I'm sorry, but this idea is just wrong on so many levels."

He relaxed a little then. His eyes softened, and I caught a ghost of a his old smile.

"I knew you'd say that."

"Can't you let her go?"

"No, I can't. Not this way. There are things I need to say. And things I need to hear." His sigh nearly broke my heart. "She just disappeared, Bay. One day she was here, and we were talking about whether or not to have a big wedding or maybe just sneak off to some island in the Caribbean, and then wham! She's gone." He paused as if to gather his thoughts. "I need her to look me in the eye and make me believe it's over."

By the end of his explanation, my anger had melted into a profound sadness. Alain Darnay, Interpol agent and my one-time lover, had done exactly the same thing—disappeared with nothing but a hastily scribbled note. Sometimes, in the dead of night, I used to fantasize about hopping on a plane to Paris and banging on the door of his family apartment, demanding explanations. Maybe I had too much pride. Or too little courage. In either case, I'd never acted on those impulses, other than to imagine everything from a tearful apology and passionate reunion to the slam of the massive door in my face.

And besides, now there was Red.

I chose my words carefully. "I absolutely understand that. I know it's not the same, but I felt betrayed by Stephanie as well. So why don't you take a couple of weeks, fly out there, and see if you can get some answers." I softened my voice even more. "But they may not be the ones you want to hear. Are you prepared for that?"

I watched a lot of the tension drain from his shoulders.

"I know, but I feel as if I can't get on with the rest of my life until I find out exactly where I stand."

"So go! You don't have to leave the agency over this, Erik. You're irreplaceable, in case you hadn't noticed. But I'm sure we can struggle along without you for a little while."

The idea of his going for good filled me with such sadness I almost couldn't speak, and I blinked back tears.

"I just feel as if I'm treading water, you know? And something else." This time it was a genuine smile. "I'm kind of bored."

I felt the world righting itself, just a little. "Me, too," I said, and we both laughed.

A few seconds of silence settled over us before I came to a decision. "We'll stop turning down clients just because there might be an element of . . ." I balked at the word *danger*, mostly because it sounded so melodramatic. "Just because we think they smell like trouble. I'll tell Alex we're back in the game when she needs some work done for her criminal defense clients." Alexandra Finch and Claudia Darling ran the all-female law firm whose offices stood just across the street from the agency. "Or even some of her more interesting divorce cases."

"What about Red?"

My husband had been the driving force behind our retreat from the more tumultuous—and interesting—problems Alex had offered us. I knew it had more to do with my safety and well-being than any lack of courage on his part.

"I'll bring him around. When did you want to leave?"

He shrugged. "I guess I hadn't thought that far ahead." His eyes held some of their old mischief. "I was mostly worried about whether or not you'd just toss me out on my ear."

"Not a chance. But there is something I need from you before you go."

"I'll make sure everything is up to date."

"I know. But I want you to spend a couple of days and get Sharese at least familiar with some of your more esoteric techniques. If something comes up, I want to be able to count on her to get me information when I need it."

"Happy to, if she's willing."

"Oh, she's more than willing. I'd say she'll be thrilled."

"So how about if I plan to head out the first of next week?"

"That give you enough time?"

"I think so. She's a pretty quick study."

"And you won't be gone for more than two weeks?" I had a sudden premonition that shook me to my core. "You won't decide to stay out there and just mail in your resignation?"

Erik sobered. "I wouldn't do that to you, Bay. I hope you know me well enough by now not to worry about that." He rose. "I'll be back," he said in a very bad imitation of Arnold Schwarzenegger. "In two weeks at the most. You have my word."

"Go with God," I said with a smile, but the fear had already settled into a tiny vacant spot in the center of my chest, and I knew it would now be keeping close company with my worries about Lavinia.

I wondered when—or if—I'd ever run out of room.

CHAPTER SEVEN

Thankfully, Red stayed out of the office for the rest of the day, and I left early to prepare for my meeting with Pudge and Bebe. I'd already told him he was on his own for dinner, so I assumed he'd just go on to Jump & Phil's or Bubba's when he finished up whatever he was doing. I needed time to figure out how I was going to explain my decision—well, Erik's and mine, actually—about accepting some of the seamier cases we'd been turning down over the past few months.

I knew he'd understand about my partner's need to confront his former fiancée, but I was certain the rest would be an uphill battle. *Tomorrow*, Scarlett—the real one—whispered inside my head, and I took her advice to heart.

So, armed with my briefcase stuffed with a couple of legal pads and the mini tape recorder from the office along with the files on all the players, I finally located Pudge's nearly hidden drive and made my way through the overhanging vegetation. It sort of reminded me of the narrow, twisting road out to Sanctuary Hill, and I sincerely hoped there would be no more strange encounters with conjure-women in my future.

The drive opened up to reveal a spectacular Lowcountry home, its wood siding weathered until it almost blended in with the overhanging branches of the towering live oaks whose Spanish moss dripped nearly onto the roof. It was two stories, with dormers, and a wide porch that appeared to wrap around the entire house. Beyond it I could just make out the shimmer of water reflecting the deep oranges and purples of the sun setting over the mainland. I pulled the Jaguar up behind an Audi convertible already parked in the semicircular pad of concrete that led back to the dirt driveway.

Light filtered out from the windows on the lower floor as I

stepped out and hefted my bag onto my shoulder. I paused a moment to savor the nearly absolute silence, broken only by the chirruping of tree frogs and the occasional rustle of a soft wind through the trees. You couldn't get much farther from the incessant noise of the big city, and I thought I understood what had appealed to Pudge about this obscure location. I wondered how long it would be before some developer, emerging from the terrible economy and housing bust, would discover this beautiful spot and destroy its serenity with manicured landscaping and swimming pools and high-rises.

I heard the door open, and a rectangle of light spilled out into the surrounding darkness.

"You gonna stand out there all night admiring the view?" Pudge held a bottle in her hand. "The wine's already fading, so get your butt in here, Bay Rum."

I wondered how long it would be before I didn't cringe every time I heard her use my old nickname as I negotiated the wide staircase onto the verandah. A couple of battered old rocking chairs bracketed a small round table, and pots of fern hanging from hooks spilled greenery onto the railings. I couldn't imagine that the house was that old, but it had certainly settled comfortably into its surroundings.

I had only a moment after Pudge's brief hug before she hustled me into an open great room with high ceilings and soft lighting. The furniture was arranged into groupings, all of it looking well-worn and comfortable, although it was obvious from the wide plank floors and elegant fireplace that no expense had been spared. I had little talent for—or interest in—interior decorating, but it looked to me as if it had probably cost a fortune to create this high-end look of casual comfort.

"Bebe's in the loo. She's been fussing and primping for the past half hour." She raised her glass and tossed back the remains of her wine. "She wants to make a good impression. What are you drinking?" she asked, whirling toward the open kitchen on the far end of the room.

"Just iced tea. Or a diet soda if you have one."

"That's it?" she called, her head in the refrigerator.

I set my bag down next to a buttery leather recliner and followed her. "Yes, that's it."

She turned and raised an eyebrow, and I forced a laugh.

"Remember why you-all added *rum* to my name?"

Pudge had the grace to blush, just a little. "That doesn't mean you can't have a glass of wine to celebrate the old gang getting back together."

"Yes, actually it does."

We stared at each other for a moment before she shrugged and pulled out a pitcher. "Suit yourself."

She was just dropping ice cubes into a tall glass when I sensed movement behind me.

Beatrice Ballantyne Bedford uttered a little shriek and threw her arms around my neck before I had a chance to open my mouth.

"Oh, Bay," she gushed, and I swore I could feel tears dampening the shoulder of my blazer. "Oh, I can't believe it!"

She pushed herself back and dashed her hands across her eyes. Carefully, because I was certain she didn't want to disturb the layer of makeup, eye shadow, and mascara that sat like a mask on her round face. Up close, I could see that all the effort she'd expended hadn't been able to camouflage the crow's feet at her faded brown eyes or the parentheses of discontent that bracketed her mouth.

Bebe hadn't aged well.

"You look marvelous, Bay, absolutely gorgeous! I swear, you two make me feel like an old hag!"

"Nonsense," I said automatically, the lie leaping effortlessly to my lips. "You look just the same."

In a way, it wasn't entirely untrue. Her dark blond hair was still shoulder-length, pulled back into a large clip to lie neatly against her neck. The pressed khakis and shiny penny loafers were certainly just the sort of thing she always wore in school, but now the oxford shirt hung untucked over a slightly bulging midsection, and even the beautifully tailored linen jacket couldn't hide all the pounds she'd accumulated over the past couple of decades. It was sad. Whatever weight Pudge had lost, Bebe seemed to have found.

"Well, now that we've got the bullshitting out of the way . . ." Pudge handed me my glass of tea and reached for a bottle of red wine on the granite countertop. "You need a refill, Beebs?"

She poured for herself and held the bottle poised in mid-air.

"I shouldn't, really," Bebe chirped.

"You're not driving back to Charleston tonight, so why the

hell not?"

"I suppose," she murmured and held out the nearly empty balloon glass. "Just one more little one."

We trooped after Pudge back into the great room where she draped herself across the recliner, her bare feet dangling over the arm. She wore black yoga pants and an oversized pink T-shirt that proudly proclaimed her support of the fight against breast cancer. Maybe that was why she'd decided against a bra. Even so carelessly dressed, she exuded glamour and the kind of self-assurance she'd never possessed in the old days.

Bebe and I took separate overstuffed armchairs. I was just about to get the discussion underway, when Pudge suddenly jumped back up.

"Are you guys chilly? I'm going to light the fire."

She fumbled around in a drawer of the table next to her and came up with a small remote control, which she pointed at the fireplace. A moment later we heard a *whoosh* as the gas ignited, and that sort of sickly smell hovered for just a second. I wasn't sure if I envied her the ease of the process. Although Red and I frequently groused about the whole rigmarole of dealing with paper and kindling, I really loved the ambiance of a real wood fire.

It did feel good, though, and I settled back into the soft cushions. "So tell me about—"

Again Pudge shot out of her chair. "Damnation! I forgot about the food."

Bebe and I exchanged a smile while out in the kitchen we could hear our hostess muttering to herself amid the clang of plates against the stone counters.

"She's always like this when the girls get together," Bebe said in her soft drawl. "For all her New York City sophistication, she still gets flustered when it's just us."

Pudge reappeared carrying a large tray. I'd figured we were in for something along the lines of pickled artichoke hearts and quinoa, but I was delighted to discover my error.

"Hush puppies and honey butter, cheese straws, and those chocolate covered strawberries we used to devour by the pound. I can't believe that little candy store in Beaufort is still there, but it's worth the trip. Dig in."

Pudge popped a strawberry in her mouth and pulled out the naked stem as she once again sprawled into her chair.

We munched and drank in silence for a few minutes, the only conversation centered around the wonderful Lowcountry delicacies. Somewhere in the house a grandfather clock began it's slow tolling of eight notes, and I wondered if it was the same one that had graced her parents' antebellum home in the historic section of Beaufort. Maybe that accounted for the eclectic collection of furniture. I gave a fleeting thought to asking her about it, but we'd been sidetracked by the past long enough.

"So tell me about Mary Alice."

As I spoke, I rose and retrieved my bag from where it sat next to Pudge. I pulled out a legal pad, pen, and the tape recorder.

"You're not going to tape us, are you?" Bebe sounded as if I'd just suggested we go skinny dipping out back in Skull Creek.

"You have a problem with that?" I swiveled my gaze between them. "It's just an adjunct to my taking notes, and that way I can be certain I've gotten all the information down correctly."

Pudge shrugged. "I'm cool with it."

Bebe fidgeted, massaging the fingers of her right hand with her left. "I don't know. It seems so . . . *formal.* Like we were being interrogated by the police."

Her shudder made me wonder if she'd had some real-life experience, but her file hadn't indicated that she had. Maybe her husband?

"I can just take notes if it bothers you that much," I said.

"No, no! You're here to help us . . . I mean, to help Scarlett. You do what you think best."

I skipped the business of naming the participants as I would have done in the office and set the tiny machine on the table between us.

"Okay, who wants to start?"

My two old friends exchanged a glance full of a meaning I couldn't decipher, but neither one spoke.

"Would it help if I asked a few questions first?"

"I think I told you everything I knew yesterday," Pudge said, her voice somber. "I wanted Bebe to verify things so you'd know I wasn't just blowing smoke."

"I never thought that," I said, turning to Bebe. "But it would help if you'd just tell me in your own words why you think I can be of help. Just ignore the recorder."

Again I watched her work her right hand with her left, and I wondered if she was suffering from arthritis or if it was just a nervous habit. I slumped down in the chair and mimicked Pudge by draping one leg over the arm.

"Come on, Bebe, talk to me."

She postponed replying by gulping down the last of her wine, whether for courage or to put me off for a few extra seconds I wasn't sure.

"Well," she said, again shooting Pudge that enigmatic look, "I'm sure you know that we love Scarlett—Mary Alice, that is— like a sister. We only have her best interests at heart."

I nodded and resisted the urge to snap at her to get on with it. If memory served, Bebe could burst into tears at the slightest provocation, and I really wasn't in the mood for histrionics.

"You're worried about her," I prompted.

"Yes, of course we are. All of us. It's just that the others are so far away. It's up to Sylvie and I to carry the banner, so to speak." She looked down at her hands clasped tightly in her lap. "I don't want you to think that we'd just butt into her life like this if we didn't care. We're not gossips. We're her friends."

"Understood." I glanced over at Pudge to find her staring off into the fire as if mesmerized by the flames, and I wondered if she'd checked out of the conversation altogether.

When Bebe didn't continue, I decided enough was enough.

"You two think her husband is beating her. Regularly. And you're concerned for her safety. Does that about sum it up?"

The silence held for a long while before Bebe nodded.

Again I waited, and I was just about to start what could only be classified as Bebe's feared interrogation, when Pudge suddenly slammed her empty wineglass down onto the table.

"James is a monster," she said, staring directly into my eyes. "If we don't do something, one of these days he's going to kill her."

The words hung in the air for a long moment before Bebe burst into tears and bolted from the room.

CHAPTER EIGHT

"She can't help it," Pudge said into the silence. "Her own life's a hot mess."

I remembered the mention in the files of Bebe and her husband's having moved into a condo, but it suddenly occurred to me that I had seen no record of the sale of their large home in downtown Charleston.

"Does she have money trouble?"

Pudge studied me from her perch on the recliner. "What makes you think so?"

I patted the briefcase next me on the floor. "Research."

"You checked them out?"

"I told you I would. It's the first step in almost any investigation. Get to know the players."

She grinned. "Oh, Beebs is going to hate that!" A moment later she cocked an eyebrow at me. "Am I included in your little game of digging up dirt?"

Her snarky tone stung. "Of course. Why? You have something to hide?"

The change in her expression made me wish I'd resisted the urge to fire back. Somehow the evening had already deteriorated into the sort of schoolgirl sniping that used to punctuate our conversation back when we were fourteen. One of us—specifically *me*—needed to rise above.

"I noticed that she and her husband had moved recently. Maybe they're just downsizing."

Pudge dropped her challenging gaze and glanced over her shoulder to where Bebe had disappeared. "Yeah, but not because they wanted to. Ralph is . . . charming, I guess, in an oily sort of way. And unbelievably good-looking. A born con man. He's always got some scheme going that requires large infusions of cash. Usually someone else's. He's hit on a couple of them, but lately he's had a bad run. They had that place on Tradd Street mortgaged to the hilt, and they lost it last year to the bank." She sighed. "Poor Beebs was devastated. She loved that old place, even if it was a constant money pit."

"Is what he does legal? I mean, is there any chance——?"

I broke off when Bebe, patting the end of her delicate nose with a tissue, moved cautiously back into the great room.

"I'm sorry," I said immediately. "The last thing I want to do is upset you-all. I really do want to help."

Bebe rewarded me with a beaming smile, and for a moment I was taken aback by how much of the skittish girl still remained in her creased, puffy face.

"Ignore me, Bay honey. We're here for Scarlett. You just ask any old thing you want. Lord knows at my age it's time I grew a backbone."

Pudge reached for her hand and gave it a squeeze as she settled once again into her chair.

"Okay," I said. "Tell me about these injuries you've observed. Where? How many? How serious? Are we talking an occasional black eye or something worse?"

Pudge swung her long, elegant legs around and planted them firmly on the floor. "Lots of bruises—arms, neck, shoulders. Even when it's ninety outside she wears long-sleeved tops. But I've made it a point over the past couple of years to catch her coming out of the shower. I swear, Bay, she's got marks all over her body."

"And last summer she had a badly sprained wrist. She made the weekend, but it was so painful I had to brush her hair for her." Bebe dabbed at the end of her nose again. "And the year before that she had a broken collar bone." She lifted her chin. "Now you have to remember how much she loved her dance classes. There's no way she suddenly got so clumsy she started falling down stairs and running into walls so often. She really wanted to be a ballerina, you know, but her daddy wasn't havin' it."

I was surprised by the vehemence of Bebe's outburst, and astounded when she added, almost under her breath, "Mean old bastard."

"Way to go Beebs!" Pudge crowed, and we all laughed.

"Well, I'm sorry, but he was." Bebe preened a little under our appreciation for her daring. "He had his sights set on James for her from the second she was born, and we all knew it. Even her mama wasn't all that keen on the match, but she never had much to say about anything that went on in that house."

It was a strange remark and one I wanted to explore, but just then music began to blare somewhere in the direction of the kitchen. It took me a minute to recognize the tune: Cyndi Lauper's *Girls Just Want to Have Fun.*

Pudge shot out of the chair muttering, "Oh, damn," and marched off across the heart pine floor.

Bebe and I exchanged a look. "It's Annie," she said with just a hint of disapproval in her voice. "That's her ring."

Annie. Anne Elizabeth Gilchrist, I thought. New York socialite, divorced, one daughter. There'd been more in the file, but I hadn't really spent much time on her. I thought about pulling the folder out of my briefcase, but I didn't want to spook Bebe any more than she already was.

Pudge walked slowly back into the room, her iPhone held tightly against her ear and a frown on her lovely face.

"Of course there's room," she said, rather crossly I thought. "Why the hell wouldn't there be?"

As she listened to the response, her scowl deepened. "Where the hell are you?"

A moment later she laughed, that loud bray that made Bebe and me both break into smiles. "Well get your bony butt in here, right this minute, you hear me?"

She tossed the phone onto the recliner and moved toward the foyer. "Company," she called over her shoulder as she flung open the front door, and one of the most shockingly thin women I'd ever seen glided into her embrace.

"I know I should have called first," the woman said in what I took to be the upper crust version of the usually harsh New York accent, "but what are friends for if you can't just descend on them with no warning?"

"How long have you been lurking out there?" Pudge threw her arm around the pitifully narrow shoulders and guided her guest into the room. "Anne Elizabeth Gilchrist, Lydia Baynard Simpson Tanner. Affectionately known as Bay."

I stood and held out my hand. "Very nice to meet you."

She hesitated a moment before allowing her claw-like fingers to brush against mine. "How lovely," she murmured, then turned to where Bebe had remained seated. "Beatrice. How nice to see you again."

"Annie."

I could tell the use of her nickname irritated the newcomer, and I was surprised to see a small smirk of triumph on Bebe's face. *Undercurrents here*, I thought. *Interesting*.

Anne removed the beautiful cashmere shawl that nearly covered her and draped it carelessly over the back of the recliner. Her unnaturally black hair was cut in a severe style that accentuated her sharp facial bones and hollow cheeks. Her makeup had been applied by an expert, but it failed to hide the deep, dark circles under her startling blue eyes. They seemed so out of keeping with the rest of her coloring, I wondered if they might be contacts.

"Drink?" Pudge asked into the growing silence.

"Darling, of course! And quickly. I am absolutely exhausted." To prove the point, she folded herself into the chair Pudge had been occupying. She glanced languidly across at me. "I couldn't get a direct flight, not in first class, so I had to change in Atlanta. I absolutely abhor that airport! So many people, and those hideous trams they force you to take. Packed in like sardines. It's barbaric."

"Welcome to the real world," Bebe said, making no effort to disguise her contempt.

"Well, of course, I understand that's how *most* people travel, but if you're used to things being a little more *civilized* . . ."

Bebe blushed, and I realized she'd probably been losing this war of words for a long time now. But I had to give her credit. She took one more shot.

"Maybe you should have held onto Devon and his private plane."

"Is it my fault Sylvie decided to create her pied-a-terre in this backwater? It was so lovely when we had our get-togethers in New York."

Thankfully Pudge interrupted what might have turned into a hair-pulling melee by handing a champagne flute to her newest guest. "You might want to think about replenishing your stash," she said, folding herself gracefully onto the floor at my feet.

"That's the last bottle."

"Tomorrow," Anne said and downed a third of the glass in one long swallow. "Ah, bliss." Her eyes darted among us. "So what's going on here? Did someone call a meeting of the sister-hood?" She narrowed her gaze on me. "And do we have a new member?"

"No and no," Pudge answered. "It's a long story." She glanced up and caught my eye. "Do you want to fill her in, Bay?"

I wasn't certain why it should fall to me to explain the situation to this unpleasant beanpole of a woman, but I nodded. "Sure," I began. "Pudge—"

"Oh no, not you too?" Anne interrupted me. "Sylvie, make them stop using that horrible nickname for you." Her attention swiveled back to me. "This woman was the top fashion model in New York—maybe in the *world*—for longer than anyone in his-tory, with the possible exception of Heidi Klum and Tyra Banks. She was named the most beautiful face in America by *Couture* three times. Three! And even at her age she makes most other women look like absolute frumps by—"

"Enough!" Pudge softened the interruption with a laugh. "Come on, Annie, give it up. These two have known me since I looked like the Pillsbury Doughboy. We went through pimples and training bras together. They can call me whatever they damn well please."

Even Anne Elizabeth Gilchrist's snort was elegant. "If you say so, darling. I just feel as if proper respect should be paid to your accomplishments."

"Thanks, but I don't need a cheerleader." Pudge pushed her-self to her feet. "And I'm not sure being born with an acceptable face really qualifies as an accomplishment." She stretched. "After all, I had absolutely nothing to do with it."

Before the brittle woman could mount an argument, Bebe rose from her chair. "I suppose you have enough luggage to last a month or two. I'm ready for bed. Do you need any help?"

I was certain the offer had been made out of politeness and not from any sincere desire to be of service. Besides, from the look of the bony wrists sticking out from the sleeves of the cream-y cashmere sweater, Anne would have difficulty lifting anything heavier than her glass of champagne.

"How thoughtful," Anne responded, a little of the ice melting from her voice. "Just four bags. This was a spur of the moment lark, so I didn't have time to plan in any detail. I asked the limo driver to leave them by the front door."

Pudge laughed, and I had to smile. I could picture the horror the driver must have felt when he saw the narrow lane down which he had to negotiate his long, unwieldy vehicle. Not to mention turning around so he could head out.

"I should be going," I said, torn between wanting to continue the thwarted conversation about Mary Alice and my growing desire to escape the unsettling atmosphere created by the arrival of the third member of the *sisterhood*. I made a mental note to ask Pudge about that strange appellation when I had a chance to talk to her alone. Maybe Red hadn't been so far off in his assessment, I thought as I gathered up my briefcase. I suddenly realized that the tape recorder had been running the entire time, and I turned my back on Anne as I scooped it up and dropped it into the pocket of my blazer. I wouldn't mind going back over the exchanges of the past half hour when I could give it my undivided attention.

Red would have a field day.

"So nice to have met you," I said, nodding in Anne's direction.

She forced a semblance of a smile. "Yes, you, too, of course. I trust we'll meet again."

"Oh, you can pretty much count on that," Pudge said with a grin. "Come on, Bay, I'll walk you out."

I sidestepped the matching Louis Vuitton luggage and turned to Pudge. "Thanks for arranging this," I said.

"Not much accomplished, I'm afraid," she answered, leaning against the railing. "I had no idea Annie would show up out of the blue."

I cast a quick look toward the door which stood slightly ajar. "She and Bebe don't get along?"

Pudge snorted. "You think? Actually, once they get the sniping out of the way, they do all right. Annie is loaded. Her first husband was a lot older and died suddenly a few years ago. He's the father of her daughter. Devon had the bucks, and she latched onto him almost before poor George was in the ground. Unfortunately, he had difficulty keeping his pants zipped, and she took him to the cleaners in the divorce." She touched a bare toe to one of the elegant bags. "Thus all this, and the first class stuff and the attitude. Underneath it all she's just scared that it will all go away, and she'll end up back where she started."

"Very insightful. I take it you've known her a long time?"

"I used to model for one her favorite couturiers. She bought almost everything I wore, so that was the start of it."

"Darling, are you coming back soon?" Anne's voice drifted out the partially open door. "I really need my bag with the meds. I have a splitting headache."

Pudge smiled. "Hostess duty calls. So what happens now?"

"Is there some way the three of us can get together and finish our conversation? I still have questions, and I can't proceed in any meaningful way until you give me some place to start."

Pudge hesitated. "I have an idea," she said, "but it may not pan out. Give me until tomorrow evening, and I'll call you. We definitely want some resolution to this mess. I don't want the next time we get together to be at Scarlett's funeral."

I cringed at her statement, but she seemed convinced she was right. Based on what little information I'd been able to glean before Anne barged in, they had valid reason to be concerned. I'd just have to wait and see what Pudge's plan turned out to be.

"Sylvie? Did you hear me?" The plaintive voice floated out into the still night air.

"I'll wait then to hear from you," I said, turning toward the steps. "Thanks again."

"You might want to wait on that," Pudge said enigmatically before she hefted a bag in each hand and pushed open the door with her hip. "You could end up cursing me instead."

CHAPTER NINE

I found Red sound asleep on the sofa, the TV blaring a college basketball game.

Gently I lifted the remote from where it lay on his lap, and he stirred. I muted the sound but left the video on the screen, and he settled back into his steady breathing. I carried my briefcase into the bedroom, exchanged clothes for pajamas, and emptied everything out onto the desk. I had just rewound the tape when my husband appeared in the doorway.

His rumpled hair stood out in several places, and he rubbed the stubble on his chin. "I didn't hear you come in."

I smiled. "I know. I just got home a few minutes ago."

"I guess I dozed off."

"Alert the media. Man falls asleep watching television."

Red stretched and yawned widely. He padded over, planted a kiss on the back of my neck, and flopped down onto the duvet. "So how did it go?"

I shuffled everything into a pile and flipped off the desk lamp. "So-so. Why don't we leave it until tomorrow when I can have the benefit of your entire brain?"

"I'm okay."

I reached over and ruffled his spiky hair. "It can wait. I'm going to brush my teeth."

In the intervening five minutes, Red had stripped down to his shorts, climbed under the covers, and was fast asleep. I smiled as I eased in beside him. It always amazed me how he could go from semi-coherent conversation to completely zonked out in a matter of seconds. I usually read before turning out the light, but the new Inspector Gamache lay closed on the bedside table. Too much on my mind, which would translate into a restless night if my customary pattern was anything to go by.

I bunched a couple of pillows up behind my head and let my

mind drift back to the strange evening. While I firmly believe that most people grow and change over time, I also knew that basic personalities, well established by the time puberty hit, really didn't alter all that much. We acquired whatever veneer was necessitated by our jobs and peripheral relationships, and often did our best to hide the real *us*. If you were lucky, you found someone who could see past all that and love and accept you for who you really were, warts and all. I let my hand rest on Red's shoulder for a moment. I had been fortunate. Twice.

But it was easy to see that the same insecurities and strengths that had marked us out as teenagers still lurked behind the pseudo-sophistication and polish we'd acquired—or manufactured —over the past couple of decades. Of course, I hadn't known Anne Gilchrist in her youth, but Pudge's words seemed to confirm my basic philosophy.

I scootched down a little and pulled the covers up over my shoulders. I wondered again what the obviously anorexic woman had meant by "sisterhood." It was a relatively innocuous term on its own, but the way in which she'd said it . . . I couldn't put into words why her tone and inflection had engendered in me a feeling of unease, except that it had. I turned onto my side, feeling the tug of weariness. I thought about the things I needed to do in the morning, including a little more digging, especially on Bebe's finances. I'd have Erik— My eyes popped open as I remembered our conversation and how his absence would affect not only the agency but my own sense of wellbeing. We'd been together longer than Red and I had, building the business from ground zero to something we were both quite proud of. I refused to think about running it without him, at least for any longer than his promised two weeks.

I felt my eyelids drifting closed and gave myself up to it. Tomorrow . . .

It was hard to imagine a more perfect day in the Lowcountry. Or anywhere else, for that matter.

A rich blue sky, unmarred by even the hint of a cloud, the sun bathing everything in a soft glow. Everywhere I looked on the short drive from my home in Port Royal Plantation to the office just outside Indigo Run the plantings were flourishing. Bright bursts of color mingled with the fresh green of grass and leaf. I put down all the windows in the Jaguar and inhaled the sweetness of the light breeze that smelled of spring and the ocean.

I'd had a surprisingly uninterrupted night, and if I'd dreamed I had no recollection. Red had been up before me and had even started breakfast. I glanced in the rearview mirror to find his restored Ford Bronco right on my tail. I waved, but I wasn't sure he saw me.

A moment later we pulled into the parking lot and our usual adjacent spaces.

"Is this an unbelievable morning or what?" I asked, levering myself up out of the low-slung car.

"Wanna play hooky?" my husband replied with a grin.

"Don't tempt me." I locked the car and caught up with him at the door to the office.

"Last chance."

Inside we found our customary Starbucks cups on Sharese's desk and picked them up as we passed. "Good morning," I said, moving toward my office until Erik's absence finally registered, and I stopped short.

I whirled back toward Sharese. "Did he call?"

"Oh, yes, ma'am," she said, and my heart began beating again. "He said he had some errands and that he'd be a couple of minutes late."

As if on cue, the outer door opened, and my partner strode in. "Sorry. Did I miss anything?"

The world righted itself, and I cautioned myself that his not sitting hunched over his keyboard would be something I'd have to get used to. For a while.

"Not a problem," I said and continued to my desk.

Red followed and settled into one of the client chairs. "Are we going to talk about what went down at your little get-together last night?"

I nodded. "Let Erik get organized. I'd like him in on this as well. But there's something we need to discuss first."

With as little embellishment and emotion as possible, I told him about my partner's decision to take a sabbatical and try to resolve things with Stephanie. Red nodded throughout my brief recitation.

"I think it's a good plan. For him, I mean. You've said

enough times that he doesn't seem to be getting over her. Maybe if they hash it out face to face he can get some closure."

"You seem pretty sure he's not going to be able to talk her out of it."

"I am. Seriously, can you see her coming back here and just taking up as if none of it ever happened? You wouldn't want her, in the office I mean, would you?"

I shook my head. "No way. Trust is something you can't just turn on and off like a faucet. Besides, I'm really happy with Sharese, aren't you?"

"Absolutely."

"Erik's going to work with her for the next couple of days to get her up to speed on some of the things he does. I know it won't be the same as having him here, but I think she'll be up to the challenge."

"And it's not as if he's going to Outer Mongolia," my husband said with a grin. "I believe they have Internet access and cell towers in Arizona."

I smiled back. "You could be right." Then I sobered. "He and I also discussed getting back into business with Alex Finch." I saw his shoulders tense and hurried on. "Look, Red, the bottom line—and I mean the *literal* bottom line—is that we could use the income. And just because we're dealing with accused criminals or battered wives doesn't mean that it has to be dangerous. We can pick and choose. Most of it will probably be just boring stuff anyway, but Alex and Claudia always pay on time and never squawk about the bill."

I waited for an outburst that never came.

Surprisingly calmly my husband said, "I can see where you're coming from. You're right, this is a business. It has to make a profit. I don't have any problem with working with the ladies again." He pointed an index finger in my direction. "But you need to promise me you'll take it easy. That's all I really care about. *You're* all I really care about."

I stuck out my hand. "Deal."

We shook, and I felt myself relax.

"So how about last night?" he asked. "You didn't sound thrilled about how it went."

I pulled the recorder from my bag and set it on the desk. "Complications." I lifted the phone and buzzed Sharese. "Will you and Erik please come in?"

"Both of us?"

"Yes. I think it's time you got your feet wet. Metaphorically speaking, of course."

"Yes, *ma'am!*" she nearly shouted, and Red and I exchanged a smile.

Erik brought in an extra chair, and I had to admit it seemed like old times with all four of us ranged around my desk. True, one of the players had changed, but I felt as if that was a good thing. If my partner managed to convince Stephanie Wyler to give in and marry him, I'd have to make the best of it. My biggest fear was that, as Red had suggested, she might not want to come back to the island, not after everything that had happened. Which could mean Erik would be making his home in the desert, and *that* I couldn't let myself contemplate.

I realized the three of them were all waiting for me to get the show on the road. I cleared my throat and gave them a thumbnail of the events at Jordan Point the night before, then clicked on the recorder. The men settled back to listen, but Sharese had her iPad in her lap and was taking notes. I let the tape run to its conclusion and held out my hand to invite comment.

"You had some strange friends." Red was shaking his head as he spoke. "Weirder than I thought just from looking at the files."

"I'm guessing you want me to dig a little deeper," Erik said, "especially on Mrs. Bedford. Her husband sounds like the kind of guy who might have skated a little too close to the edge. I didn't check any of them—the men—for criminal records. Except for the Stuart guy."

I nodded. "Exactly. Also the Bedford finances. Pudge said they'd been foreclosed on, so that should be easy enough to track down. Maybe these additional searches will provide a good way to get Sharese some practice."

"Ma'am?" Her voice sounded both hopeful and wary at the same time.

"Erik has to be away for a couple of weeks, starting on Monday, and I'd like you to take a crash course in some of his search methods." I swiveled my gaze to my partner. "I'm assuming you'll be available for consultation while you're gone?"

""Sure. I plan to check in every couple of days to see if you need anything." He turned toward Sharese. "You've got a really good grasp of the kinds of information we usually need, and all I have to do is show you some shortcuts and a couple of tricks for getting around any roadblocks you encounter. And you keyboard so much faster than I do. It'll be a piece of cake."

She beamed. "Thank you, thank you *so* much! I really want to learn everything. I want to be a real part of the agency, a real help to all of you." Her breath came in short gasps. "Oh, God, I'm so excited!"

Red laughed, and Erik and I exchanged a grin.

"Mind you, a lot of it's boring, too," I said. "And confidentiality, especially with your increased access to sensitive information, is especially critical. You don't talk about anything client related to anyone. And that includes Byron."

"Yes, ma'am, I understand that. I signed that agreement when I first came to work here, and I've honored it. I swear."

"I believe that, otherwise you wouldn't still be here." I softened the implied threat with a smile. "Now, I'm kind of stuck until I hear back from Pudge about this so-called plan she has, so I'm going to run some personal errands myself after I check out a couple things. Anyone need me for anything?"

Three heads shook in unison. "Okay, let's get to it."

The two young people hurried off, their heads together over the game plan for Sharese's training, I guessed.

Red stood and stretched. "I'm sort of at loose ends myself," he said. "Any of these errands I can help with?"

"No thanks. If you're up for it, I'd like you to take another look at the Tennyson business." I picked up a pink message slip from the top of my desk. "She called this morning."

"You didn't want to discuss it with the others?"

"No, I want them concentrating on getting Sharese up to speed on the computer stuff. I'm going to take a quick look at it, but I hoped you'd give it a good going over. Erik has exhausted his searches for the gardener. If he's illegal, he's probably moved on to somewhere else, maybe using another name. One of the things I want to do this morning is to speak with Dolores, see if she's ever heard of him." I checked my watch. "She should be at the house by now. Then I think I'll call Neddie and see if she's free for lunch."

"Julia?"

"Yeah. But if you'd go over all the details one more time I'll feel better about telling Mrs. Tennyson we can't help her any further. We both know it was probably her own kid—he and his friends—who emptied her wallet, and she's never going to accept it. If you give me the okay, I'll call her tomorrow and blow her off."

"Sounds like a plan, honey."

"Call me on my cell if anything comes up. I'll catch up with you later here or at home if I'm running late. Jump and Phil's tonight?"

"You got it."

I swiveled around when he left and gazed out the window at the bright sunlight sparkling off the shiny leaves of the shrubs that lined the side of the building. Too nice a day to be inside. I quickly booted up my laptop, scribbled a few notes, and stuffed them into my briefcase. In less than ten minutes I was outside, breathing in the soft spring air, and thinking that maybe things were going to work out, on a number of fronts. I stepped around in front of the Jaguar, glanced over my shoulder to make sure I wasn't being observed, and knocked on the trunk of one of the towering crape myrtles that flanked the parking lot.

No use flying in the face of fate, I thought.

Of course, as events unfolded, it had been a complete waste of time.

CHAPTER
TEN

"Dolores, it's me," I called as I dropped my bag on the floor just inside the foyer.

The garage door had been closed, so I'd used the short steps in the front. I could hear the whine of the vacuum cleaner in the back of the house as I let myself in. Up in the kitchen, I poured myself a glass of iced tea from the bottomless pitcher. The thought made me smile. Dolores had come to me after I'd been released from the hospital. The physical injuries I'd suffered as a witness to the explosion of my first husband's sabotaged small plane had healed to some extent by that time, but the mental anguish nearly overwhelmed me. Dolores Santiago had been nurse, companion, housekeeper, cook, and one of the staunchest friends I would ever have the good fortune to acquire. She had—both literally and figuratively—saved my life.

Silence abruptly descended, and I carried my glass down into the dining area. "Dolores, don't get spooked! It's only me."

A moment later the diminutive woman, her warm brown skin glistening from her efforts, bustled down the hallway.

"Ah, Señora, you are here! Is there the *problema?*"

"No, nothing's wrong, my friend. I just wanted to ask you about something. Well, some*one*, actually. Would you like some tea?"

"*Sí, gracias.* I get."

She hated being waited on, especially by me, so I let her pour herself a glass.

"Let's go out on the deck. It's a glorious day."

She followed me through the French doors without comment, waiting until I had sprawled myself on one of the chaises before taking one of the Adirondack chairs. She was so tiny her feet dangled a couple of inches off the deck boards, but she smoothed the skirt of her apron and regarded me with interest.

"I want to run a name by you. I don't know why I didn't think of it before this, but there have been a lot of things going on at the office."

"*Sí?*"

"I hope it won't be upsetting to you."

Dolores and her family, especially her husband Hector, had been involved in a clash with ICE, the immigration people, a while back. It appeared that everything had been resolved, thanks in part to the attorney I'd hired to represent them. I didn't want to dredge up any bad memories, but one thing I'd learned from that unfortunate incident was that the Latino population on the island kept pretty good track of one another.

"No, Señora. You ask."

"I'm trying to locate someone, an Hispanic man who works —well, worked—for a woman over on Bram's Point. Since Hector operates a landscaping business, I thought maybe you might have run into him."

Dolores continued to study me with her huge dark eyes. "This man, he has the trouble?"

I'd always done my best to be scrupulously honest with this sweet woman. "He's accused of something, but I don't think he did it. If I could talk to him, I might be able to make the whole thing go away."

"His name?"

"Manuel Cruz. He worked part-time for a woman named Tennyson. Isabel Tennyson."

"I do not know these names. I ask Hector."

"Great! Remember, I only want to talk to him. It won't involve the authorities, at least not at this point." I made sure I had her eyes locked on mine. "But if he's guilty, then I'll have to turn him over to the sheriff. I want to be very clear about that."

"I understand." She scooted forward until her small feet reached the floor. "You like the lunch? I can make."

"Thanks," I said, rising as well, "but I've got some things to do. You can leave me a note if you find out anything. Or call my cell number. It's on the pad by the telephone. I really appreciate it."

"*De nada*, Señora." She followed me to the front door. As I reached for my bag, she said, "You eat, yes?"

I laughed. Dolores had spent the entire length of our relationship trying to fatten me up. I thought about Anne Gilchrist and wondered what my friend would make of *her*.

"Yes, I'll grab something, promise. Thanks again."

She picked up the glass where I'd set it on the table and wiped away an imaginary speck of dust. "*Sí*, Señora," she said, her voice dripping with skepticism as I trotted down the steps.

I had to settle for a brief and entirely unsatisfactory conversation with Neddie Halloran as I sat in the Jaguar in my driveway. She intended to eat lunch at her desk, preparing for an especially sensitive case arriving in the early afternoon. She was completely swamped, her assistant said, but I bullied my way into stealing five minutes of her time between patients. She'd seemed distracted and not much interested in discussing my fears about Julia and the wisdom of continuing to allow her free run of Presqu'isle.

"What do you expect me to do?" she asked amid the rustling of papers in the background. "I can't exactly lock her in her room."

"I can," I said with a hint of a laugh.

"Against the law," she said. "Not to mention a really bad idea."

I heard the murmur of voices and realized she had put her hand over the receiver.

"Neddie?"

"Yes, fine. Sorry, Bay. It's just a zoo around here this morning."

"Well, I know you give me the old college roommate hourly rate, but I'm a paying customer, too."

"Don't get pissy. I'll be happy to discuss your concerns about Julia's behavior, but this isn't the time. What have you got going this weekend? I'll be at the condo late tomorrow night."

Neddie had recently purchased a fabulous oceanfront unit at the Sea Cloisters off Folly Field Road. She drove up from Savannah most weekends unless the weather was lousy, which it had been for most of January and February. The unusually cold, rainy winter had us all panting for the kind of days we'd been blessed with so far in March.

"I don't know. The kids, of course, on Saturday. Want to come to dinner?"

"Maybe. Can I let you know?"

"Of course. It won't be anything fancy. Probably throw something on the grill."

"I'll call you."

"Hot date?" I asked with a smile in my voice. After her divorce, Neddie had reclaimed both her name and her independence, but she'd been wary of getting involved again. There'd been a series of short-term flings, but nothing serious.

"Maybe," she said, almost distractedly, and my radar began pinging.

"Anything I should know about?"

"Listen, I have to run. I'll call you Friday night or Saturday morning. In the meantime, lighten up a little on Julia. Give her some space and let me work my magic. Bye."

I listened for a moment to the silence before clicking off my cell.

So much for that.

I debated whether or not to head back to the office, maybe hunt down Red and see what he was doing for lunch. I told myself I probably should drive over to Presqu'isle and scope out the situation there, but Neddie's advice to back off for a while seemed worth heeding. At least for the time being.

I drummed my fingers on the steering wheel, glancing from the driveway back up toward the bay window in the kitchen. Dolores would fix me something, I knew, but I wasn't really hungry yet. I searched through the contact list on my phone and pushed the Talk button.

"Finch Law Firm," the brisk voice responded after one ring.

"Bay Tanner for Alex Finch, please."

"One moment."

The wait was minimal.

"Bay? Hey, it's Claudia. Alex is in court this morning. It's good to hear from you."

"It's been a while. How's everything?"

"Fine. You know how it is. As long as there are bad guys and slimeball husbands, we're cracking right along."

I laughed. "I hear that. I wondered if you had any time to see me this morning. I have a couple of things I need to discuss."

"Case things?"

"Sort of. I need to pick your brain." I paused. "And I thought you might have something for us as well."

The hesitation was brief, but significant. "We don't at the moment, but do I take you to mean that you'd be willing to help us out in the future?"

"Yes, we would. If you're still interested in retaining our services."

"Oh, I'm sure we are. Of course, that's ultimately Alex's call, but I know she's missed being able to shoot some of the background and leg work over to you-all. I'll talk to her this afternoon when she gets back. I think you can count on hearing from us quite quickly."

I let out the little breath I'd been holding. "That's great. I appreciate it."

"But you said something about a case?" I heard the ruffling of paper. "I could meet you, say, around two? Or are you free for lunch? I was just going to grab some Chinese and bring it back here, but I'd be glad to meet you somewhere."

"That would be great. How about Crazy Crab? In an hour or so?"

"Perfect. See you there."

I clicked off, happy to have two items on my agenda taken care of in one shot. In the meantime, I had an hour to waste. I inhaled deeply of the warm air drifting in off the ocean and decided playing hooky was exactly what was called for.

I left the car where it was and skirted the house to the boardwalk that floated over the dunes toward the ocean. Sea oats waved beside me as I made my way down onto the beach. The tide was coming in, but there was still plenty of hard-packed sand. I left my shoes alongside the steps and set off on a leisurely stroll accompanied by the rhythmic *shush* of the soft rollers and the occasional sharp screech of a gull.

The Crazy Crab restaurant sits alongside Jarvis Creek overlooking the wide marshes on the north end of the island. The original old single-story building had burned a long time ago, and its replacement rose above several steps onto a wide verandah that encircled the place and provided breathtaking views. I spotted Claudia Darling at an outside table in the sun and made my way around to join her.

"This okay?" she asked after we'd exchanged greetings. "I hate being cooped up inside when the weather is this fabulous."

"Finally," I said. "For a while there last month I thought I was back at Northwestern. Except for the snow, of course."

"How did you stand it?"

"The cold? You get used to it, after a while."

I flashed back to a similar conversation Stephanie Wyler and I had had, back before she'd come to work for us. She'd spent most of her life in and around New York City, and her introduction to the Lowcountry had come in the sweltering middle of July. I suppressed a pang of regret for how things had turned out for her. And her father.

We ordered and sat back, both of us turning our faces up to the warmth.

"Ah, that feels good," Claudia murmured. Her long brown hair hung loosely down her back, and in the brilliant sunlight I noticed a few strands of gray. Lately I'd acquired a lot of experience in spotting them in my own mirror.

"So business is good?" I asked, shrugging out of my jacket and draping it over the back of the chair.

"Very. Alex has won a couple of high-profile cases lately, so that always draws in new clients."

"She got that woman off who was accused of embezzling from her employer, didn't she? I read about it in the *Packet*."

"Yeah, that was one she could have used your expertise on, but she's been hesitant about calling you."

I flushed a little at the implied criticism, but I had to admit it was warranted.

"After that whole thing last fall, we—*I*—felt as if we all needed a break."

"I read about it. So sad. My aunt is suffering from Alzheimer's, and my mother does her best to help out, but it's getting too much for all of them, including my uncle. It seems so unfair that a debilitating disease like that strikes when people are already vulnerable just from the process of getting older."

I nodded, happy when the server interrupted us with the arrival of our food. Even after several months, recalling the kindly, confused face of Malcolm St. John still made me sad.

Over my fried shrimp sandwich and Claudia's grouper, we made small talk, mostly about some of the changes being wrought on the island. Too much building, we both agreed, and we lamented the demise of the Mall at Shelter Cove.

"It was nice to have somewhere enclosed where you could wander around on rainy days," she said, sitting back in her chair.

"I know. Although thankfully Belk's is still there. I hate the idea of having to trek off-island to the outlet places."

"They're so spread out you have to wear your running shoes, but I have to admit there are some wonderful bargains."

We fell silent while the table was cleared, and both of us reached for our bags.

"My treat," I said, slapping my American Express card down on the table.

"Thanks. What was it you wanted to ask about? You mentioned a case."

"Right." I smiled at our server as he whisked my card away. "Just some general information, at least for the moment. It's about domestic abuse."

"I hate that term! We encounter so much of it, as you can imagine, since we specialize in women's issues. Most of the time it's assault, pure and simple. I mean, if a man came up to some stranger on the street and slapped her around, he'd be in jail so fast it would make your head spin. Somehow, it's not viewed as so heinous when the woman is his wife or girlfriend. Calling it *domestic* makes it sound almost benign."

"But isn't part of the problem that the women won't press charges?"

"Absolutely. And that's what complicates things for us when something really nasty goes down—broken bones, concussion. Even attempted murder. We spend a lot of our time trying to convince our clients that it isn't going to stop unless they have the courage to take—"

The waiter returned with the check for me to sign, and Claudia finished off her iced tea while I took care of business. I tucked the receipt into my bag along with my card.

"You were saying?"

She smiled. "Sorry for the rant. I get fired up on this issue way too often, as Alex will attest. I just never understand how a woman can allow herself to be turned into a punching bag and then keep letting the bastard back into her life."

"I suppose there's some twisted psychological aspect to it,

but I agree. Someone would lay hands on me one time, and he'd never get the opportunity to do it again."

Claudia snorted. "If Ray ever tried it, he'd be auditioning for the Vienna Boys' Choir."

I had been in the process of finishing off my own tea, and I nearly spewed it across the table. "Good one," I said between coughs and sputters.

"You okay?"

I nodded and wiped my face with my napkin. "So here's what I wanted to ask you about. Let's say—hypothetically—that a woman lives in another state with her husband, but they spend a lot of time here on the island. There's a strong suspicion by her friends that's she's being battered. What's the jurisdictional status? I mean, if she wanted to prosecute him, would she have to prove in which state the abuse took place?"

"There's no reason she couldn't press charges in either jurisdiction, providing she called the cops right at the moment the abuse happens. I mean, if she's at home or here, the local authorities would have the right to arrest and prosecute, at least for the crime that occurred at that time."

"Makes sense. So what about the pattern, some of it in one state and some in another?"

"That probably wouldn't come into it unless it went to trial. It would mostly affect sentencing—or lack thereof, as is too often the case."

"It might not be an issue, but I like to have as much information as possible going in," I said.

"Well, we'll be glad to partner with you if this *hypothetical* client needs representation. If it comes to a divorce, though, that would have to be in her legal place of residence."

"Got it." I pushed back my chair. "Thanks so much for all your help. I'll let you get back to work."

"No problem. I know Alex will be thrilled that you and the agency are available again. I'm sure we'll be in touch soon."

I followed her slim back around the verandah and down the steps.

"Thanks for lunch, by the way," Claudia called as she stepped up into her big SUV.

"My pleasure."

I watched her pull out onto 278 before I slid into the Jaguar.

It was on days like this one that I missed my old convertible. I recalled the Audi parked in the driveway in front of Pudge's place on Jordan Point, and I wondered if it was hers. But she'd said Bebe was driving down from Charleston, so I'd guess it would belong to her and her husband, although it was hard to imagine how they'd let their home be foreclosed on and still managed to hold onto a car that had to retail for, at a guess, somewhere around sixty grand. Maybe it was a lease. In any case, the speculation spurred me back to the office in the hope that Erik had been able to scare up some additional information on that front.

And what the hell was taking Pudge so long to come up with her so-called plan? Talking with Claudia had made me eager to get to the bottom of Mary Alice's problem, to begin priming her to kick James's aristocratic butt to the curb.

My cell rang just as I pulled into the driveway, and I managed to pick it up and maneuver into my parking space without mishap.

"Hey, it's me."

"Pudge?"

"Of course. Don't you check your caller ID?"

"Not when I'm driving."

"Oops, sorry."

"No problem. I'm in the lot in front of the office now. What's up?"

She sounded less chipper, less confident, than at any time since we'd renewed our acquaintance a few days before.

"I think I have this all set up, but keep in mind that it could blow up in my face with very little effort. Everyone says they're on board, and I've taken care of the tickets for Gill and Jen. It's just such short notice that it wouldn't surprise me if one or both of them backed out at the last minute."

I opened the car door and swung my legs out, letting the sunshine bathe me in its warmth while I sorted through Pudge's rambling. Gillian McDonald and Jenny Carson were apparently coming to town, courtesy of my old friend's generosity in footing their plane fares, which because of booking at the last minute must have cost a fortune. I figured I knew what was coming next.

"And Mary Alice?" I asked, reaching back for my bag and slinging it over my shoulder as I stood.

"You're quick. I like that in my PI," she said with a laugh. Her next words belied her attempt at humor. "Yes. I confirmed that she and the monster are coming down for the weekend. As usual, he's entertaining some corporate bigwigs on the boat on Saturday, so she'll bunk in with me that night. They'll sleep on the boat on Friday. Annie's already here, and Beebs is staying on." She paused. "Now all we need is you. I thought maybe you could stay over, too. I have plenty of room. That way we can all hash this out and come up with a plan."

I sighed, wondering what Red would make of my joining the middle-aged version of a sleepover, but that wasn't the real issue.

"I'm not sure it's a good idea to have so many . . . I don't know, irons in the fire? Cooks in the kitchen? I pretty much work alone, Pudge, no offense. I know you all have the best of intentions, but all I really need is some background. I can take it from there."

I paused when she didn't respond.

"So that's a no? I went to all this expense and trouble for nothin'?"

I almost smiled at how the hint of a drawl had crept back into her carefully constructed sophistication. I stood outside the door to the agency, basking in the warmth of the waning sun, and gave it some thought. I reminded myself that Pudge, old friendship or not, was footing the bill.

"No, not exactly," I finally said. "I guess I could meet with everyone, hear what they have to say. And you and I can then discuss what's the best direction to take. Would that work for you?"

"I suppose. So you'll come? And stay the night?"

What the hell, I thought. *In for a penny . . .*

"What time should I show up?" I asked, and my old friend let out a resounding, "Yes!"

CHAPTER
ELEVEN

I pulled open the door to the agency still pondering on how to break the news to my husband that he would be on his own again, at least for Friday night. I had no idea if my participation would spill over into Saturday, but the possibility existed. I didn't think he'd have any problem dealing with the kids. If this weather continued, they'd be happy to spend the entire day on the beach right outside our back door. And pizza or burgers on the grill would be more than okay with all of them. I made a mental note to get in touch with Neddie to postpone my dinner invitation, just in case I got held up.

I greeted Sharese and Erik, both of them huddled at his desk.

"Any luck on the Bedfords?" I asked on my way into my office. I paused and turned back when no one responded. "Hello? Is anyone home?"

Erik nudged Sharese. "Go ahead. You found the information."

She nodded. "Okay. Ralph Jessup Bedford and Beatrice Tremayne Ballantyne Bedford. Their home at 4257 Tradd Street, Charleston, South Carolina, was foreclosed on last October 23 by the Trans-Union Mortgage Company of Dover, Delaware. Amount owing was eight hundred thirty-two thousand nine hundred forty-six dollars." She looked up. "And eleven cents."

The amount staggered me a little, but I had to smile. "Fine work. Anything else I should know about?"

Sharese had lost her hesitancy, her voice steady and confident. "No other big outstanding debt except a couple of credit cards that are current, although they haven't always been in the past. They lease a new Audi A5 convertible through the dealer leasing program. Their payment is four hundred and nine dollars a month."

Again I shot her a grin. "Even?"

She smiled back. "No, ma'am. And eighty-six cents."

"Good work," I said and finished my trip into my office. "Add that to the file and send me an updated version, please."

"Yes, ma'am."

I sat in my father's old swivel chair with the high back and waited for the *ping* of my laptop to alert me to the arrival of the new file. While I had it on my mind, I picked up the phone and called Neddie. Of course she was with a patient, and I left a message on her voice mail asking her to accept a rain check on my dinner invitation. I told her I'd explain later. I added that I hoped her date turned out well and fully expected a tart response before the day was over.

Which wasn't too far away, I noted, glancing at my watch. Somehow time just seemed to disappear of late, the weeks flying by. I thought about how all of us—Pudge, Bebe, Scarlett, and I— had talked endlessly about what we would do with our lives, who we'd marry, how many kids we'd have. It was impossible that any of us would have come close to predicting just exactly how the intervening years had played out, except maybe for Scarlett. Poor Mary Alice.

And who could ever have figured James would turn into some wife-beating lowlife? I remembered him as brash, confident, even arrogant. But then, he had it all—looks, brains, and money— so why shouldn't he have been a little overbearing? And, according to the file, he'd become just as successful as everyone had assumed he would. He'd sailed through undergrad at Clemson, moved on to law school at Auburn— Strange he hadn't gone to some big time Ivy League place like Yale or Harvard, I thought. His parents could certainly have afforded it. At any rate, he'd zoomed right to the top of his profession, trading in his father's small-town practice for the big money lure of Atlanta and its dozens of corporate opportunities. Unlike Ralph Bedford, James hadn't overextended himself and his family. Except for the house in Buckhead, which carried a relatively modest mortgage balance, he owned everything outright. Including the fifty-four foot Off-shore yacht he kept docked at Skull Creek Marina. I remembered the name, and it suddenly registered on me how apt it was. *Tiger Pause*. Both Clemson and Auburn had the big cat as their mascot. Clever James. Or maybe clever Scarlett.

My laptop *dinged*, and I opened the amended file. Other than the updated financial information on the Bedfords, there wasn't much more for me to go on. I'd have to rely on whatever evidence, such as it might be, the girls could provide me. And then I'd have to tackle Scarlett. I wondered what kind of women Jenny Carson and Gillian McDonald would turn out to be. I noted that Pudge had pronounced the latter's name with a hard *G*, Gill, like in a fish. I made a mental note to remember that.

I looked up as Red stepped into the office, pausing to speak to both Erik and Sharese. A moment later he folded his tall frame into a client chair.

"You look beat," I said, noting his disheveled hair where he'd undoubtedly been running his hands through it. "I thought you just intended to review the Tennyson file."

"I did. And I came to the same conclusion as you. So I thought I'd spare you the aggravation of dealing with her. When I got her on the phone, she refused to talk to me, kept insisting that I speak with her in person. So I went over to Bram's Point." He shot me one of his boyish grins. "I swear, she's something else."

"Tell me about it. The first day she came in I practically had to chase her out of here with a broom."

"She's a talker, all right. Read me the riot act about wasting her time, taking her money under false pretenses. I pointed out to her that it says right in the contract that we can't guarantee success. I told her all the things we'd done trying to locate this Cruz guy, but she wasn't buying it." He wiggled his eyebrows at me. "Attorneys were mentioned."

I shrugged. "She doesn't scare me. Let her try it. Anyway, are we done with her?"

"As far as I'm concerned, but I have a nasty feeling she isn't going to go away. She's just the type that could institute some kind of legal action just to have the satisfaction of causing us grief."

"As I said, let her try. We've got records of the hours spent trying to track down her suspect, and lots of circumstantial evidence that the only ones with the opportunity to rifle her wallet were her loser son and his loser friends. That reminds me," I said, "speaking of attorneys. I had lunch with Claudia today, and I let her know we were back in the game."

I rightly interpreted his change of expression. "I told her it would be on a limited basis. We can cherry-pick the cases we want to get involved in. She said Alex would be in touch."

"Okay, I guess. So what's going on with the ladies' club?"

That made me smile. "Well, you're going to have to fend for yourself tomorrow night, and maybe part of Saturday. Big pow-wow at Jordan Point. The rest of the group is flying in, so I'll be hanging with them. It's a chance to get everyone's take on what's going on with Mary Alice before she shows up on Saturday. So I want to take every advantage of the opportunity. I'll probably be staying the night."

"What about the kids?"

"Oh, I have every faith you can handle your own children for a few hours."

"Cute. I meant they'll be expecting to see you. What should I tell them?"

"The truth. I'm at a sleepover with a few of my BFFs. Elinor will understand."

"That's good, because I sure as hell don't," my husband said.

"Yes, you do. Now quit acting like some jilted schoolboy and take me to dinner. It seems as if lunch was a week ago."

"Isn't it a little early?"

"We can go sit on the deck for an hour or so, soak up some of this wonderful sun."

"An offer I can't refuse," he said with a genuine smile, holding out his hand.

I took it, and we made our escape.

Jump & Phil's is a delightful bar/restaurant on the south end of Hilton Head, just outside the main gate to Sea Pines Plantation. Even after our little catnaps on the chaises on the side deck, we were still relatively early, and only a couple of tables were occupied. This time of year it was mostly populated by locals, although there was always a smattering of golfers escaping the last gasp of winter up north. The bar had begun to fill up by the time Red's beer and my Diet Coke materialized in front of us. Tucked in at the Moose Table, underneath Waldo's glittering antlers and watchful eyes, we sat in relative silence, occasionally commenting on the sports news being broadcast on most of the overhead TVs.

When we both had medium-rare burgers—Red's with fries and mine with coleslaw—grasped in our hands, conversation stopped altogether. Until my cell phone rang. I checked the Caller

ID and punched the Talk button.

"Neddie," I mouthed at Red, swallowing before I said, "hello, there. You got my message?"

"Yes, Miss Smartass, I did. I never said I had a date for Saturday. You know what happens when you assume?"

"Old news. And old joke. Anyway, sorry to yank back my invitation." I paused a moment. "Are you up for a consultation? Not now, but maybe one day next week?"

"Is this about Julia again, because I really—"

"No, nothing to do with my sister. This is a case. Possible domestic violence, although I've been told recently that expression is objectionable to some people."

"Like it or not, it's an accurate description. You dealing with the abuser or the victim?"

"I'm on the side of the angels, but I know them both. From high school."

"That could get sticky. How can I help?"

"Just be on hand in case I need to run something by you. I just have a hard time understanding how a woman can tolerate a situation like that for years and not do anything about it."

"You and a good many members of law enforcement. And the mental health community, as well. Every case is different, but there are a lot of hypotheses."

"Like what? Bad childhood, low self-esteem?"

"See, you really don't need me at all. Listen, I have to run. I'm meeting some friends for dinner before I head for the island. Give me a shout if I can be of any help. It's certainly not my specialty, but I'd be glad to offer whatever advice I can."

"You're the best. Enjoy your evening."

"You, too," she said and disconnected.

Red wiped his mouth and pushed back his chair. "I didn't know you'd asked her to dinner. That would have been fun. She's so good with the kids."

"Occupational expertise," I said, finishing the last scrap of coleslaw on my plate. "Plus she really likes them. I wish she'd get married again and have some of her own."

"Not likely at this stage of the game, is it?"

I looked up to find him studying me intently, and I knew I hadn't missed the subtle but deliberate double meaning of his question.

"We're the same age, Neddie and I, as you well know. And yes, it's probably a done deal in that department." I looked directly into his eyes. "Problem?"

"Not for me," he said, reaching for my hand. "I like our life just the way it is."

"Amen, brother," I whispered around a deep feeling of relief.

CHAPTER TWELVE

Friday disappeared in a flurry of activity, most of it centered around Erik's imminent departure. He spent quite a bit of time with Sharese, and I tried to identify any loose ends that might need his attention before he took off. We sent out for lunch, Red volunteering to fly as he was the only one not directly involved in all the computer work. Even I pitched in and managed not to screw anything up too badly. By the time we hit four o'clock, we were all exhausted but happy with what we'd managed to accomplish.

"You'll be fine," Erik assured Sharese as he shut down his laptop and slipped it into its carrying case. "You can email me if you get stuck, but just use your head, and I know you'll be able to figure out just about any problem you run across. You think logically, which is one of the most important parts about understanding computers and software." He grinned. "You guys won't even know I'm gone."

"That's a crock, and you know it," I said, forcing myself to smile. I had to exercise a great deal of restraint to keep from throwing a rope around him and hogtying him to his chair. "But we'll muddle through." I sobered. "Take the time to get things worked out, if you can. I don't know how it will all shake out, but my only concern is that you're happy at the end of it. No matter what the outcome."

Erik smiled. "I know that. And I'm prepared for whatever happens." He laughed, a short, mocking sound, and shook his head. "At least that's what I keep telling myself."

"Travel safely," I said and resisted the urge to hug him.

We'd never had that kind of relationship, although I often thought of him as the well-loved younger brother I'd never had.

"I'll be in touch," he said, hefting the computer bag onto his shoulder. "Take care."

Both Sharese and I sniffled a little after the door closed behind him. Red had said his goodbyes earlier in the afternoon
before he took off to try and run down a deadbeat dad we'd been
hired to find. That had been one of Erik's last lessons for Sharese,
and they'd come up with a lead that needed to be checked out.

"We'll be fine," I said to the room in general, and Sharese laid
a tentative hand on my shoulder.

"We will," she said with conviction, and we exchanged a
smile.

"Well, I'm out of here," I said, checking my watch. "I have to
pack a few things for my sleepover gig."

"Anything I can do to help?"

"Thanks, but no. I hope to have a lot more useful information by the time I see you again on Monday." She followed me
back into my office. "You and Byron have plans for the weekend?"

"No, ma'am, nothing special. He's got a lot of work to do,
and I thought maybe we'd walk the beach at some point, if the
weather holds."

"It's supposed to be nice," I said, hoping the weatherman
knew what he was talking about. I shuddered to think about Red
having to entertain two restless tweeners on a rainy Saturday.

"You go ahead. I'll lock up," she said, standing aside. "I hope
everything goes okay with your friends."

"From your lips to God's ear," I said on my way out the
door.

At home, I retrieved a small overnight case from the attic and
rummaged in the dresser for a pair of modest flannel pajamas.
Although the days had been wonderfully warm the entire month
of March so far, the nights could still be chilly. I added a change
of underwear, a pair of slippers, and the least disreputable of my
robes. I've never been much for makeup other than brows and
lashes, so I just needed to throw in a spare toothbrush, and I was
set to go.

I'd printed off a clean copy of all the files before leaving the
office, and it was tucked inside my briefcase along with the tape
recorder, a couple of legal pads, some pens, and my iPad. After
pondering for a moment, I spun the tumblers on the tiny combi-

nation lock. I didn't think any of the other ladies would stoop to snooping, but a lot of the information Erik and Sharese had gathered was highly personal, maybe even things they hadn't shared with the others. I reminded myself to be careful how much I revealed in casual conversation. Pudge hadn't liked the idea of being investigated, and I had no reason to think the others wouldn't balk as well.

I showered and changed into clean jeans and an oxford cloth shirt and slid my feet into my old Bass loafers. With the sleeves of a Marine Corps sweatshirt tied around my shoulders, I felt as if I looked like a coed again. Well, except for the gray strands in my chestnut hair. And the encroaching crow's feet around my mother's bright green eyes.

I smiled at my reflection in the full-length mirror on the bedroom wall. *Not bad for an old broad,* I told myself, almost believing it.

I carried everything out to the door leading to the garage and dropped it in the foyer. Up in the kitchen I pulled open the refrigerator and peeled off a couple of slices of provolone from the package. Lunch had been fast food in more ways than one as we all scurried around before Erik's departure, and I had a little hollow spot that needed filling. Pudge had said not to eat dinner as she had it all arranged. I wondered if she cooked. The kitchen in her Jordan Point home, as I conjured it up on my way out the door, had looked well-used, not just some granite and stainless showplace meant to impress guests.

I threw everything in the backseat and drew a long breath, letting it out slowly, as I fired up the Jaguar. I had no idea what to expect at the end of my short journey, but I couldn't suppress a feeling of anticipation. And, if I were being honest, maybe a little shiver of concern. It wasn't a class reunion with a couple of interlopers thrown in. This was serious business. Mary Alice needed our help, and the rest of the group was looking to me to provide the game plan.

I hoped I wouldn't let them down.

I pulled in behind what I now knew for certain was Bebe's bright red Audi convertible, which was parked behind a dusty black Range Rover. The door opened before I'd even managed to set my feet on the ground, and Pudge bounded down the steps.

"Finally! The party's already in full swing."

"Party?" I asked, hauling my bag and briefcase out.

She immediately grabbed them out of my hands. "Of course. The first night of our weekends always begins with everyone getting pretty well smashed. Takes the awkwardness out of it. Come on."

She whirled and dashed for the stairs, and I had to trot to keep up with her.

Great, I thought, as I climbed up to the verandah, *a bunch of drunks to deal with.*

Not that I didn't have some experience in that regard, what with my mother and all. But I thought this was supposed to be about putting our heads together, which wasn't going to get very far if mine was the only sober one in attendance. I sighed and followed Pudge into the great room.

"The guest of honor has arrived!" she announced in a voice just short of a shout, and heads swiveled in our direction. She nudged me. "You remember Annie from the other night?"

Anne Gilchrist managed to look both slightly dazed and disdainful, no mean feat, I thought. Bebe squealed and came rushing across the room to grab me in a bear hug.

"Oh, Bay, it's so wonderful! We're all here together again."

I pushed gently on her shoulder to disengage myself. "Except for Scarlett," I said, loudly enough for everyone to hear, and the noise immediately abated.

Bebe looked crestfallen. "Oh, honey, of course you're right!" She arranged her face in what I'm sure she thought of as the proper look of solemnity. "I'm so sorry!" The effect was spoiled by a high-pitched hiccough, and she giggled. "I think I may have had just a tiny bit too much wine."

"You could have something there," I said, straining to keep the snarkiness out of my voice. I gave serious thought to wrenching my bag and briefcase out of Pudge's hands and beating a hasty retreat.

"Come on, Bay Rum," our hostess said in that same booming voice, "we'll sober up over dinner. Get the stick out of your ass and come and meet the rest of this disreputable bunch."

The sick feeling that always curled like a snake in the pit of my stomach whenever I had to deal with my mother on one of her binges rose like bile into my throat.

"I came here to help you help Scarlett, not to party. What in the hell is the matter with you, Pudge?"

As if someone had flipped a switch, my old friend shed her tipsy persona. "I know what we're here for, Bay. We just need to let off a little steam before we get down to the whole unsavory business. Lighten up a little, okay?"

I let out a long breath. "Okay. But we're going to need to have all our wits about us—not just half of them."

She laughed. "Fair enough. Ladies, this is our illustrious private investigator Bay Tanner." She took me by the elbow and guided me farther into the room. "Gill McDonald, former model and longtime friend."

The woman who looked up at me from slightly bloodshot eyes had certainly once been beautiful. It was there in the cheekbones, the large dark irises, the nearly perfect oval of her face. But it was also obvious that drinking—or maybe drugs—abused over a long period of time had taken its toll on her looks and her body. Her skin sagged, and its gray pallor told a story of overindulgence and neglect.

"Hello," she said in a soft voice, and I could tell she'd read my assessment of her on my face. "*Former* being the operative word here. I never made it to the heights Sylvie did. She's just being kind."

"I'm pleased to meet you," I said, nodding. She had both hands wrapped around a brandy snifter and didn't seem inclined to let go of it.

"And this is our den mother, Jenny Carson. Lord knows she tries to keep us on the straight and narrow, but it's a losing battle, right Jen?"

She was older than the rest of us, or at least she appeared so. *Comfortable* was the first word that popped into my head. She wore no makeup, and her clothes were a size too large even for her hefty frame. A round face, chubby actually if I was truthful, with a pert nose atop which perched John Lennon glasses that magnified her eyes and made them hard to read. Everything about Jenny Carson was neutral, from her hair to her complexion to the scruffy tennis shoes that must once have been white.

And she looked vaguely familiar. I hadn't spent a lot of time with her file, but I remembered it said she was a schoolteacher in northern Virginia, so the possibility that our paths had crossed at some time in the past didn't seem likely. Still it nagged at me, and I knew I would spend the rest of the evening trying to figure out the connection.

She was the only one who stood, offering her hand. When I took it, she clasped the other around it and smiled benevolently. "I'm so glad to finally meet you. Sylvia just never stops talking about you and your exploits. I'm so hoping you can help us. We're worried to death about Mary Alice."

At last, I thought, a sane voice. "I'll do whatever I can to resolve the situation." I nodded my head to encompass the whole room. "With your help."

"I know you will. I can tell by your aura that you're a serious person with a good, true heart."

Aura? Dear God.

"So what are you drinking?" Pudge asked at my shoulder as Jenny settled back onto the loveseat with a beatific smile.

"Uh, nothing right now. I'm good."

"Party pooper," she said with a laugh. "Listen, I have to take care of stuff in the kitchen. You want to give me a hand?"

"Sure," I said, eager for any excuse to escape from the strange atmosphere of the great room. Drunks and clairvoyants. What the hell had I gotten myself into?

"Listen," she said over her shoulder, "I've put you in the guest quarters over the garage. It's bigger than the other rooms, with its own bath, because I thought you might want to have a little distance from the rest of us. I can tell by that tight upper lip that you don't approve of most of us, and besides we're liable to be up until all hours." Pudge dropped my bag and briefcase on the floor next to a doorway. "You can take those up later. Hang a left at the top and there's another door at the end of the hallway." She grinned at me. "It locks."

That made me angry. "Come on, Pudge, get off my back. I don't drink, okay? You and Bebe certainly know why. If you want to have a middle-aged version of a frat party, that's your business, but that's not what I'm here for. If things are as bad as you say they are with Scarlett, I need to formulate a plan to get her out of that situation. I need some clearheaded input from those of you who know her better than I do. I'd like to arrange to meet with her tomorrow, and I'd like to be armed with as much ammunition as possible." I paused. "If you-all would rather party, maybe I should just go on home."

"Don't be ridiculous! I know we have serious business to take care of here, despite what you think." Her eyes held mine. "And in case you've forgotten, I'm paying for your time."

"And I can refund that money to you, every last damn penny, if you don't knock off this bullshit, Pudge."

She surprised me by backing down almost immediately. Her face crumpled, and for a moment I was afraid she might break down into tears.

"I'm sorry, Bay. Really." She reached out and captured both my hands in hers. "Let's start over, okay? Give us a chance to prove we're serious about this. I absolutely guarantee you that we are." She managed a watery smile. "And I promise we'll behave."

I thought of Mary Alice—Scarlett—and forced the tension out of my shoulders. "Fine."

"Good!" She nodded once and whirled toward the wall of double ovens. "Now, let's see. I have a prime rib just about ready to come out, and it has to rest for about fifteen minutes. The salad is all cut. Can you toss that for me? The dressing is made and chilled. And give the lobster bisque a quick stir." She pointed to the stovetop. "I'll be right back."

In a whirl of her signature scent, the one I assumed Sharese was so fond of, she dashed out of the kitchen back to the great room.

"Refills anyone? Last call before dinner!"

I shook my head and pulled open the refrigerator.

Chapter Thirteen

The meal, prepared entirely by Pudge, was fabulous. For a model, former or not, she certainly knew her way around the kitchen. And she could put the food away. I held up my end of the table as well, and Jenny insisted that her foraging from the plate of the anorexic Annie was to prevent the unpardonable sin of waste.

Over coffee, which I declined and which the others definitely needed, we devoured an entire key lime pie. With the last fork deposited in the dishwasher, we got down to business.

Thankfully, the drinks cabinet had been shut down, at least for the time being, and everyone seemed in reasonable control of their faculties.

While Pudge was putting the finishing touches on dinner, I'd carried my bag and briefcase up to the guest quarters over the garage. The thing was the size of a hotel suite, complete with sitting area and a beautifully appointed bath featuring a walk-in shower. The wide windows on the bedroom side looked out over the waters of Skull Creek, across Hog Island to the wildlife preserve on Pinckney. I would be more than comfortable there, and I had to admit to feeling as if I were ensconced in an aerie.

And the door did lock.

As we all resettled ourselves in the great room, I set the small cassette recorder on the table and turned the volume up to full.

"I'd like a glass of champagne, Sylvie. Just to settle my stomach."

Anne Gilchrist had commandeered the lounge chair—again —and waved her bony hand in Pudge's direction.

"What, for the teaspoon of food you ate?" Bebe made no effort to keep the note of disdain out of her voice or off her face.

"Let's just stick with coffee for now," I said, not looking at Anne.

"I'm sorry, did someone suddenly appoint you house mother?"

The footrest of the recliner snapped down, and I wondered for a moment if the woman was about to leap across the narrow space and slap me.

"Ladies, ladies!" Pudge stepped between us. "Bay's right. She wants our input about Scarlett's situation. We can worry about drinks later." She directed a frosty smile at Anne. "It is, after all, why we're here, right?"

"Some of us," Bebe mumbled from across the room and earned herself a withering glare from the occupant of the lounge chair.

I decided to ignore the quivering tension in the room and get things going. I made a show of pushing the record button, named everyone present, and leaned back in my overstuffed chair.

"Who wants to start?" I glanced at Pudge. "We've already discussed your observations. And you, too, Bebe. Both of you have noted injuries that Scarlett has either offered flimsy excuses for or denied altogether. Anyone else have firsthand knowledge of abuse?"

The silence stretched out so long I almost decided to shut down the recorder. Finally, Jenny Carson raised a tentative hand as if we were all back in the classroom.

"Yes, Jenny?" I said, smiling directly at her.

"I know she hasn't been my friend for very long, but I've come to care about Mary Alice over the years of our getting together. Even before any of us ever raised the issue of abuse among ourselves, I sensed there was great strife and unhappiness in her life. Her aura was dark and cloudy—"

"Oh, for God's sake, Jen, will you give that crap a rest?"

Surprisingly, the outburst came from Gillian, who had been the most subdued of all of them throughout dinner. In fact, she'd barely spoken a word, toying with her food much as Anne had, although she'd managed to down a few bites.

"Come on, Gill," Pudge said softly, "lighten up. Jen means well. And there's no denying she's been right on about . . . some things in the past."

I saw Gillian color and drop her head, and I wondered just what observation—or prediction—Jen had made that caused the other woman such embarrassment.

"Other than that, Jen, this feeling of trouble you sensed, is there anything more concrete, more . . . substantial you observed?"

She seemed totally unruffled by Gill's outburst. "Just the same as the rest of you, I suppose," she said waving her hand around to encompass all of them. "She's had a black eye twice when I've been here, and there's that thing about covering up her arms all the time." She graced Gillian with a smile full of understanding and pity. "And I'm sorry if my reading upset you, Gill. You did ask, if you remember. And I don't censor my findings. Things are what they are. I just report."

"Which is no doubt why you're stuck in that dumpy little town in the middle of nowhere," Annie purred. "How the mighty have fallen."

Rather than seeming upset by the obvious insult, Jenny Carson simply smiled at the brittle woman glaring across at her. "I understand why you need to strike out at me, Anne. It's okay."

"Could we get back to business?" I asked, that niggling feeling that I'd met Jenny before growing stronger by the moment. "Gillian, do you have anything to add?"

She shook her head, and silence settled over the room. I began to think that this had been a total waste of time and Pudge's money, but I'm nothing if not persistent.

"Has any of you ever seen James actually strike her? Or push her?" I let my eyes wander across the group. "How do they interact when they're in company?"

Pudge spoke softly. "I've been to their house in Buckhead, a couple of times, for holiday parties and so on." She took her time, seeming to have difficulty gathering her words. "James is charming, no doubt about that." She looked up at me. "You remember. All the teachers loved him. Mr. Polite. And he got along fine with the other guys, at least as far as I could tell."

She paused as if inviting comment.

"I never paid that much attention to him," I said, glancing at Bebe. "He was good to look at, but there was always something off-putting about him, at least in my book. He was definitely possessive of Scarlett." I managed a weak smile. "And he really hated it when we called her that."

Bebe gave a little titter. "He used to call us the Unholy Alliance, remember? I never did understand where that came from, but he would have been thrilled if Mary Alice had dropped us. I guess he didn't think we were good enough for her."

I nodded. "I'd forgotten about that. The Unholy Alliance.

Maybe he thought we'd bring him down. Guilt by association and all that."

"Well, as it turns out, the son of a bitch didn't have anything to feel superior about, did he?" Pudge leaned back into the cushions of the loveseat and tucked her long legs under her. "What I observed over the few days I spent with them is that he pretty much ignored Scarlett unless he wanted something from her. He treated her like a servant, although they had plenty of those in evidence when they gave a party."

She leaned forward. "'Honey, I need a drink.' 'You need to circulate, Mary Alice. Quit hiding in the corner.' 'You've lost an earring again. Go get another pair.'" Pudge sighed. "It was nothing but constant criticism. And the worst part is that Scarlett just knuckled under. She'd *yes dear* him and scurry off to follow orders. Sometimes I just wanted to shake her, tell her to stand up to him, but she never did."

"Maybe she was afraid of the consequences," I offered. "But you never saw him get physical with her."

"I did. Once." Gillian spoke so softly I wasn't sure she'd actually said it.

"What happened?" I edged the tape recorder a little closer to where she sat.

"We'd had one of our weekends, one of the first ones here, actually. He came to pick her up on Sunday, and we'd gotten— Mary Alice and I—into a pretty intense conversation about . . ." She faltered, and her gaze dropped to her lap where her fingers worked at each other, much as Bebe's had done a couple of nights before.

"About?" I asked softly.

"It doesn't matter. Nothing to do with . . ." She waved her hand in our direction. ". . . this. We were just very involved and not paying attention to the time."

I saw tears pooling in her eyes, and Bebe reached across to lay a hand softly on Gillian's. "And?" I prompted.

Her shoulders drooped for a moment before she straightened them and continued. "And she wasn't outside when he pulled up. He came storming into the house without even knocking and yelled at her for making him wait." She glanced at Pudge. "Remember?"

"Yes, I do, but I didn't see anything. I was throwing sheets in the laundry, but I certainly heard him. He screamed that she was a thoughtless bitch, and he had a five-hour drive ahead of him, and that she never thought about anyone except herself." She looked at Gillian. "Did something else happen? You never told me. By the time I got in here, they were pulling out of the driveway."

Gillian sighed. "It was so upsetting. He grabbed her by the arm and yanked her out of the chair. She cringed, as if maybe she was already in pain, grabbed up her suitcase, and let him march her out the door." She looked at Pudge. "I just let it drop, because I didn't want to cause her any more embarrassment in front of the rest of you." She shivered. "The look she gave me, over her shoulder, was so . . ." She fumbled for the word. "Pathetic. Like a dog that someone kicked." A sob escaped, and she buried her head in her hands. "I should have stopped him! I'm such a freaking coward!"

Jenny was the first to reach her, encircling her in an embrace. "It's not your fault, Gill. We've all been watching from the sidelines. It's everyone's fault for not doing something about it." She caressed the scrawny woman's short-cropped hair. "But we're all here now, ready and willing to make this right. And Bay's going to get it done for us." She looked over Gillian's bent head and made direct eye contact. "Aren't you?"

I was saved from making a promise I wasn't sure I'd be able to keep by the pealing of the doorbell. Everyone, including me, jumped at the clanging intrusion.

"It's about time." Pudge swung her feet onto the floor and stomped toward the foyer.

We all followed her progress as she threw open the heavy oak panel, but I was the only one who gasped at the tiny woman who stepped tentatively through the doorway.

"You're late," Pudge said, ushering her new guest into the room. "We started without you."

Bebe rushed to offer a welcome hug, and over her shoulder I caught the woman's gaze locked directly onto mine. She disentangled herself and stood for a long moment, her stare never wavering, before she seemed to draw herself up to her full five-foot height.

"Hello, Bay," she said. "It's been a while."

And Bitsy Elliott, my best friend from birth and betrayer of my trust, headed resolutely in my direction.

CHAPTER
FOURTEEN

She stopped a little in front of me and stood, arms down at her sides, as if she were approaching a snarling dog. I almost expected her to extend a tentative hand for me to sniff. A thousand thoughts careened around inside my head, but Emmaline Baynard Simpson hadn't wasted all those hours drumming proper etiquette into her only child.

"Hey, Bitsy." Okay, it wasn't profound or elegant, but it seemed to do the trick.

All the tension drained from her shoulders, and a wide smile split her still pretty face.

"I've missed you."

I sat back in my chair, rightly interpreting her intention to close in for a conciliatory hug. I wasn't prepared to go that far. Not yet.

"You look well," I said and meant it.

Despite bearing four children and having had to endure too many years with the overweight, overbearing ox of a man she'd married, Elizabeth Quintard Elliott had managed to hold onto her slim frame and cheerleader prettiness. We couldn't have been more different, in a host of ways, but our friendship had been forged as toddlers, and we'd been each other's safe harbor through the vagaries of childhood and our teenage years and into adulthood. I'd been relieved to find her absent from any of Pudge's tales about the group of women who met in New York and later here on Hilton Head, although she'd been a part of our *gang* as much as I had. I certainly hadn't expected her to show up unannounced. But apparently not uninvited.

I looked at Pudge to find her studying my reaction. She had obviously been privy to the circumstances that had caused the rift between Bitsy and me—at least one side of it—and I knew in-stinctively that her omission had been deliberate.

Everyone except Anne murmured greetings of one kind or another, and Bitsy dropped her bag next to the loveseat. She and Pudge settled in side by side, and I'm pretty certain I didn't misinterpret the conspiratorial look that passed between them before our hostess finally spoke.

"So, Bits, we've been relating any firsthand knowledge we have about Scarlett's . . . situation. Bay wants facts, not speculation."

The look my oldest friend turned on me sent a chill down my arms. "That's *usually* how she operates," she said, her thin smile doing little to temper the underlying harshness of her words.

Or maybe I was the only one who caught the implication of her stress on the word *usually*. But I had no intention of getting sidetracked into a discussion of our personal falling out. Time for that later. Much later, if I had my way.

"Do you have anything to contribute, Bitsy, or are you just here for the booze? Sorry to disappoint, but the bar's been shut down for the time being."

The moment the words were out, I wanted to snatch them back. It's so easy to wound when you know someone as well as I did Bitsy, and my remark had been cruel and thoughtless. She'd had a drinking problem many years ago, pretty well concealed from those who weren't as tuned to her as I was, but she'd managed to work her way through it.

And it was apparent my barb had struck its mark. Her face colored, and she turned away from me. The defiant set of her shoulders dropped, and Pudge laid a hand on her arm while blasting me with a look that could have stripped wallpaper.

"I'm sorry," I said, hoping she could see how much I meant it. "That was unnecessary."

Bitsy turned back and offered me a tentative smile. "We've both been a little too bitchy. Shall we start over?"

I couldn't resist her. Truth is, I never could. "Consider the hatchet buried," I said, and she laughed.

"Okay, now that we've got the true confessions portion of our program out of the way, could we get back to business? Bits, what have you got? About Scarlett, I mean."

Immediately my friend sobered. "She talks to me. We follow each other's kids on Facebook, and we exchange emails and phone calls. Other than Bay—" She shot me another of her pixie grins. "—she and I have stayed the closest, I guess because of the stay-at-home mom thing." She waved in a manner to encompass the whole room. "Y'all have led such much more glamorous lives." Her face clouded. "I can tell you for a fact that James beats her, regularly and viciously. I can't count the number of times I've told her to leave him, to call the police, to take the kids, when they were little, and go to a shelter."

My ears had perked up at the mention of emails. "Do you have any of her correspondence? I mean the ones in writing?"

Bitsy reached for her bag and extracted a flash drive. With a flip of the wrist, she tossed it across the space between us, and I caught it in midair.

"I knew that would be what you wanted, so I downloaded them onto the drive. I don't have every single email she sent me, but I just had a feeling that the ones about the violence might come in handy some day. If I ever managed to convince her to do something about that monster."

It was the same word Pudge had used to describe James Madison Stuart the Third, and I marveled again how none of us had ever seen that side of him in all the years we'd shared the joys and traumas of high school. Maybe that was why domestic abuse seemed to flourish unchecked, except for the occasional celebrity or professional athlete who made headlines. No one wanted to believe their neighbor, friend, son, brother was capable of battering a woman.

"This could be the smoking gun," I said. "We have a great law firm here on the island, all female attorneys, and they'd love to take on James in court. If you're all willing to testify, we just might be able to hang the creep out to dry."

"But doesn't Scarlett—Mary Alice—have to file a complaint first?" Jenny's question hung in the air for a moment.

"Claudia—one of the lawyers I mentioned—says yes, that's the first step." I clutched the flash drive in my hand. "But I think this might just be the ammunition we need to get Scarlett off the sidelines and into battle." I turned to Pudge. "Can I use your printer?"

Her head tipped toward the kitchen. "There's one in the alcove where my laptop is. Just pull out the drawer on the right."

"I'll do it before I head upstairs. Anyone else want to add something?" When no one met my gaze, I said, "Then the last thing is to figure out how I'm going to get an opportunity to talk to Scarlett one on one. You say she's coming here to spend the night tomorrow?"

Pudge nodded. "Ever since we moved the weekends down here, I go pick her up on Saturday at the Skull Creek Marina where they keep the boat. The creep generally spends the morning drinking and screwing around with his friends, getting all the fishing gear in order while she fixes them food and makes sure everything's clean and organized for their trip. Then she waits for me outside if it's a nice day or in the little office on the dock if it isn't. You could go in my place."

"Wouldn't that frighten her, if Bay just shows up out of the blue when she's expecting Pudge?"

Bitsy had a point. Before I could mull it over, Bebe offered the solution. "We'll all go!" she said, clapping her hands like some excited five-year-old. "We can take a couple of cars. Then we can all go to lunch someplace wonderful."

I opened my mouth to say, "It's not a party," but the glowering Anne beat me to it.

"We're trying to extricate the woman from an abusive marriage, not plan a debutante ball," she said, sarcasm dripping from every word.

"It might not be a bad idea, though." I'd had a moment to run the possible scenario through in my mind. "If we make it seem like some sort of social occasion, James won't be alerted, assuming he might still be around, and with everyone talking and so on, it might be easier for me to get her alone." Again I gestured to the flash drive still clutched in my hand. "I'd love to spend a few minutes with her bastard husband, too, but I don't want to tip our hand."

"Are you carrying?"

Bitsy asked it with a smile, one that told me despite her blunder in the Canaan's Gate debacle, she still lusted after being a part of my investigations.

"Not at the moment," I said, holding my hands out to my sides. "Besides which, I have no intention of threatening James with a gun." I smiled. "Not that the idea doesn't hold a certain amount of appeal, but I really don't want to spend the next six months in the Beaufort County Jail if it's all the same to you."

"But how do you plan to convince her?" Bebe's voice had

gone plaintive.

"I haven't had a lot of experience in dealing with this problem," I said, "but we did do some work for the woman who operates a shelter, and I'm afraid I learned way more than I ever wanted to about how reluctant wives are to turn in their husbands. It's not just about the violence. There's a psychological component that most of us can't understand, a sort of Stockholm-syndrome kind of thing that binds them to their abusers. And there's also the huge element of shame. But I think that once I confront her with this—" I waved the memory stick. "I think then we can surround her with enough love and support as a group to get her at least to throw him out. We have evidence, thanks to Bitsy, and she should be able to use that as leverage. I'm sure her injuries have forced her to use a clinic or emergency room, especially for the broken bones, and they'll have records as well."

I stopped for a breath. "The main thing is getting her to admit to the problem. I hope, in part because I haven't been as close to her as the rest of you, hearing it from me will shock her into taking action. I think right now that's the best we can hope for. And I'm not above threatening a little blackmail, if it comes down to it. I'm sure James's corporate bosses wouldn't be too thrilled to find out that their high-powered attorney is a wife-beater. But the most important thing will be to convince Scarlett that she's not alone, that we're all here to support her, but only if she's willing to find the courage to set herself free."

Silence settled over the group until Bebe gushed, "It'll be an intervention, just like the ones they have on TV."

"Dear God, I hope not," Gillian muttered, her face a study in despair, and I wondered if she'd had some personal experience in that arena.

"So we're agreed?" Pudge asked, scanning the room. "We'll all go tomorrow, surprise Scarlett, and just sweep her away. I hope the creep is still around. It wouldn't hurt to let him know that his wife has friends who aren't afraid to take him on." She stood and stretched. "Damn, it makes me angry that it's taken us so long to get to this point. If we'd had the courage to act a long time ago, we could have saved Scarlett a lot of grief and pain."

There didn't seem to be anything to say to that, so I clicked off the tape recorder. "What time do you usually head over to the marina?"

"She calls me when she's ready. Most of the time it's mid-morning, ten or after."

"So we'll wait until we hear from her." I rose, too. "Thank you all for your input. I think among us we just might be able to pull this off."

"We needed you to point us in the right direction," Gill said softly. "Thank you."

I'm not good at receiving compliments. "Let's wait and see how it turns out."

"I'm sensing a good outcome," Jenny said from her place next to the fireplace.

"Alert the media," Anne mumbled, and Pudge laughed.

"Don't knock it if you haven't tried it," she said, an enigmatic smile on her face. "Okay, enough gloom and doom for one night. I officially declare the bar open!"

Which was my cue. I felt drained and certainly in no mood for any drunken shenanigans. I nodded to Bitsy, picked up the recorder, and headed for the kitchen. Behind me I heard the clink of ice in crystal and the chatter of conversation. I found Pudge's laptop, loaded the flash drive, and hit Print. While the pages spit out, I nuked a cup of hot water to make tea to carry up to my room. From the volume of paper piling up in the printer tray, I figured I had at least an hour of unpleasant reading ahead of me.

When the machine fell silent, I gathered the considerable stack, tucked it under my arm, and made my escape. I had half-expected Bitsy to corner me in the kitchen for some sort of re-conciliation talk, and I was both pleased and disappointed to have been left in peace. In my room, nothing of the goings-on down-stairs penetrated my aerie. I showered, donned my pajamas, and settled into the comfortable queen-size bed. I had just perched my reading glasses on the end of my nose when I heard the soft knock.

"Damn," I muttered under my breath. More loudly I called, "Come in."

But it was Pudge, not Bitsy, who stuck her head around the partially opened door. "Everything okay?" she asked. "Anything you need?"

"I'm fine. Just settling in to go over Scarlett's emails."

"Not exactly my choice of bedtime reading." She glanced at the cup on the bedside table. "I'll bet that's gone cold. Let me get you a fresh one."

I shook my head. "It's fine."

"No bother," she said, crossing to retrieve the mug emblazoned with the Harbour Town lighthouse. "Be right back."

"Pudge, really—" I began, but she cut me off.

"Hostess with the mostest, that's me."

I heard her scurry down the stairs, returning a few minutes later carrying a delicate, nearly translucent cup and saucer, the rims of both banded in gold, steam rising from the tea.

"The mug was fine," I said. "You didn't have to break out the Reynolds heirloom china on my account."

"You deserve it," she said. Her face held a strange mix of sadness and excitement. "We're all grateful, even though some of us don't express it well. I hope you won't be sorry you agreed to help us."

It was an enigmatic remark, one I would ponder over in the days to come, but at the time just seemed quintessentially Pudge.

"I'll see you tomorrow," I said.

She nodded and backed out of the room, closing the door softly behind her.

I blew across the rim of the fragile cup, inhaling the aroma of something herbal and strangely soothing, maybe chamomile with a hint of lavender, I thought. I'd opted for decaf Earl Grey in my mug, but this was definitely an improvement. I sipped, blew some more, sipped again, and set the cup carefully back in its saucer. I slid down against the bunched-up pillows and picked up the first printout.

I was prepared to be appalled, but the shocking revelations contained in Mary Alice's accounts of her husband's brutality were almost too much to comprehend. I'd only waded through about half of them when I saw a mention of Jenny Carson that let that last little piece of one of the day's puzzles click into place.

She had been Jennifer *Lane* then, even that probably a pseudonym, a favorite guest on the late-night talk shows, and, if I remembered correctly, had once had her own syndicated radio program. She talked to dead people, among many other talents, including the reading of auras and divining of the future. She'd been about forty pounds lighter and quite good looking, as I recalled. There'd been a scandal, the disappearance of some celebrity's child, and she'd claimed to know the whereabouts of the kidnappers. Resources had been concentrated based on her claims, and she'd been completely and disastrously wrong. The child had been found in another state some months later, and the original suspect the authorities had zeroed in on had been the abductor. Had they pursued their own leads, the young girl might have been spared weeks of torture and degradation. The only real saving grace was that she'd been found alive.

So our mousy little schoolteacher had once been the darling of Hollywood superstars, top runway models, and big-time athletes. That explained Anne's catty remark about the falling of the mighty. Weird.

I yawned widely. I'd meant to call Red and report in, but the bedside clock read after midnight, and I didn't want to get into a long discussion about our plans for the next day. I'd reach him on his cell on his way to pick up the kids. I felt my eyes drifting closed, the events of the evening running through my head in a kaleidoscope of voices and emotions that seemed to drain the last of my energy. I set my glasses on the nightstand, tossed the stack of papers onto the opposite side of the bed, and let exhaustion claim me.

No light seeped around the edges of the plantation shutters when something woke me. It might have been a car engine. Or a boat out on the waterway that hugged the rear of the property. I hung suspended for a moment in that gray zone between waking and sleeping, trying to pinpoint what it was that had disturbed me, finally decided it had been a dream, and let myself drift back to sleep.

The next time I came to life, someone was pounding on my door. This was definitely not some product of my subconscious, I thought, rolling over and pushing myself into a sitting position.

"Come in." It came out more like a croak, and I cleared my throat. "Come in," I called more forcefully.

"Bay, open the door! Hurry up!"

It was Pudge's voice, hard to recognize at first, I guess because I'd never heard her sound panicked before.

"It's not locked." I swung my legs over the side of the bed, shook my head to clear it, and shuffled toward the other side of the room.

"It damn well is locked!" I heard the rattle of the knob, reminding me for a confused moment of my actions at Presqu'isle earlier in the week.

I fumbled with the catch on the knob and finally managed to jerk the door open.

"Well, I didn't do it," I began, trying to focus my fuzzy mind on my actions of the previous night. Maybe I'd done it automatically, without thinking, but that didn't make any sense. I never locked my bedroom door at home. Never. And I'd been in bed when Pudge left me, and I hadn't approached that side of the room the rest of the night. So how in hell—?

Pudge's face stopped my thoughts in their tracks. Her eyes were huge, the pupils expanded as if she'd seen a ghost.

"What's the matter?"

"It's Scarlett. I mean James. She's downstairs. Scarlett."

"Slow down. You're not making any sense."

Pudge drew in a deep breath. "Scarlett is downstairs. She can't find James."

"What do you mean, she can't find him?"

"What the hell do you think I mean? He's gone. Vanished. Disappeared."

"From the boat?"

"Get some clothes on. We've got to figure this out." She whirled away and clattered down the stairs, leaving me to stand, open-mouthed, astonished, and more than a little afraid.

CHAPTER FIFTEEN

They were all there, huddled around a chair at the breakfast nook table. I assumed it was Scarlett who sat surrounded by the chattering mob, but I couldn't see anything other than the top of her blond head, obviously bowed.

I had thrown a robe on over my pj's, not wanting to waste time getting dressed. Pudge twisted around at my entrance.

"Bay's here. Let her ask the questions."

I had no clue what I was supposed to be asking questions *about*, but I let Pudge lead me into the center of the melee. Scarlett had her head resting on her folded arms, and her shoulders shook with what I took to be sobs, although she wasn't emitting any sound.

"Scarlett? It's Bay. Bay Simpson."

She looked up then, her face grim, but no hint of any tears. "Bay? What on earth are you doing here?"

"Long story," I said. "Tell me what happened."

She drew in a long breath, and I had an opportunity to study her in more detail. The hair was still blond, but it definitely looked as if it had some assistance from a very talented stylist. I was surprised to see that she wore full makeup, including eyeliner, a skill I'd never been able to master. Though her skin was somewhat splotchy, as if she'd been crying earlier, it seemed smooth and slightly tanned. In total, she looked a whole hell of a lot better than the rest of us probably did, fresh from sleep and without the artificial armor most of the others donned daily.

Although, that wasn't entirely right. Pudge was fully dressed. Bebe wore a robe and, incongruously, her penny loafers, and I wondered if she couldn't afford a decent pair of slippers. The others were in robes, and most held coffee mugs. I was the only one who looked as if she'd just rolled out of bed. I glanced across the room, surprised to find the clock over the stove reading 9:45. I never slept that late. Well, almost never. I jerked back when Scarlett began talking.

"We went to bed about eleven, because James's friends were coming early." Her voice shook only a little. "We sleep in separate cabins. He snores." She said it as if it was something she'd memorized. "Sometime in the middle of the night I heard the dinghy, or at least I thought I did, but then I thought I must be mistaken. I went back to sleep." She lowered her eyes. "I . . . I don't usually sleep well, so I take something. When I woke up, about six, the dinghy was gone. And James, too. I waited, not sure what to do, because he's never done anything like this before. But he didn't come back."

"What about your car?"

She frowned at me. "What about it?"

"Was it still there? At the marina?"

"Of course. I drove it over here."

"Okay. So the only thing missing is the dinghy?" She nodded. "Where do you keep it?"

"On the yacht. That's the whole point. If you have to anchor somewhere rather than dock, you need some way to get to shore." She spoke as if she were addressing a not very bright child.

"Sorry, but I don't know a lot about boats. So go on. Then what did you do?"

"Then his friends showed up, and they insisted on searching the yacht, but of course he wasn't there, so I said no." She sniffed loudly. "They're out looking for him."

"Where?" I asked.

"What do you mean?" Scarlett's chin rose a fraction, as if I'd challenged her in some way.

"Where are they looking for him? Did they have some idea about where to start? On land? Or did they hire a boat?"

She looked me then—really looked into my face—and I thought for a moment I detected the bare hint of a smile. "I wouldn't know. They don't confide in me."

That sounded incredibly strange, but I let it go.

"We should call the sheriff."

It was Bitsy, and I wondered if she'd also stayed the night. I found it hard to believe she'd have left her kids to fend for themselves, but they were getting to an age when that might not have been a problem. And there was always Big Cal, her oaf of a husband, although I'd never noticed his being particularly helpful in the parenting role.

"They won't do anything," I said. "He's a fully capable adult man, and there wasn't any evidence of foul play." I locked my gaze onto Scarlett's. "Was there?"

Her hand went to her throat, and her fingers ran the obscenely large diamond drop along the fine gold chain, back and forth, back and forth.

"I don't know what you mean."

I drew in a long breath and ordered myself to be patient. "Was his bed disturbed? Any stuff thrown around as if there'd been some sort of struggle?" I didn't see any point in pulling punches. "Blood?"

Jenny gasped. "You think someone attacked him?"

"I have no idea. Well?" My eyes never wavered from Scarlett's.

She met my stare without flinching. "No, nothing like that. His bed had been slept in, but his pajamas and robe were on the floor. As if he'd dressed in a hurry."

"This makes no sense." Pudge stood a little apart from the group hovering around Scarlett. "Why would he get up in the middle of the night, get dressed, and take the dinghy out? He certainly couldn't have gone fishing. Could he?"

Scarlett uttered a sound somewhere between a sob and a laugh. "He doesn't even like to fish. He just does it because his bosses expect him to entertain their clients and business associates. They pay for the upkeep of the yacht."

I made a snap decision. "Scarlett, you need to take me over there. I'll throw on some clothes."

As I turned away, Bebe said, "We'll all come."

"No." I whirled back around. "Let's not make a big production out of this until we know for sure what's happened. I'll report back as soon as we know anything."

"I'm coming." Pudge spoke softly, but there was no denying the steel in her voice. "The rest of you wait here. There's plenty of food, and Bebe has her car if you need to go out for anything. Bay's right. There's no sense in turning this into a circus until we have more information."

Surprisingly, no one disagreed. Except for Bitsy.

"I need to get on home, at least for a little while. Y'all can call me if . . . when I need to come back."

I didn't wait for any more discussion, but trotted up the stairs. In less than ten minutes I had brushed my teeth and hair, thrown on the clothes I'd carried with me, and was back downstairs. I'd also managed to talk briefly to Red. I knew he'd be tied up with collecting the kids and getting them back to the island, but I wanted him to know at least the bare bones of what was going on. He told me to be careful and to keep him posted. I promised on both counts.

"Okay," I said, "Pudge, Scarlett, let's go."

"I'll drive," Pudge offered, and I shook my head.

"I've got it." I didn't mention that, for reasons I couldn't explain, I'd decided to keep my S&W handgun locked in the glove compartment of the Jaguar. I'd been carrying it around for the past several months, eschewing its usual storage space alongside the Seecamp in the floor safe in my bedroom. I hadn't examined my motives, and I'd be hard pressed to put them into words. I only knew I felt better knowing it was there within reach when I was on the road, out of touch with either home or office.

If Red knew—or objected—he'd never mentioned it.

It seemed, under the circumstances, like a good idea to have it close by.

As we made our way down the front steps, the rest of the group trailed along behind. They huddled together behind the railing, some with arms linked, no one speaking, and I thought again of Anne's use of the word *sisterhood*. Maybe I'd read way too much into it. Maybe all she'd meant was that this strange mix of women, some with long ties to one another, had formed a familial bond that went beyond friendship. That they would care for and support each other no matter what.

I pulled away, watching them recede in the rearview mirror, and felt a momentary pang that I'd never been invited to join the club.

CHAPTER SIXTEEN

Skull Creek Marina is nestled inside the back gate of Hilton Head Plantation, almost across the street from the country club and golf course. I'd never had occasion to visit either, mostly, I supposed, because I didn't boat or golf. It was one of the continual surprises of living on this small barrier island, that these pockets of activity could exist and flourish almost unnoticed by outsiders, including those of us who called it home.

We had a little hassle at the gate because I didn't have a resident sticker or visitor pass. Luckily, Scarlett recognized the woman in the uniform that stretched across her considerable chest and managed to cajole her into granting us admittance. We had the same procedure at Port Royal Plantation, and I always wondered why it was so important to some people to be huddled behind gates and guards. It was a false sense of security, at least to my mind, as anyone really determined to get in would find a way.

In only a couple of minutes I had pulled into the parking area at the foot of a long boardwalk. We piled out of the car and followed Scarlett across the short stretch of marsh and open water where another expansive dock formed a T. There were a lot of sailboats tied up to the various slips, along with smaller craft. Lots of empty spaces, too. I wondered if people had taken advantage of the beautiful spring Saturday to get out on the water. We kept on going, through a locked gate that Scarlett opened with a code, straight to the end where a long white yacht lay gleaming in the morning sunshine.

"It's beautiful," I said without thinking, turning to Scarlett.

"I suppose so," she said without enthusiasm. "To me it's just something else that has to be cleaned."

"Don't you have—?" I began, but Pudge cut me off.

"It's like having to two houses to take care of, that's what she meant. Hell, the inside of this thing is nicer than most people's homes."

We reached the end of the pier. "So you've been here before?"

Pudge nodded. "Scarlett gave me a tour when they first brought it down." She cast a glance sideways at our companion. "James was off somewhere."

The mention of his name focused me. "Can I look around?"

"There's nothing to see."

I turned to see that Scarlett had hung back, coming to a dead stop a few feet from the gangway.

"Where is the dinghy kept?"

"Up there." She pointed to the higher of the two decks where something that looked like an arm hung out over the side.

"Got it. And you use that . . . sort of derrick thing to put it in the water?"

"Right."

"Does it have a motor or do you have to paddle?"

"There's a small outboard."

"So you probably did hear it last night. Does the mechanism make any noise?"

Scarlett had been slowly edging her way back from the side of the boat until she stood several feet away.

"Why are you asking me all these questions?"

I drew in a calming breath. "I'm trying to figure out what happened. Isn't that what you want?"

"Of course I do! My husband has just fallen off the face of the earth. Don't you think I want to know where he is?"

It was a strange turn of phrase—*fallen off the face of the earth*—but I supposed she was entitled. I was having a difficult time deciding exactly how to characterize Scarlett's reaction. If everything the girls had said about her relationship with her husband was true, then I could sort of understand why she wasn't wailing and moaning. Still, there was definitely something odd about her behavior.

"Of course," I said. "But you need to help me. I don't know the first thing about yachts like this. My only experience was with those johnboats the Judge and his cronies used to take out into the marshes when they went duck hunting. I think your father used to go along once in a while, didn't he?"

"I have no idea what he did. Nor do I care."

With that, Scarlett pivoted and took off at a brisk walk that turned into a trot.

"Jesus, Bay, lay off her for a while, okay?"

Pudge shot me a scathing look and headed after Scarlett's retreating back.

"Okay," I said to no one in particular, turned, and stepped aboard the *Tiger Pause*.

The interior proved to be as stunning as the outside. Brightly polished wood was everywhere. The seating in the main room looked plush and comfortable, a built-in U-shaped sofa and several individual chairs. A flat screen TV was encased in a cabinet, and there were tables, many with storage, bolted to the floor. *Or deck*, I corrected myself. Probably to keep them from sliding around in rough weather. Wide windows spilled light over everything, including a compact but fully equipped galley, with what looked to be granite countertops, a full range and oven, and lots of cabinets. *You really could live on board this thing*, I said to myself, as I negotiated a narrow hallway toward the front.

"Bow," I said aloud, then added, "oh the hell with it!"

I'd never get the terminology right. My mind flashed back to the nightmare of my one other encounter with a boat this size in Palmetto Bay Marina. The layout had been similar, but that one had been considerably larger. Or at least that's how I remembered it, much as I tried not to.

The bedrooms both showed signs of occupancy, although the one that held Scarlett's clothes had been straightened. The bed was made, and a peek in the nearest bathroom also showed evidence of having been cleaned, faucets gleaming and towels neatly folded. In the larger cabin I found James's pj's and robe crumpled on the floor, just as Scarlett had described. The duvet was neatly folded back, but the sheets looked rumpled.

There was certainly no sign of a struggle of any kind.

Back outside, I climbed a ladder to the deck that had held the dinghy, but there wasn't much to see except the spot where the little boat must have been secured when the yacht was out to sea. I looked back along the boardwalk to see Scarlett and Pudge ambling slowly back in my direction, their heads together in what looked like serious conversation. I shimmied down the ladder and hopped back onto the dock.

I waited for them to approach, but they stopped a few yards short of me. Whatever it was they were conferring about apparently wasn't meant for my ears, a situation that always sent my antennae quivering. I glanced past them to the small building attached to the docks. It looked like some sort of office, and I wondered if someone manned it 24/7. Probably not. The marina wasn't exactly a hive of activity, at least not at this time of year. Maybe in the height of summer, when I guessed there'd be a lot of visiting boat traffic, people stopping off on their way to or from other spots along the East Coast. I knew the Intracoastal Waterway ran smack through our little slice of paradise, and the island had a lot to offer visitors, whether they came by road or water.

I set my shoulders and walked directly toward my two former classmates. Strange, I thought as I approached Pudge and Scarlett, how those relationships lasted through years of separation and change—marriages, children, triumphs, disasters—our adult personae never quite able to excise the bonds formed during our floundering teens.

I was a few steps away when my cell phone chimed from the pocket of my jeans. I stopped and checked the caller ID and picked up when I saw Red's name flashing on the screen.

"Hey," I said, turning my back, "what's up?"

"Where are you?" he said without preamble.

"At the marina. I've been through the boat, and he's definitely not here. No sign of a struggle, and the dinghy is missing." I paused. "And Scarlett—Mary Alice—is acting a little strange."

"You think she knows more than she's saying?"

I glanced over my shoulder. Both women had abandoned whatever they'd been discussing and were now staring directly at me.

"I do, although I'd be hard pressed to give you anything concrete." I took a quick look at my watch. "Are you home? Everything okay with the kids?"

"Fine. Scotty's game ran a little long, so I took the opportunity to give Malik a call, see if there'd been any reports of a boating accident."

Even though Red had been gone from the sheriff's office for quite some time, he still maintained a good relationship with most of his former colleagues, especially the man who's life he'd saved out at Sanctuary Hill. Despite regulations, Malik could almost always be counted on to slip us information when it didn't compromise any ongoing departmental investigation.

"And?"

"Nothing. Any hint of why he might have taken off? Did they have some kind of blowup or something?"

I shot another look behind me. "Not that she's saying. And besides, it seems that James's reaction to any marital friction is to beat the crap out of his wife, not take off for parts unknown."

"Point taken. Anyway, I just wanted you to know." He paused, then seemed to turn away from the phone. "I don't know where your sneakers are, honey. I didn't wear them last."

I smiled. *Elinor.* "Red? Tell her they're in her closet. Dolores cleaned them up after she wore them to the beach last weekend. She probably doesn't recognize them since they're not caked with mud and sand. And not lying in the middle of the floor."

He laughed. "You gotta love the kid." His voice sobered. "So what's your next move?"

"I don't have a clue. I thought maybe I'd check with the dock master or whoever it is that keeps track of things around here, if I can find anyone on a Saturday morning. Sorry, but I don't know when I'll make it home."

"Not to worry. We're going out to the sporting goods store to stock up on some things the kids need, then I'll take them to lunch. What do you think about dinner?"

"Don't count on me. There's spaghetti sauce in the freezer if you want to mess with it."

"And the pizza delivery guy on speed dial," he said. "I wish I could help, honey, but . . ."

"Understood. I'll try to keep you posted, if there turns out to be anything to report. There's no use getting anyone official involved at this stage, right?"

"You know the drill. Forty-eight hours. But now that Malik is aware of the situation, I wouldn't be surprised if he hasn't quietly passed the word for the guys to keep an eye out."

"That's great, but not much help if he's out on the water."

The South Carolina Department of Natural Resources did most of the patrolling on our waterways, at least as I remembered it. And the Coast Guard, but their station was in Charleston. Still, if it came down to it, they had helicopters.

"True. You be careful, you hear me?"

I smiled. "Not to worry. Apparently the most dangerous thing I'm going to be involved in is trying to keep a house full of women from turning on each other."

"Better you than me."

"Thanks, pal. Give the kids a hug. I'll be home when I can."

"Love you," he said, and I cut the connection without responding.

The moment I shoved the phone back in my pocket, Pudge and Scarlett surrounded me.

"You have any news?" Pudge asked.

"No, not really. That was Red. He alerted a buddy of his at the sheriff's office, but there's been no word of any boating accidents. What were you two so engrossed in back there? Something I should know about?"

"I'm really getting a bit tired of your attitude." Scarlett spoke in what I immediately labeled her *Queen of Buckhead* voice. "You sound as if you think I'm lying to you."

I held her gaze for as long as she was able to sustain the eye contact. When she finally looked away, I said, "Maybe not lying. But you're not telling me the whole truth either. My bullshit meter has been pretty well developed over the course of my careers, and you're making it jump off the scale." The decision was a snap one, but it felt like exactly the right response. "Call me when you've decided to come clean," I said, shouldering my way past them and marching down the dock.

I hadn't made it more than twenty yards when Pudge's hand fell on my shoulder. It took a great deal of self control not to slap it away.

"Listen, Bay, come on. She's upset. She didn't mean anything by that."

I stopped and turned to face my old friend. "This is getting ugly, Pudge. Scarlett is hiding something, and she's obviously more comfortable confiding in you than she is in me. I get that. But this whole thing is starting to feel off to me. Maybe she dumped James's sorry ass in the creek last night. Or maybe he just decided to do a runner. Maybe he's embezzling from his firm or maybe he has a new girlfriend and doesn't want to have to give up anything in a divorce. The possibilities are boundless, and I can't do a damn thing to help you and Mary Alice if she keeps skating around the truth. If you know what she's hiding, now's the time."

I watched the mental battle rage in Pudge's eyes for less than a minute.

"Okay. Okay. Just give me some time to talk to her. Wait right here."

With that she turned and hustled back to where Scarlett stood, her arms resting on the weathered railing, her gaze seemingly locked on the endless stands of trees across the creek on Pinckney Island.

I thrust my hands into my pockets and thought about how tough it would be to admit that Red had been right about this whole mess. The somnolent quiet of the golden spring morning was suddenly broken by a shout, and all three of us turned to watch two men come striding purposefully up the dock. One of them was gesticulating, and his words were being carried away from us on a brisk offshore breeze, but the angry set of his mouth as he got closer made his intent pretty clear. Both of them whipped by me and zeroed in on my two friends leaning against the rail.

"Okay, what's going on?" I heard the larger of the two say, although neither of them could have been called a small man. Former offensive tackles gone a little to seed was my first impression, but all that flew out of my head when the bigger one grabbed Scarlett by the arm.

She squealed, not loudly, but more like a frightened puppy. I automatically reached for the gun I might have had tucked into the waistband of my jeans only to realize that it still lay unreachable in the glove box of the Jaguar. I pulled out my phone as I sprinted in their direction, ready to punch in 911, when Pudge stepped back and landed a right jab to his gut, doubling him over. His companion made a move toward her, and I hesitated only a moment before leaping into the fray.

CHAPTER SEVENTEEN

I am not a small woman, but I knew instinctively that none of us would be a match for the two burly guys if they decided to turn this into a real fistfight. Either of them could have tossed us into the water without breaking a sweat, but somehow sanity prevailed. Before I'd even had an opportunity to get in the game, they had stepped back, hands out in surrender. I knew it wasn't from fear of three middle-aged women but obviously some spark of their upbringing that dictated it was bad form to engage in hand-to-hand combat with females.

A lesson James Madison Stuart the Third had apparently never absorbed.

"Who the hell are you?" I asked, slightly winded after my sprint and the rush of adrenaline.

"Who the hell are *you?*" the one who hadn't been decked by Pudge snapped back.

"They're James's . . . *associates.*" Mary Alice fairly spat the word, and the wounded man forced himself upright, his face twisted in anger.

"And you're supposed to be his wife," he fired back. "We're out scouring the whole damn island trying to find him, and you're here partying with your friends?"

"Back off," I said with as much authority as I could muster. "Let's everybody just settle down." I scanned the area of the dock, surprised that the commotion hadn't attracted any attention. At least no one had come on a dead run to offer assistance. I waved my phone. "I have the sheriff's office on speed dial, and they can have someone here in about two minutes."

"You don't scare me, lady," the shorter one said. He flipped his gaze to Scarlett. "And you need to come clean about what the hell is going on here, missy."

The epithet stung, as if Mary Alice had heard it before.

"Go to hell," she said, her chin rising a fraction. "I don't answer to you."

The one Pudge had decked took a step forward.

"If either one of you lays a hand on her again, you're going to be enjoying the hospitality of the local lockup. I'm sure your employers or your families wouldn't be too keen on having to drive all the way down here to bail your sorry asses out."

That seemed to sink in. I held his gaze, and his shoulders relaxed. I waited a beat then slid the phone back into my pocket. I held out my hand.

"I'm Bay Tanner, and this is Sylvie Reynaud. We're friends of Mary Alice's. She asked us here to help her find out what happened to James."

The shorter—and younger—of the two men was the first to accept the peace offering. "I'm Larry Ferrell." He cocked his head in the direction of his companion who continued to rub at the spot just below his breastbone where Pudge's jab had landed. "This is Hank Edison."

I gave his hand the proper amount of pressure, enough to show him I didn't shake hands like a girl, just the way the Judge had taught me. Edison hesitated and finally begrudgingly allowed his fingers to brush against mine.

"Why don't we make ourselves comfortable and talk this through?" I gestured toward the yacht, then turned to Scarlett. "Okay?"

Without a word, she pivoted on her heel and led the procession down the few yards of dock and up the gangway onto the *Tiger Pause*. Once inside, we lined up like fighters in their respective corners, the men on one side of the large seating area, the three of us women clustered opposite them on one of the sofas.

"Did you find anything?" I asked just at the same moment Larry said, "This is getting really weird."

We both stopped, each waiting for the other to continue. Finally, I said, "Go ahead, Larry. Tell us where you've been and what you've found out."

"Why should we?" Hank Edison still glared in spite of his apparent acquiescence to the sit-down.

"Bay's a private investigator. She works *very* closely with local law enforcement, so I suggest you cut the attitude and answer her question." It had been Pudge's first contribution since her punch landed, and Hank bristled.

"No one's talking to you, babe," he said with a sneer.

"You want me to kick your ass again, buster? You may be big, but you're slow. I have a brown belt, and it would do my heart good to knock some manners into your flabby butt."

I whirled on her. "Knock it off, Pudge. This isn't getting us anywhere."

"No one calls me *babe* and gets a chance to do it again," she said.

"But you let her call you *Pudge?*" Hank's voice dripped contempt.

I laid a warning hand on Pudge's arm. "It's a childhood nickname," I said. "And I would seriously suggest you not use it again. Now, can we all take a giant step back and try to conduct ourselves like semi-reasonable adults? We're all after the same thing here, right? We need to find out what happened to James. If you like, I'll go first, although I don't have much to offer. Mary Alice heard what she thought was the dinghy in the middle of the night, but then figured she'd been mistaken. She didn't realize her husband was gone until about six this morning." I leaned forward so I could see Scarlett's face. "Right?"

She nodded, refusing to meet my gaze.

"She and Sylvie are old friends, and I . . ." I faltered for a moment. "I happened to be at her house this morning when Mary Alice came to ask for help, so I volunteered to come along. So far there doesn't appear to be any evidence that James left other than under his own power. No sign of a struggle. So what do you have to contribute?"

I looked from one to the other of them. Larry Ferrell seemed to have been elected to speak for both.

"We were supposed to meet James here around seven thirty. When we showed up, she—" He cocked his head in Scarlett's direction. "Mrs. Stuart said he wasn't here and she didn't know when he'd be back. We've made plans to go out on the boat dozens of times, and James has never done this before. We waited around out on the dock for about an hour, and I tried his cell every fifteen minutes, with no luck." His jaw tightened. "She wouldn't let us wait in here."

"I wasn't dressed," Scarlett said in a small voice. "James wouldn't have liked it if I let you onboard when he wasn't here."

"Way I hear it," Hank said in a voice that dripped with innuendo, "James wouldn't have been surprised at all."

Scarlett's face colored, and she dropped her head as if she'd been struck.

Pudge slid to the edge of the sofa cushion, and I laid a restraining hand on her arm.

"That's a rotten thing to say." I forced the words out through clenched teeth.

Larry gave Hank a hard stare, and he, too, dropped his head.

"Sorry," he mumbled. "It's just that . . . I mean, we've heard things, okay?"

"I don't give a damn what you've heard. Let's just stick to the issue. Where exactly did you look for James?"

Pudge leaned back and placed a protective arm around Scarlett's shoulder. She slumped against the taller woman, a marionette whose strings had suddenly been cut. Her brief flare of independence seemed to have been short-lived.

Larry cleared his throat and focused his attention on me. "Well, we noticed the dinghy was gone, first thing, so we figured he was out trolling or maybe scouting out some fishing holes. But that didn't make a lot of sense because James isn't really into the whole fishing thing, you know? He likes being on the boat and hanging out with the guys, enjoying the experience so to speak. He'll drop a line in once in awhile, especially if they're running pretty good, but most of the time he just sits on the bridge and watches the rest of us." He glanced at his companion. "Right, Hank?"

"Yeah."

After his unforgivable slur on Mary Alice's character, he had apparently decided to drop out of the whole conversation.

I repeated my question. "So where did you look?"

Larry shrugged. "We drove around to some of the places where we've dropped anchor before, you know, along the creeks. Over by the May River. Pinckney. I have binoculars in the Escalade, and I checked out any small boat we saw, but there were only a couple. I can't figure why he's not answering his cell. He keeps the damned thing glued to his ear most of the time." Again he cast a look at Hank. "I mean, we didn't think anything had happened to him, not until we'd been out there running around for a couple of hours. If something came up to make him need to cancel, he would have called. Hell, we came down last night. He knows we're at the Westin, just like always. It's not like him, right?"

This was directed to Scarlett, but she ignored him.

"Right?" he said again, turning to Hank.

"James is anal. I guess that's what makes him a good attorney. When he says to be here at seven thirty, you damn well better be on time because the boat's leavin' at seven thirty-five, with or without you."

He managed a smile, and the expression changed his whole demeanor. It almost made him attractive. Almost.

"Listen," he went on, "I'm sorry about that crack, Mrs. Stuart. I was out of line. And I'm sorry if I scared you out there." He paused to run a hand through his thinning brown hair. "It's just that we've known James a long time. I wouldn't say we were best friends, but we've been doin' this for a lot of years. We're worried about him, same as you."

Scarlett finally raised her gaze from the floor. "I accept your apology, although what you said was extremely hurtful." It was Mary Alice Pierce Stuart at her haughtiest. "I appreciate your efforts to locate my husband, but I believe we can handle it from here." She tilted her head in my direction. "We have professionals involved, and the police will be notified. I think it would be best for all concerned if you left us alone now. Thank you for coming."

She rose, her back ramrod straight, and disappeared in the direction of the staterooms. With a quick glance at me, Pudge hurried after her.

"So," I said after an uncomfortable silence, "I guess that's that. As Mary Alice says, we'll take it from here."

Neither one of them made any move toward rising, so I stood and held out my hand. "If you leave me your numbers, I'll be sure to let you know what transpires."

They both hesitated, whether it had to do with genuine concern about their friend or more likely that they hated being bested by a bunch of women. They struck me as that kind of men, which might explain their close relationship with James. It didn't really matter to me. Either way, they had become expendable, at least as far as my investigation was concerned. Still, I didn't want to alienate them completely. If it came down to a real disappearance, possibly involving foul play or maybe the bastard just deciding to ditch his life and start over, their insight into James might come in handy.

Larry lumbered to his feet and shook my hand, then reached into his wallet for a card. "You can get in touch with me. I'll keep Hank up to date." He paused. "How about you?"

"Simpson and Tanner, Inquiry Agents. We're in the book."

There didn't seem to be anything else to say. I followed them out as they made their way onto the deck and down the gangway. I watched them plod back up the dock, not speaking, until they disappeared into the parking lot. A few moments later I saw a gleaming black Escalade whip out onto the street and speed away.

Back inside, I flopped onto the couch and stretched out my legs.

This is turning into a real mess, I told myself. From the companionway I could hear what sounded like an argument between Pudge and Scarlett, but I didn't have the energy or inclination to jump into whatever was going on with them. I thought about Hank Edison's crack about Mary Alice and wondered how much truth there might be in it. On the surface, it made no sense. I didn't know a hell of a lot about the psychology of battered women, but I found it hard to believe that someone who had suffered physical abuse at the hands of one man would seek out another one. Still, who knew? Maybe that was perfectly natural. I needed to consult with Neddie.

I remembered then that she was on the island for the weekend. I'd drop these two back at Pudge's house and pay a call on my old roomie, see if I could pick her brain. I had just risen to get them moving when they suddenly materialized in front of me. Both of them looked as if they'd been put through the wringer.

"What?" I asked, rising to meet them. "What's wrong?"

"Scarlett wants you to go now," Pudge said. I noticed that she'd stepped away from our friend, physically as well as emotionally, or so it seemed to me.

"Why?"

"She just does. She says she wants to be alone."

"Why?" I repeated, and Mary Alice's head snapped up.

"You're just making things worse. I need to think."

"About what? Either you want to find your husband or you don't. What's to think about?"

"Just go," she said with a weariness that tugged at my heart a little. "Please."

"Fine." I paused on my way toward the deck. "What about your car?"

"It's not your problem. None of this was ever your problem."

I stepped outside and waited for Pudge to join me. When she didn't, I shrugged and walked slowly back to where I'd left the Jaguar, slid behind the wheel, and let out a long breath.

If I wasn't mistaken, I'd just been fired.

CHAPTER EIGHTEEN

I stomped up the stairs from the garage and into my bedroom, flinging my bag onto the bed.

When we'd dashed out of Pudge's house, I'd had the good sense to throw all my things—including the pile of emails Bitsy had offered—into the Jag. I wasn't sure if it was because I didn't trust the others not to snoop or if I'd had some inkling of how the morning was going to play out.

Which was ridiculous, I thought, as I separated my clothes from the files and papers, tossed the former into the hamper and dumped the latter onto my desk. How could I possibly have foreseen that Scarlett would throw me out on my ear after all the time and effort I'd expended on her behalf? Hell, I'd nearly gotten into a fistfight with a couple of over-the-hill football players, and she shows her thanks by dismissing me like some unsatisfactory servant?

I forced myself to take a deep, cleansing breath. Time to calm down.

I should have written up a report for Sharese to add to the file, but I was too agitated to think about it right then. I peeled off my jeans, pausing to pull Larry Ferrell's card from the pocket before I dropped them on top of all my other dirty clothes.

"Lawrence T. Ferrell, Executive Vice-President of Sales," I read aloud. The company was one I'd never heard of, headquartered in Atlanta. I'd Google Stoney Brook Recreation and Management after I'd had a shower and a chance to cool off. As I set the body sprays on full, I realized I didn't really know anything about what James's outfit did either. Some sort of conglomerate with their hands in a lot of pies, if I remembered correctly. Apparently it was big enough to warrant an in-house counsel.

I stepped beneath the pounding cascade of water and tried to empty my mind. I felt as if I'd been well and thoroughly jerked around for the past few days, and I didn't like it. Not one bit. Pudge had played me, using our old relationship, parlaying it into a sort of benign form of blackmail, if I was honest about it. And I'd let her do it. That pissed me off more than any of the rest of it.

Well, I'd calculate just exactly how much time we'd all spent on this nonsense and send Pudge—*Sylvia*—a refund from her retainer. James could go to hell, or wherever he'd decided to end up on his little jaunt. I felt sure he'd show up when he was damn good and ready. And if Mary Alice was stupid enough to take up her role as resident punching bag again, then that was her problem. *Not* mine, as she'd so rudely pointed out.

I let the water beat on my head for a long time, feeling a lot of the tension melt out of me. By the time I heard the Bronco in the driveway, I'd dressed, straightened the papers into some semblance of order, and thrown a load of clothes in the washer. Having missed both breakfast and lunch, I wolfed down a couple of English muffins with peanut butter and pulled the spaghetti sauce out of the freezer.

The kids came trotting up the three steps into the kitchen, Scotty laden with shopping bags. Elinor flung her arms around my waist, and I suddenly realized how much she'd grown in the past few months. Those hugs used to involve my legs.

"Hey there, you two," I said, smiling at Red as he followed them up. "Did you leave anything for anyone else to buy?"

"Hey, Aunt Bay," the gangly boy said. "I needed new soccer cleats. I can't hardly get my feet in the old ones anymore." He glanced over his shoulder. "And Dad *insisted* I get some new T-shirts and stuff."

"You can see the bruises where I twisted his arm," my husband said, planting a brief kiss on my cheek.

"And I got some new stuff, too," sweet Elinor offered. "Want to see?"

"Sure," I said, "in a minute."

Red rightly interpreted the look I gave him. "Why don't you guys go lay everything out on your beds for inspection? We'll be there shortly."

They bounded back down the steps, and I smiled after them. It was wonderful to see that exuberance after the awful months of waiting to find out if their mother would manage to win her battle with breast cancer. They'd been sullen, mostly out of fear, and I completely understood, although it had been painful to watch. Seeing them happy again made my heart a little lighter. I just hoped Sarah's good outcome would hold.

"So what happened?" Red moved around me and pulled the iced tea pitcher out of the refrigerator. "I didn't expect to see you back so soon."

"Let's sit down."

We moved to the round table set into the bay window, and I told him the whole story. Condensed, of course, because the kids were waiting for us, but I felt I hit all the salient points.

"So I guess we're fired," I said. "I have to say it's an experience I don't care to repeat if I can help it."

Red clasped my hand where it rested on the table. "Well, technically, you don't work for her, right? I mean, it was your friend Tubby—"

My hoot of laughter cut him off in mid-sentence.

"What?" he asked with a grin that told me he knew exactly what he'd said.

"It's Pudge, not Tubby," I said and saying the words out loud sent me off again.

Red smiled. "That's better." His face sobered. "But we need to talk about this. The man is still missing."

"And frankly, my dear, I don't give a damn," I said. "At least not today." I rose and took his hand. "Come on, let's go see what those kids of yours have wheedled out of you this time."

Hand in hand we walked down the hallway toward the bedrooms.

We stuffed ourselves with spaghetti, salad, and garlic bread, followed by ice cream halfway through a silly movie the rest of them had been dying to see. I had half an ear on the antics of two incredibly stupid men who continually put themselves in incredibly stupid situations and the other half tuned to my cell phone.

I had expected to hear from Pudge. She owed me an explanation—if not an outright apology—and I felt certain she would have figured that out over the course of the day. But not a peep. I wasn't sure if I was more angry or relieved.

Red and I kicked it around for a while after Scotty and Elinor had reluctantly trooped off to bed. I showed him the emails from

Mary Alice to Bitsy, and he had the good sense not to inquire too closely into how my oldest friend and I had managed to mend our rift so quickly. He was appalled at the descriptions of James's brutal treatment of his wife.

"You know, though, we only have her word for it," he said after a while, his free hand stroking my back as we sat side by side on the sofa.

"The others—the girls—have seen the bruises. And the broken bones. So it isn't just a he-said, she-said thing. And you don't have to spend a lot of time around Mary Alice to see that she's been beaten down emotionally. When that Hank guy touched her arm, she just whimpered like a puppy." I shook my head. "It was difficult to watch."

"I hear you. But if it ever came to a court case, could she prove he was the one who injured her? It sounds as if she's never called the cops on him, at least according to what Erik and I found. Or didn't find, more like it. Don't you wonder why she's put up with it all these years?"

"Of course I do, but I'm guessing that's part of the . . . psychopathy? I'm not sure if that's the right word. I'll ask Neddie."

The idea of being in touch with her had flown right out of my head, basically, I supposed, because I no longer had a client. Or did I? Red had a point. It was Pudge who'd hired me, not Scarlett. I didn't like feeling in limbo, and I wished to hell she'd just call and get it over with.

But she didn't.

Sunday passed as it usually did. The kids went grudgingly to Sunday school. After Red picked them up, we all decided to go out for pancakes. The weather had cooled a little, but we bundled up and took a brisk walk on the beach before it was time for them to gather their things together for the trek back to their mother's.

I toyed with the idea of riding along and making a side trip to Presqu'isle, but in the end I didn't. The thought of facing Julia and all her shenanigans on top of the other upsets of the weekend just seemed too much to handle. I settled for a long chat with Lavinia. She sounded cheerful, regaling me with stories of their Saturday spent working the ground for the spring flower beds, of battles with moles and their tunnels and with especially recalcitrant weeds. She said that the pair of ospreys who for years had nested in the same place in the old dead tree near the dock had returned and were busy adding to their home. I loved those birds, a certain sign that spring had returned to the Lowcountry, and I promised to stop by soon to check on their progress.

Monday morning had a surreal aura about it. I kept glancing out to where Erik normally sat. Even though the privacy screen blocked my direct view of his desk, I would have known that he wasn't there. A sort of emptiness pervaded the office, although I would have been hard pressed to articulate that feeling without sounding like Jenny Carson. I wondered if the others had gone back home and what Pudge and Scarlett were doing about James's disappearance.

Or maybe he came back, I thought, finally ordering myself to knock it off and get some work done. The deadbeat dad hadn't been where Sharese's research had thought he might be, so we needed to get back on that case. With Erik out of the picture, Red had picked up the legwork and had called in a short time before to report no luck. I was reaching for the phone to buzz her and ask for an update when she appeared in the doorway. I sat up a little straighter when she stepped inside and pulled the door closed behind her.

"What is it?" I asked. "Is something wrong?"

She glanced over her shoulder. "There's a sheriff's guy here to see you. Mike Raleigh? He says you'll know what it's about."

She reached out and handed me a card, but I didn't need it. Mike and I had crossed paths a couple of times in the course of our investigations, and I both liked and trusted him. And he was right. I was pretty certain I knew why he'd come.

"Send him in."

"Yes, ma'am."

A moment later the tall, well-dressed detective reached across the desk to shake my hand. "Good to see you, Bay."

"You, too, Mike, although I'm afraid you don't come bearing glad tidings."

He smiled, a boyish grin that reminded me of Erik's. At a guess he wasn't much older than my partner, but he had always conducted himself with professionalism and good manners, unlike his nasty-tempered cohort, Lisa Pedrovsky.

I indicated the chairs in front of the desk, and he nodded before seating himself. He adjusted the sharp crease in his pants leg before crossing his ankle over his knee. While he gave the appearance of being relaxed, as if this were a social call, the notebook he pulled from the inside pocket of his suit jacket told me it wasn't.

"I've got a problem I'm hoping you can help me with."

"Does it have anything to do with James Madison Stuart the Third?" I asked and watched one corner of his mouth turn up in a half smile.

"Why do I always feel as if you're one step ahead of me?"

I shrugged. "Lucky guess."

His expression sobered almost immediately.

"His boat turned up."

"The dinghy?"

He nodded. "A couple of early morning fishermen spotted it. Pulled up in the trees on the west side of Pinckney Island. They wouldn't have seen it at all if one of them hadn't needed to take a—" He colored a little. "Didn't need to relieve himself."

"And James?"

"No sign of him. Well, that's not completely accurate."

I was pretty sure I knew what was coming.

"Blood?" I finally asked, and Detective Mike Raleigh nodded.

CHAPTER
NINETEEN

The story didn't take too long to tell.

I left out a lot of the details of the two evenings I'd spent with the members of the Unholy Alliance and their new recruits. I figured Mike didn't need to hear about all the catty undercurrents running through the group. I concentrated on why I'd been hired by Pudge, my limited actual knowledge—which even then was mostly hearsay—and my observations of Mary Alice Stuart. I kept my one piece of solid evidence—the emails—to myself for the time being. I didn't have time to analyze my reasons. It just seemed like the right thing to do.

"So you're saying this Stuart guy was a wife beater?"

I had known that particular information would rise immediately to a greater level of importance than anything else I'd told him. Even without that, a spouse is almost always at the top of the suspect list when foul play is suspected. In spite of my ranting and raving over the weekend, there was still some vestige of the old loyalty I couldn't quite shake. There was no point in throwing Scarlett under the bus, especially when we still didn't know exactly what had happened to James.

"Any signs of how he was injured? You think something occurred in the boat itself?"

"Too soon to tell. We'll have the forensics people take a look. My gut feeling is that he was attacked—or whatever—somewhere else and transported in the dinghy, although as I say, that's just my initial take on it."

"How much blood?"

"I don't know how to judge that. Let's just say it was more than a nosebleed."

"I checked his room on the yacht Saturday morning. There was no sign at all that something happened there. A struggle or an attack. I mean, even if someone tried to clean it up, there would have been signs—wet spots, a bleach smell, that sort of thing. I didn't see anything like that."

"Did you check the whole boat?"

"No, not completely, but I think I was in every room. Except the bridge."

"Well, the experts will be taking a look at it this afternoon." He paused and fiddled with the pen with which he'd been jotting notes. "Look, I know the wife is a friend of yours, but what's your take on this? Any gut feelings of your own?"

One thing I'd learned over the course of running an inquiry agency for the past few years was that cooperating with the authorities was almost always the best choice, unless doing so compromised a client. We didn't have any protected privilege, unless we were working in conjunction with an attorney. I'd played hardball a few times when I was convinced of my client's innocence, but for the most part it was in our best interests to work with rather than against an investigating officer.

Except in the case of Lisa Pedrovsky. Her I'd block every chance I got, if for no other reason than that she was a loud-mouthed, overbearing pain in the ass.

And she hated my guts.

"Who told you about me?" I asked, momentarily deflecting his question.

"The wife. Mary Alice, right?"

I nodded. "What did she say?"

"That you'd been around when she came to tell her other friends that she couldn't find her husband, and you'd offered to help. She didn't mention that one of those ladies had actually hired you."

I wondered why, although I'd been up front with Mike about Pudge's visit to the office the week before. Maybe trying to protect her? But from what?

"She might not have known. About Pudge—Sylvia, I mean. I never really had a chance to talk one-on-one with Mary Alice, although that was the plan."

"Convince her to throw the bum out?" He said it lightly, but I could tell by the tightening of the skin around his eyes he really wanted to hear my answer.

"Something like that. I'm no expert, but her friends thought I might be able to make her face up to the fact that, odds were, it wasn't going to end well." I paused, weighing whether or not to add anything, but I felt it needed to be said. "They were all afraid the abuse might escalate into a serious injury."

Mike, too, seemed to choose his words carefully. "Well, from the amount of blood in the bottom of the boat, I'm guessing she won't have to worry about that anymore. If it was her husband's, he could be hurt pretty badly."

He didn't add *or worse*, which were exactly the words I'd left out of my own assessment of Scarlett's situation.

Which was the ultimate in good news/bad news, I was afraid, at least as far as Mary Alice Stuart was concerned.

I pushed the implications of that aside for the moment. "So what happens next? Are you conducting a search of the island?"

"As we speak," he said briskly, rising. "And I should get back out there. Thanks a lot for your candor, Bay. I know it must be difficult to have to . . . you know, sort of rat out a friend."

"On the contrary," I said with a bite of anger in my voice. "I don't think I've done any such thing. I assume you've interviewed Mary Alice?"

He nodded.

"Can you seriously see her bashing her husband over the head, dragging his body into that dinghy, lowering it into the water, and then dumping him someplace? First of all, she isn't physically capable of it. Secondly, why now? She's put up with his crap all these years. She knew he had friends coming first thing in the morning and that his disappearance would raise all kinds of alarm bells. She's not a stupid woman, Mike."

"Maybe he hit her one too many times. Maybe she just snapped."

I shook my head. "I know you have to look at all these possibilities, but I'm telling you now Scarlett—Mary Alice—didn't do this. That dog just won't hunt."

He smiled at the expression, a favorite of my late father's.

"We'll see. Anyway, thanks for your time and the information. I'll be back in touch if—*when*—we locate Mr. Stuart."

We shook hands again, and he spoke to Sharese on his way out of the office. As soon as the door had closed behind him, I picked up the phone.

● ● ●

Pudge didn't answer, so I left a voice mail message for her to call me immediately. I guessed she was with Scarlett. I wondered what her reaction had been to the discovery of her husband's boat such a short distance away from where the yacht was moored. I shook my head. It would have been incredibly stupid of her to have dumped his body so close to home. Unless she'd thought the dinghy wouldn't be found for some time. But Pinckney Island was a renowned wildlife preserve. Locals loved its quiet walkways along the marshes with partially hidden ponds where all manner of shore birds nested and congregated. Visitors as well often made it a stop on their itineraries of must-see places when coming to the island. There were other more isolated islets, like Corn or the Harrys—Big and Little—where the boat might have escaped notice for a longer period of time.

But how would she get back? I asked myself, scootching down in the Judge's big, comfortable chair. Pinckney was the only one with a causeway back to solid ground. Unless she swam? But it wasn't open water, not until you got across a lot of squishy marsh and pluff mud. And Scarlett didn't strike me as the kind of woman who would voluntarily go tromping through the stinky, slimy stuff if she didn't have to. Of course, if it was high tide . . .

I shook my head. Despite my heated defense of her to Mike Raleigh, here I was concocting scenarios in which Scarlett had murdered her husband and disposed of his body. No way. The biggest impediment to such a theory was the first one I'd offered Mike: she just wasn't physically capable of it.

I looked up as Red walked into my office.

"You heard?" He dropped down into a chair and studied me across the wide expanse of desk.

"Yes. Mike Raleigh was just here."

"I know. Malik called me and said Raleigh was on his way. I thought maybe I might make it back before he left."

"Something you wanted to ask him?"

My husband shook his head. "No. I wanted to be here for you." He ducked his chin, as if embarrassed by his show of concern. "I know it wasn't entirely unexpected, but . . ." His voice trailed off.

"I'm fine," I said, realizing that I meant it. "Of course they're looking at Mary Alice, but she's just not capable of it."

"Everybody's capable of violence, Bay. You of all people

should know that."

I wasn't quite sure how to interpret that remark, but I set it aside for later consideration and gave Red my perfectly logical take on Scarlett's lack of physical ability to have carried out her husband's murder.

"There's no reason to assume she acted alone."

I had to admit I hadn't considered that scenario, and I knew the name that leaped instantly into my head was also rattling around in Red's brain.

"Pudge may be an ungrateful pain in the butt, but there's no way she would involve herself in a murder."

"Are you sure?" He spoke softly. "I mean, how well do you really know these women? It's been a lot of years since you've been in touch. People change."

"Not that much," I fired back. "And besides, it makes no sense. Why would she drag me in to the point that I was actually sleeping in her house if she had plans to commit a murder practically right under my nose?"

He shrugged. "Alibi?"

"Well not much of one. I was asleep until Scarlett came banging on Pudge's door. It's not as if we were all camped out in sleeping bags on the living room floor."

That made him smile. "Point taken. Anyway, I think you're well out of it. *We're* well out of it."

I wasn't sure he was right about that, but there was nothing to be gained by hashing it around. The chips would fall where they fell.

"So what's happening with this guy who's been making a habit of cheating his kids out of their support?"

Red settled himself back in the chair. "He's slippery. Sharese came up with a good lead, found him working off the books at one of the landscaping places, but he's already bugged out. I took another run at the manager, with zero success, but I have a feeling the guy could be one of his buddies. He claimed not to have known him, but I had a chat with one of the girls in the office. The boss isn't one of her favorite people on the planet, and she was very eager to share the information that the skip and the manager spent a lot of time together—lunch, cigarette breaks, that kind of stuff. I think he just might lead us to the deadbeat, eventually. It's going to take keeping an eye on him after work hours, so I might not be around much in the evenings for a while. Especially with Erik going AWOL."

I hadn't thought much about how Erik's absence would affect that aspect of the business. He'd spent more and more time in the field, at least until Stephanie's defection. The two of them had been a good team. I sighed and leaned back in my chair.

"Well, I'm available. We could tag-team it." I forced a smile. "Apparently I don't have a client at the moment."

Red leaned in and reached across the desk to pat my hand. "Probably a good thing, honey. If someone did knock off this Stuart guy, I mean. Don't you think?"

Logically, I had no comeback. But in my gut, I knew we hadn't quite finished with the Unholy Alliance.

Or with James Madison Stuart the Third.

CHAPTER
TWENTY

On Tuesday morning, Red and I sat over breakfast at the round table in the bay window sharing the *Island Packet* over scrambled eggs and sausage.

Normally, we grabbed something on the run, but we hadn't been able to do much more than that the night before, and we were both starving. We'd gone together to tail the manager—Doug Smith—from his small building on Route 278 to his home in a newer development off Buckwalter Parkway, not far from the Bluffton schools campus. It was a densely residential area that afforded us little in the way of places to conduct surveillance, so we'd basically wandered the neighborhood at about fifteen miles per hour. The Jaguar, although not one of the sportier models, nevertheless garnered its share of attention, and it soon became obvious that we couldn't just hang out without someone deciding to stop us and ask what the hell we were up to. Or call the cops.

We found a spot in one of the school parking lots that gave us a decent vantage point on the main entrance to Smith's place and settled in to wait. I'd stopped at home earlier to change and to throw some water and energy bars into a tote bag, and we sipped and munched in silence for the better part of an hour before our mark's dusty pickup with the company logo on the side pulled out.

Red had been driving, so I'd concentrated on keeping the white vehicle in sight. The problem was that night was rapidly falling, Daylight Saving Time still being a few days away, and in the end I had to resign myself to watching his taillights in the gathering dusk. Thankfully, he didn't go far. When he turned abruptly into a sketchy looking bar, Red eased on past, turned around in a gas station, and arrived in time to see Smith striding inside.

"So now what?" I'd asked as my husband stopped the Jag on the far side of the lot, under some overhanging branches of a scruffy live oak that looked to be on its last legs.

"So I'll go in and see if our guy is there." He'd pulled a photo from a folder alongside his seat.

"Do you know this place? I mean, have you ever been here— officially?"

"Yeah, a couple of times when a few pool-playing jerks got out of hand or someone took offense to the outcome of a USC-Clemson game. It's normally a decent crowd, if that's what you're worried about."

"I'm more concerned with your being recognized. And even if they don't, you still sort of scream *cop*, you know."

He'd looked at me in the gloom and smiled. "I do not."

I punched his arm. "Of course you do. It's the way you carry yourself, even without the uniform."

"All we want to do is see if he's there. We can't do anything about it, right? I mean we tail him back to wherever he's staying and let the ex-wife know so she can have papers served on him. Or have him picked up. We aren't going to arrest anyone."

He'd pushed open the door and headed for the bar before I'd had a chance to reply . . .

"Stuart made the front page, I see."

Red had made it through the first section of the paper and moved on to the sports while I was at the stove. Not that a mid-week *Packet* took that long to read unless, of course, you needed to study the ads along the bottom half of every page.

I looked up from the article on the disappearance. Not a headline or above-the-fold mention, just a short description of the discovery of the boat, a quote from the fisherman who stumbled on it, and a terse response from the sheriff's office spokesperson that the investigation was ongoing. There was also a request for anyone with information about James or his whereabouts to come forward.

We had entered day three of no contact, either from Pudge or Scarlett, and I had to admit it was beginning to get to me. I'd postponed my plan to have Sharese make out a check for the balance of Pudge's retainer, hoping, I suppose, that she'd change her mind. I wasn't certain why I entertained the possibility of getting back on the case. She hadn't answered my voice mail from the day before, the one I'd left right after talking with Mike Raleigh. I'd felt strongly that the discovery of the dinghy would have shaken both her and Scarlett, and my ego was undergoing a decided drubbing that neither one of them had contacted me for help or reassurance.

"What's on your mind?"

Red's voice jerked me out of my pointless speculation.

"Nothing. Why?"

He smiled. "You look as if you're ready to rip somebody's head off."

"Really? I suppose I could come up with a few candidates if I put my mind to it, but no one in particular at the moment."

"I thought maybe it was our illustrious deadbeat dad. I have to tell you, I could cheerfully wring his neck myself. Nothing pisses me off more than guys who flake out on their responsibility to their kids."

"That's because you're an exceptional father yourself."

"No, not exceptional. I just do what's right because it's . . . *right*," he said, his face coloring a little.

I carried our plates to the dishwasher. "And, unfortunately, in this day and age, that makes you exceptional."

I knew I'd embarrassed him, but I'd only spoken the truth.

"So which one of us is going to deliver the good news to Teri Walton?" he asked in an obvious attempt to change the subject.

When Red had emerged from the bar the night before, he'd been smiling so widely I could see it in the darkness. He'd slid into the Jag and handed the photo to me.

"He's in there. The two of them are knocking back Buds as if someone was going to come and rip them out of their hands."

"Good work. And no one made you?"

He shook his head. "Nope. Had a beer, chatted a little with the bartender, and here I am. All we have to do is wait them out."

Which is why we'd made a dinner out of energy bars and tepid water. We'd waited nearly two hours before both men emerged from the bar, a brief flash of light and loud music cutting the dim silence before the door swung closed behind them. Smith waved and wove a little unsteadily to his truck. Red and I had turned our backs as his high headlights swept across the windows of the Jag, but he never hesitated before pulling out and heading back down Route 46 toward home. Our mark, one Brian P. Walton, had no trouble as he unlocked a fairly new Camry and wheeled out in the opposite direction. At ten o'clock on a March Monday, we had little trouble staying back far enough to keep him in sight for the few minutes it took to make his way to one of the inexpensive motels that bordered Exit 5 on the interstate. He parked and climbed the outside stairs to a door about halfway down the building. Red cut the lights as we pulled into the lot, and I had bounded out to trot up the steps and make note of the room number a moment before a dim lamp came on behind the thin curtain . . .

"You may have the honors if you like," I said, closing the dishwasher and wiping my hands on a towel. "You did most of the legwork."

"It's not a contest," he said with a hint of annoyance in his voice.

"I know. It's just that I've got a couple of things to handle this morning, so you can make the notification. No big deal."

"It will be to Teri Walton."

"What's your problem?" When he didn't reply, I turned and slid my arms into the blazer I'd left hanging on the back of a chair. "Let's get going. We're already going to be late."

"So what?" I heard him mumble as he followed me out the door. "You own the place."

I filed that remark away as we each slid into our separate vehicles and the garage door rattled open.

And they claim women are hard to figure out, I said to myself as I pushed the gearshift into reverse and made sure I was the first one out of the garage.

Sharese was dusting off Erik's printer when we walked into the office.

"Morning, ma'am. Sergeant."

I nodded and scooped up my chai tea latte from the corner of her desk. Red stopped to chat.

Our usual routine was for the three of us—Erik, Red, and I—to conference over caffeine in my office before heading our separate ways. I decided it was time for Sharese to get her baptism by fire, so I buzzed her phone and asked the two of them to step in. She did a creditable job of balancing her coffee, her iPad, and a stack of mail, which she dropped on my desk. The envelopes had been slit, their contents fastened with paper clips, along with a sticky note if any explanation was required. I glanced through it while Red brought Sharese up to date on our late night surveillance of Brian Walton.

Bills, which I would need to approve for payment, a couple of checks, which were welcome. Nothing out of the ordinary until I got to the last one. Marked PERSONAL in large handwritten capitals, it remained sealed. No return address, postmarked in Savannah, but that didn't mean much. Most of our island mail ended up there for distribution. I had just hooked my thumbnail under the flap when I realized the conversation had come to a halt.

"I'm sorry," I said, looking up. "Did I miss something important?"

"No, ma'am. It's just that I wondered what you had for me to do today." She ducked her head and consulted her iPad. "You have two appointments this afternoon. I sent the information to your computer. One new client and one . . . I guess you'd say, former one."

I raised an eyebrow. "Please don't tell me it's Isabel Tennyson."

Sharese squirmed a little in her seat. "I'm afraid so."

"Want me to take it?" Red smiled, a mischievous, boyish grin that reminded me so much of Rob. "I think I know how to handle her now."

I waffled. I would have loved to hand off the haughty woman to my husband, but that seemed like copping out. "That's okay. Maybe if she gets a chance to vent at me, she'll go away and leave us alone."

My gaze dropped to the unopened envelope. I didn't recognize the printing, but that didn't surprise me. I supposed, with the demise of cursive writing in elementary schools, the cops would soon be unable to use handwriting as a forensic tool. I wondered what these kids would do for a signature, but I'd probably be in the home by the time it made any difference to me.

I forced my attention back to my two employees. "So let her come," I said. "I see there's a request in here from one of the local charities for our list of services and charges. You can take care of that." I handed her the letter. "And you'll need to close out the Walton file and prepare an invoice. Red, were you planning on calling or seeing her in person?"

"I thought I'd deliver the news directly. Or maybe I should take the address over to Alex's office? They're representing her, if I remember correctly."

"That might be good. You can butter up the ladies with your boyish charm, see if they have anything for us."

He wiggled his eyebrows at me, and I laughed. "What about you?" he asked.

"I'm going to see what this is about." I waved the unopened envelope. "Then I'm going over to Jordan Point." I braced myself for a tidal wave of disapproval, but Red surprised me.

"Not a bad idea. See if they've got any news." He smiled at the look of astonishment I couldn't quite control. "Yeah, I know. But you're not going to stay out of it no matter what I say, not until you're satisfied, so I'm taking the path of least resistance."

"Thanks," I said softly, meaning it.

"Mrs. Tennyson is coming at one, and the new client at two-fifteen," Sharese said, rising. "I can have lunch delivered if you like."

I smiled at her earnest expression. "Do that for yourself, if you want, but I don't think the world will come to an end if you lock up the place for an hour. Or one of us may be back by noon. Either way, don't count on me. I'll grab something while I'm out."

"Yes, ma'am."

Red stretched his arms as Sharese carried her things back to her desk. "Damn," he said, "I like that girl. I think she's just perfect for the agency, don't you?"

His words made me remember the reason we'd hired her in the first place, which led naturally to my missing partner. "I wonder how Erik's making out."

"No news is good news, or so they say," my husband said, standing. "I'll try to be back by lunchtime so Sharese can get out of here for a little while."

"Thanks. See you later."

I waited about five seconds after he'd walked out the door before ripping open the mysterious envelope. To my disappointment it contained only a small slip of paper with a series of numbers in the same neat printing as the outside: 32144480460. I turned it over, but the back side was blank. I upended the envelope and shook it, but nothing else fell out. I counted the digits:

eleven. One too many for an area code and phone number. Two too many for a social security number. What had eleven digits? I leaned back in the chair and thought about it for a couple of minutes, but I came up blank.

"What in the hell am I supposed to do with this?" I muttered out loud, and Sharese materialized in the doorway.

"Did you need me?" she asked.

"No, sorry. Just talking to myself." I took one more look at the paper and envelope, then shoved them both into my center desk drawer. "I meant to ask, though, about the new client. Did he—or she—give you any indication of what the problem is?"

"No, ma'am. And it was a gentleman. English. At least I think his accent was. And very polite. He just said he wanted to consult with you about a matter of concern and asked when you might spare him a few minutes. Devlin O'Hare. That's his name."

"Sounds Irish."

"I thought so, too, but his accent was straight out of *Downton Abbey.*"

"Okay. Well, I guess we'll just have to wait and see what he wants." I took my bag from the bottom right-hand drawer where I usually stored it. "I'm off in a couple of minutes. You be sure and get yourself some lunch, hear? If you have to close up, don't worry about it. I'll be back for my one o'clock with the detestable Mrs. Tennyson."

Sharese smiled. "I hear that. She wasn't exactly pleasant on the phone this morning."

"Hopefully, this will be the last time any of us has to deal with her."

"Yes, ma'am," she said as I made my way out the door, the series of numbers running around in my head. I promised myself I'd figure it out before the day was over.

My heart rate kicked up a little when I maneuvered the Jaguar over the ruts that led to Pudge's hideaway on Jordan Point. I was relieved to see her Range Rover pulled up in the turnaround in front of the house. Bebe's Audi was nowhere in sight, but I assumed she'd gone back to Charleston. I drew in a long breath and stepped out into the cool spring air.

It was another day of cobalt blue sky and zero clouds, although some of the warmth had been pushed out by a cold front sliding down from the north. Not that we'd get anything like what those poor folks on the other side of the Mason-Dixon had to put up with, but we were spoiled, no doubt about it. After two weeks of January chilliness, we were pretty much fed up with winter and eager for our spring, which usually arrived sometime in February and lasted well into May.

It took me some time to locate the doorbell. On every other occasion that I'd approached the house, Pudge had come bounding down the steps to intercept me. I could hear the soft chimes sounding inside, but there was no responding clack of heels on the pine floors. I tried again, turning to survey the surrounding area in case she was outside doing something in the yard. Then I snorted, remembering Pudge's elegantly long, well-manicured fingers. No way could I picture her grubbing around in the dirt.

But the fact remained that she didn't appear to be at home. Funny. Of course she could be out with friends. Or maybe she was staying with Scarlett on the *Tiger Pause*. I would have thought they'd want nothing to do with the boat, especially after the sheriff's people had rifled through it, but I could be wrong about that. I fidgeted for a couple more minutes, debated about leaving a note in the door, and then decided to give it one more try. I lifted my phone from my bag and searched for Pudge's cell number. I punched it in and was surprised to hear its faint tone coming from inside the house. *Strange.* I waited for voice mail to pick up and stumbled through a message telling her I had been to the house and asking her to call me right away.

Back on the ground, I hesitated, then turned toward the side of the house. The yard was small and well-maintained, with native shrubs and grasses intermixed with azaleas, just beginning to burst into blossom. A little late, I thought, but maybe their proximity to the water somehow held them back. What I knew about plants, much to my mother's chagrin, would have barely filled a thimble.

The back of the house also sported a wide porch, and the wild vegetation that did its best to reclaim the cleared land had been cut back to open up access to the waters of Skull Creek. At ground level, Hog Island impeded the view a little, but it was still breathtaking.

And empty. But as I moved back the way I had come, I thought I heard a slight rattle, the kind the night creatures—raccoons, possums, and marsh rats—made as they scurried through the sharp leaves of low-growing palmettos. I waited, keeping perfectly still, but nothing, animal or human, made an appearance. I shrugged and walked back to the car, unable to shake off a feeling of dread.

Something wasn't right. I couldn't put a name to it, but I didn't like it.

I didn't like it one little bit.

CHAPTER
TWENTY-ONE

I stopped for a slice of pizza at Mangiamo's, one of my favorite restaurants on the northern end of the island. The walls were adorned with lots of big-screen TVs and more Ohio State banners and paraphernalia than a Northwestern grad should be forced to endure. But the people were genial and the food great.

I called Sharese to see if I could bring her anything, but the office phone went to the answering service, so I assumed she'd gone out. I dallied a little, catching up on the progress of the college basketball rankings and marveling that a lot of the sports news centered around the opening of baseball spring training camps. *Tempus fugit.*

Back at the office, I let myself in and tidied up my desk. I was just running through a probable scenario starring Isabel Tennyson when one of the outside lines rang.

"Simpson and Tanner, Inquiry Agents."

"Bay? What are you doing answering the phone?"

"Erik! It's good to hear from you. What's happening out there in the desert?"

His pause told me it wasn't going to be good news, at least for him, but he forced some lightness into his voice.

"Not too much, not yet anyway. I talked to Stephanie's mother, told her I was in town, and she said she'd get back to me. Steph has a job at one of the local magazines, so she wouldn't have been able to talk to her until last night." Again that pause. "I'm just hanging out waiting to hear back."

"How's the weather out there?" It was an inane question, but there didn't seem to be anything I could say about his situation.

"Hot. Dry. Desert-y."

I laughed. "I guess I asked for that."

"Sorry. I'm just not used to sitting around doing nothing. How's everything there?"

"Fine. Well, not exactly. I mean, the office is fine, but . . ."

I wasn't sure if I should burden him with the outcome of my short involvement with my old high school gang, but maybe it would take his mind off his own troubles for a while. As I was filling him in, Sharese arrived, waved, and settled at her desk.

"So I guess I'm out of it, at least for the time being," I concluded. "We have a new client coming in this afternoon, so I'll see what that brings. Oh, and the Tennyson woman should be here any moment. I've been trying to come up with a semi-tactful way to convince her to take a hike, but so far no luck."

"You'll think of something. So, listen, I'll let you go. Call if you need me for anything." His next words made my heart ache. "I'm not exactly accomplishing much right now."

"It's early times yet," I said, forcing as much encouragement into my voice as I could muster. "Hang in there."

"Talk to you later," he said and disconnected.

"Damn," I said out loud a moment before the front door opened and Isabel Tennyson marched into the office.

"And double damn," I muttered as Sharese ushered her in my direction.

Twenty minutes later, battered but unbowed, I leaned back in the chair, fairly confident that Isabel Tennyson would most probably not be darkening my door again anytime soon.

I'd just watched the tail of her navy blue blazer disappear in a whirl of anger when Sharese scurried into my office.

"Wow, that was something!" she said, dropping into a client chair.

I smiled and nodded. It was almost the first time she'd reacted spontaneously, or so it seemed to me. She usually held herself in pretty rigid control, always unfailingly polite and businesslike. I liked the flush of excitement on her face. I hoped it was a trend.

"I left the door open on purpose in case you had to come in and rescue me."

She laughed, and I joined her.

"I'm not sure I'd have been much help. She's really a terror, isn't she?"

"Nothing we couldn't have handled." I sobered. "I guess if I were a better human being I'd be sorry for her. She lives in a fabulous place, according to Red, and she doesn't seem to lack for anything monetary. But she's obviously very unhappy. It's too bad her kid is such a jerk."

"Maybe that's why he's the way he is. Way too much money and not enough responsibility."

"Very insightful of you."

"We had basically nothing when I was growing up, but Mama insisted on everyone getting an education and making something of themselves." A rueful smile. "You didn't want to cross Mama, so we all turned out pretty good."

"I'd say you did. How many siblings do you have?"

"Two sisters and a brother. All older."

"Ah, the baby of the family."

Again that smile. "That didn't get me any special privileges, I can tell you. Mama didn't play favorites."

"Sounds like a wonderful family."

The silence made Sharese uncomfortable. "Well, I'm sorry to be bothering you with all that. Anything I need to do about Mrs. Tennyson?"

"No, just close out the file. She owes us a few bucks, but I'm going to write it off. The less contact we have to have with her the better."

"Yes, ma'am," she said, rising.

I made a quick trip to our unisex bathroom and ran a comb through my mane of auburn hair. I'd been trying to keep it a little past shoulder length since it had grown out, and I was in desperate need of a cut. If I kept pulling out the gray ones, though, I might end up needing a transplant. That thought made me smile as I settled back in behind my desk.

With nothing important to do until the new client arrived, I pulled the envelope and its mysterious series of numbers out of the drawer. I hit Google, but that didn't give me much beyond a couple of references to some sort of math sites. I copied the string out onto a legal pad and tried breaking them up into segments. Again, there were too many for any familiar arrangement I could come up with.

But they had to mean something. I glanced at my watch, surprised to find that I had wasted half an hour doodling around. The new client would be arriving momentarily. I tore off the bottom of the legal page, carefully copied the numbers onto it, and called for Sharese.

"Yes, ma'am?"

"When you have a few spare minutes, take a look at these numbers, will you? See if you can make any sense out of them."

She stepped in and reached for the paper. "Of course. Are they something to do with a case?"

"I don't think so." I held up the small note that had arrived that morning. "This is what was in that envelope marked personal."

Her smooth brow furrowed as she stared at the paper. "Not a phone number."

"No, and not a social security number either."

"Maybe an international number? Don't they have extra digits?"

"Good idea. Check it out, please. I hate to admit it, but I'm stumped."

"Would it be okay if I asked Byron? He's a whiz at math."

I could have taken offense. I was, after all, pretty damned whizzy at math myself. I smiled instead. "Sure. Any help I can get. It's going to drive me absolutely nuts until I—or someone—can decipher it."

She turned as the outer door opened, stuffed the paper in the pocket of her sweater, and approached the newcomer. "Good afternoon, sir. Mr. O'Hare?"

"Yes, my dear. I trust I'm on time?"

Sharese had been right about the accent. Maybe a little Irish lilt there, but definitely British.

I leaned back, whisked some dust off the corner of my desk, and waited.

Sharese led him in my direction, made the introduction, then stepped back.

I rose and extended my hand. "Mr. O'Hare, I'm Bay Tanner. Please take a seat."

"It's a pleasure, Ms. Tanner. Thank you so much."

He didn't look old enough to need the intricately carved wooden cane he rested against the extra chair, but it did take him more than the usual amount of time to get himself situated. He wore a three-piece gray suit, the vest gapping a little around his middle, with a white shirt and muted navy blue tie. His black wingtips gleamed. His face was very pleasant—*kindly*, I thought, like someone who enjoyed his life, whatever it was. His brown hair had grayed considerably around his face, giving him a certain professorial look. Dark brown eyes were surrounded by crow's feet, but they looked as if they came from laughter rather than age.

I made a stab at early sixties, maybe a little more.

"How can I help you, sir?"

Instead of answering immediately, he let his gaze wander around the office. I didn't have much on the walls except for a Lowcountry landscape I'd confiscated from my father's old room and my investigator's license. The view was nice, mostly shrubs and some wilder vegetation, but it certainly wasn't worthy of that much scrutiny. I waited, letting him run his hand over the surface of the Judge's antique desk and nod sagely.

"This is a lovely piece. Mahogany never goes out of fashion."

"It was my late father's. In his law office."

"Yes. I knew Tally Simpson. Not well, mind you." He sighed. "I was actually born in London, but we moved around a lot. Father was in the military, you see."

"And how did you come to know my father?"

"He did some work for me, a long time ago. Ginger—that's my wife, you see—she and I settled here some fifteen years ago. After my retirement." He smiled sadly. "I was sorry to hear of his passing."

"Thank you." I forced myself not to look at my watch, but I wondered when Mr. O'Hare might finally wander around to the reason for his appointment. "I'm honored to be the second generation of Simpsons you've called upon for assistance."

It wasn't a question, but I hoped he got the message.

"Yes. Well, Ms. Tanner, here's the thing in a nutshell." He leaned forward and rested his clasped hands on my desk. "Yes. Well, it seems . . . I mean to say, I seem to have misplaced my wife."

CHAPTER
TWENTY-TWO

Of course I love British mysteries. I DVRed *Masterpiece Mystery* on PBS every Sunday night, and I devoured the novels featuring Morse and Poirot and Inspector Rutledge and Maisie Dobbs and countless others. So I was not totally unprepared for the understated ways of our cousins across the pond. But I have to admit to being totally stopped in my tracks by Devlin O'Hare's statement. I took more than a moment to gather myself before responding.

"You've *misplaced* your wife? Could you be a little more specific, sir?"

He had a wonderful smile. "I know how curious it must sound, Ms. Tanner, but I don't know any other way to put it. You see, we—or rather I—have just returned from a lovely holiday in south Florida. Ginger—Virginia, actually, but she hates it—doesn't like the cold, and so we generally spend most of January and February where the climate is a little warmer. We leave right after Christmas, driving two vehicles because we both like our independence."

He paused then, his head cocked to one side, as if waiting for me to reply.

"I, uh, see," I managed. "So you have both cars to drive back when your vacation is over."

"Exactly! We packed up and set out in tandem, just one week ago today, but I had a spot of trouble with the Jaguar. Something to do with the transmission, or so they told me at the garage in Jacksonville. Ginger waited with me a couple of days, but she was eager to get home, so we decided she should go on without me. I played a little golf while I was waiting for the part to arrive so the repairs could be made and finally arrived back on the island yesterday, only to find that she wasn't here."

The concern on his face was genuine, and I swallowed the urge to smile. "Did she arrive at all?"

He studied me quizzically for a moment before his face cleared. "Oh, you mean, did she arrive and then leave again?"

"Exactly."

"I'm not sure," he said, a frown crinkling his brow. "Her own vehicle isn't in the garage, so I just assumed that she had been waylaid somehow. I was so exhausted last evening that I'm afraid I fell asleep before I could do more than mark her absence. But now that you bring the possibility to my attention, it could be that she came home and left again. Although for the life of me I can't understand why she would. She's very reliable, Ginger is. Normally."

Reliable? Really? I took extra care to keep the skepticism out of my voice. "But you haven't been in contact at all? No phone calls or text messages?"

"We don't have cell phones. Hate the bloody . . . oh, I do beg your pardon! What I mean to say is we don't believe in all that nonsense of being reachable every waking hour of the day. And Ginger and I are so seldom apart . . . Well, we just don't make a habit of ringing each other, you see?"

I didn't, actually, but everyone has their foibles. And I couldn't really cast stones, being myself a charter member of the International Society of Technophobes. "She didn't even call to tell you she'd arrived?"

"No," he said with a brief smile, "I didn't expect her to. She's very competent. I just assumed things had gone according to plan."

"Have you checked for her luggage? Any of the things you remember her packing up before you headed back north?"

"No, actually, I haven't. I assumed . . . well therein lies the tale, doesn't it? I've been making a lot of assumptions."

"Yes, sir, it appears you have. What is it, exactly, you'd like me to do?"

"Find her, of course."

"Is there some reason you've come to me instead of the authorities?"

"Not a lot of faith in that lot. No, very little indeed."

I sighed and leaned back in my chair. I very much wanted to hustle Mr. Devlin O'Hare right back out the door, armed with directions to the sheriff's substation down the road. Despite his misgivings, they were far better equipped to deal with situations like this and far more likely to succeed. Unless there was something he wasn't telling me. Although his face and manner appeared guileless, I remembered my recent lecture to myself about not taking things—and especially people—at face value.

"Do you think it would make sense to check for her things before we go any farther?" He frowned, and I hurried to add, "I'd be happy to accompany you if that would make the task any easier. That way we can decide what might be the best course of action for you to take depending on whether or not your wife made it home from Jacksonville."

He rose abruptly and snatched up his cane. "Quite. Most sensible."

In a matter of seconds he was out of my office and heading for the outside door. He nodded at Sharese before pausing and turning back toward me. "Well?"

I had followed him as far as my doorway. "I'm sorry?"

"Let's get cracking, Ms. Tanner. I'm in the Jaguar. You can follow me."

Sharese and I exchanged a look before I grabbed up my bag and trotted after Devlin O'Hare.

"Should I start a file and get a contract ready?" she murmured as I passed her desk.

"Not sure. I'll keep you posted."

She smiled. "Good luck."

I trailed the dark blue XJL, a newer and fancier model than my own, down 278 to the Sea Pines circle. I hoped we weren't continuing into the plantation as I had neither a gate pass nor an owner's sticker, but Devlin O'Hare kept going, exiting instead onto Pope Avenue. We went right out of the smaller roundabout at Coligny and eventually left onto one of the small side streets that ran from South Forest Beach Drive down to the water.

Not too shabby, I thought as I followed him into a tight semicircular drive in front of an obviously renovated jewel just one row from the ocean. Fresh white paintwork gleamed in the chilly March air, made brisker by an onshore wind. Two stories rose above a double garage into which O'Hare pulled his Jaguar, tight to the right side as if to leave room for his wife's car. The gesture made my eyes mist up a little, and I shook my head.

"Open mind," I said aloud and stepped out into the sunshine.

"This way," he called, waving his free hand in my direction.

We mounted a series of steps which I noted my potential client maneuvered with a minimum of difficulty despite the cane. I began to think it might be an affectation rather than a medical necessity. In fact, I mused as we came into a spotless kitchen, maybe the whole more-British-than-the-Queen routine might be a little over the top. *Open mind.*

I had little opportunity to observe any details of the rooms through which we passed except a general feeling that it had been done by a professional decorator. There were few personal touches—photos, souvenirs of trips, knickknacks—but that could simply have been Mrs. O'Hare's taste. Having spent my childhood in a house in which the contents were more important than the occupants, I had developed a decided preference for comfort over style.

The bedroom was just as elegantly appointed and feminine in the extreme. I never understood why grown women—especially ones who had probably attained the age of Ginger O'Hare—thought pink an appropriate color for their surroundings. A Hollywood starlet of the fifties would have felt right at home amidst the glass and crystal and ruffles.

Her husband must have caught a hint of distaste in my expression.

"I know, Ms. Tanner. Not something you'd expect for an old warhorse like me. But Ginger and I have separate sleeping quarters." He smiled. "I snore abominably."

Where had I just heard that same rationalization? I wondered. Then I had it. Scarlett—Mary Alice—had said something very much the same about hers and James's sleeping arrangements.

I shook my head to clear it. "It's lovely. Where would your wife have stored her luggage if she did in fact come home and unpack?"

He led me across the plush carpet and pulled open a door. The closet could have held two of mine at the beach house. Clothes and shoes were arranged by color and season, accessories neatly arrayed on shelves obviously constructed expressly for the purpose. At the far end, he pulled open another door and stepped aside with something like a flourish.

"You were right! Her cases are here. She's been home! Oh,

I'm so relieved."

I joined him in front of the generous space where three matching pieces of leather luggage stood, perfectly aligned, side by side.

"These are the ones she had with her in Florida?" I asked.

"Yes, of course. That is, I believe they are." He turned to smile at me. "I'm afraid I don't pay much attention to that sort of thing."

"If you don't mind?" I stepped around him and hefted the smallest of three the bags. It seemed awfully heavy to be empty. "Could you open this one? Or I'll do it if you like."

Before he had a chance to reply, I knelt in front of him, slid the suitcase on its side and popped the brass latches. I dropped the lid, and Devlin O'Hare gasped.

Inside were a series of fitted compartments for makeup, jewelry, and toiletries. All of them were full.

"I don't understand," he said.

"Let's check the others," I replied without looking at him, and he stepped back out of the way so I could haul the larger two out into the wider space of the closet.

Both held clothes neatly folded, most of which looked as if they would be appropriate for the warmer weather of south Florida. I sat back on my haunches and thought about what it meant.

"Does your wife carry a handbag?" I asked over my shoulder.

"What? Oh, yes, of course. Not sure about the color. I'm so sorry, Ms. Tanner, but I'm afraid I'm not very observant of my wife's attire. But I do know she keeps it in the bottom drawer of the nightstand to the right of her bed. Yes, I do know that for certain."

I left the bags lying open and hoisted myself up. He had already marched back into the bedroom and was yanking open the appropriate drawer by the time I caught up to him. He turned to display a beautiful shoulder bag in a soft, supple brown leather that begged to be touched. It had to be Gucci or Prada or something equally outrageously priced, I thought.

"May I?"

I wasn't sure how he'd react to my request to rifle through his wife's most personal possessions, but he handed it over without a word. I upended the contents onto the frilly pink bedspread before he could change his mind. Wallet, makeup bag, glasses cased in another wonderful piece of leather. A package of tissues, uno-pened. No cell phone, as expected, but no keys either. I turned to find O'Hare staring at the small pile of things that constituted his wife's daily necessities. His face held a look of both surprise and something else I couldn't quite name. I shook off the chill that did a little dance along my spine.

"Doesn't your wife usually keep her keys in here?"

It took him a long time to answer. "I beg your pardon? You said . . . Oh, yes, keys. Of course she does, although we have one of those combination locks on the outside doors. You know, where you enter a series of numbers rather than an actual key. And the cars use those funny little fob things, remote control I suppose it is, and Ginger has the habit of storing that in the pock-et of whatever she's wearing at the time. But where's—?"

He cut himself off, and the tone in his voice made me snap to attention.

"Where's what, Mr. O'Hare? What else is missing?"

For a long moment I was afraid he wasn't going to answer me. A thought flashed through my head, and I had to check my-self from giving it voice. If it were Red standing here, looking at the contents of my oversized handbag spread out in front of him, he might pause to wonder about the absence of a handgun. True, I'd been keeping the S&W in the glove box of the Jaguar lately, but I frequently had the smaller Seecamp tucked away in a com-partment of my purse, especially if I was working a case. Okay, not so much over the past few months, but it still might give him pause. It was a fanciful thought, and yet one that wasn't entirely out of the realm of possibility. Still, I could think of no particular reason why Virginia O'Hare would go running around armed. But there was something about her husband's expression . . .

Oh, what the hell, I thought and cleared my throat.

"Does your wife own a gun, sir?" I asked softly.

Again, he took a long time to answer. When he did, his voice had dropped almost to a whisper so that I had to strain to hear him.

"She does, in fact," he said, staring at his feet. "God help us, she does."

CHAPTER
TWENTY-THREE

Devlin O'Hare insisted on brewing tea, a process which took almost as much time as we'd spent searching his wife's bedroom. I fidgeted in my wicker chair once I'd been permitted to arrange the delicate cups and saucers, linen napkins, and heavy silver spoons on the glass-topped table in what my client referred to as the sun-room, a small bump-out off the kitchen that did indeed capture the waning rays of the afternoon sun.

Apparently the British were not to be rushed in this ancient ritual of warming the china pot and steeping the loose tea, which O'Hare had measured carefully into a little silver ball with a tiny chain dangling from it. He had promised answers once we'd been properly fortified, and I was beyond antsy by the time he finally carried in the pot on a silver tray along with a plate of some sort of flat, brown cookie that looked decidedly unappetizing. I declined milk and added two heaping spoons of sugar, something of which my host's expression told me he did not entirely approve. I sipped cautiously and did my best to tamp down my impatience, pointedly ignoring his offer of a *biscuit*. I did a long, silent count to ten then set my paper-thin cup carefully back on the saucer.

"Why does your wife carry a gun?" I asked without preamble.

O'Hare studied the view out the small bay window, cocking his head to one side as if contemplating whether or not he intended to answer me. I leaned back in my chair and waited him out. When he finally turned to me, his face had lost much of the bonhomie he'd been at pains to display over the short course of our acquaintance.

"Do we have a formal relationship, Ms. Tanner?"

I understood the intent of his words, their seriousness, and responded accordingly.

"Not at the moment, sir. And please call me Bay."

He nodded.

"But," I went on, "we can remedy that, at least temporarily. You can simply give me a dollar to establish our mutual intent, and we can leave the formalities for another time." I smiled to take any sting of my next words. "If, that is, we decide to proceed."

In answer, he removed a bulky wallet from inside his coat pocket and handed me a hundred dollar bill.

"That's not necessary—" I began, but he waved me off.

"It will suffice for now. So I have now engaged your services, and by so doing I have acquired your absolute discretion, is that correct?"

I stalled by taking another sip of tea. So many people misunderstood the requirements of our profession, confusing it with that of attorney-client. While we always undertook to keep the information provided to us in confidence, we had an obligation to disclose any criminal activity to the authorities, and we could certainly be compelled to reveal what we knew in court. I had skated extremely close to that line on a few occasions in an effort to protect a client I was convinced was innocent of any wrongdoing. But I would always stop short of compromising my license or the agency. At least that's what I told myself.

"As much as is legally possible," I said. "I'd be glad to give you a complete rundown on how that works, but rest assured that it would take my certain knowledge that your wife—or you—had committed a crime before I'd willingly divulge anything to the authorities. That's the best I can do."

I held the bill loosely in my hand in case he decided those assurances weren't adequate, but he sat back in his chair. "Fair enough."

"So answer my question." I dropped the hundred alongside my spoon. "Why does your wife carry a handgun? And is she permitted?"

"Yes," he said, ignoring the most important part of my query. "We are both licensed, in multiple states, in case you're wondering."

"Why?"

"Why not?"

We stared at each other across the small expanse of table for a long moment.

"Here's the deal, Mr. O'Hare. You're proposing to retain me

and my agency to find out where your wife is. Either we trust each other, or we don't. Right now I'm tending toward the latter." I set my index finger on the bill and slid it across the glass toward him before pushing back my chair. "Thanks for the tea. I hope you find Ginger alive and well."

Before I had a chance to stand, his fingers gripped my wrist. "Wait! I'm sorry."

I glanced down at his hand, and he released his hold.

"I'm sorry," he said again, and I resumed my seat.

I waited while a range of emotions chased each other across his face, and I could almost pinpoint the moment when he decided to come clean.

"You're right. I can see it's no use my trying to pull the wool over your eyes. You're obviously a very astute young woman."

I let the dual compliments—astute and *young*—wash over me. "Just tell me the truth, sir. That's what we'll need if I have any hope of helping you. Just the truth."

He smiled then, and it changed his whole demeanor. "Ah, yes, the truth. A rare commodity in my experience. And also in yours, perhaps?"

"Sometimes. But I've found that it's the only way to conduct my business."

Again we held each other's gaze for a moment before he finally gave his head a definite nod. "Right. My wife and I both go about armed because she used to be a spy, and there are still people out there who harbor ill will toward her. Very Ian Fleming, I'm sure you're thinking, but that is the truth of it. I'm afraid they've finally caught up to her, and no one in a position of power is going to believe a damned word of it. My government—my former government, that is—believes I'm just a paranoid old has-been and Ginger a woman who regrets her exit from the clandestine life and manufactures enemies where none exist." He paused for breath and smiled sadly at me. "I expect you're thinking pretty much the same, are you not?"

I could feel my mouth hanging open, and I snapped it shut. After my recent diatribe on the subject of the truth, there was only one reply I could make.

"Pretty much," I said softly as I once again slid Devlin O'Hare's hundred-dollar bill across the smooth glass table.

And when I rose this time, he didn't try to stop me.

• • •

I had to force myself to pay attention as I steered the Jaguar back toward the parkway. Devlin O'Hare's shocked and angry face kept popping up in front of me. I knew I'd made the right decision, knew for a certainty that Red and Erik would be foursquare behind me in declining to take on a case that involved a missing former spy—real or imagined.

The thought made me smile. I wasn't certain if O'Hare was genuine or some sort of nutcase, but I had to admit to tending toward the latter. On my way out the door, I'd strongly advised him to contact the sheriff's office. If in fact his wife was armed and on the run, they were far better qualified than I to handle the situation.

I determined to put the whole thing out of my head, at least after I'd told Red the story. As I approached the turnoff for Gumtree Road, I made another decision, eased over into the left-hand lane of the Cross Island Parkway, and headed away from the office. That whole creepy thing of Pudge's cell phone ringing inside the house had been gnawing away at the back of my mind all afternoon. I'd checked my own while idling at the light at Pope Avenue and New Orleans Road, but there had still been no word. And this time my call went immediately to her voice mail.

Off-island traffic was heavy, as close as we ever got to a legitimate rush hour, and the sun had nearly disappeared over the mainland by the time I bounced along the dirt road that led back to Jordan's Point. I tried to shake off the feeling of claustrophobia the overhanging branches and densely packed vegetation engendered in me, literally sighing in relief when I broke out into the clearing in front of the house. The Range Rover still sat on the concrete pad, and not a light glowed from inside.

Without thinking too much about my reasons, I reached into the glove box and retrieved the S&W, tucking it into the deep pocket of my blazer where it bounced against my hip as I trotted up the steps. Once again I rang the bell, pressing it repeatedly for a minute or so with no response. I hit redial on my phone, hearing the short burst of noise inside the house before it abruptly cut off. I waited a moment, but it had apparently just rolled over to voice mail.

Outside porch lights suddenly popped on, raising my hopes

until I realized that twilight had fallen, and they were probably on a timer. I ducked back a little into the shadows on the porch, feeling somehow exposed in that glare of light surrounded by the deep, dark silence.

I'm usually not one to shrink from taking action, but something about this situation gave me more than a little pause. I jogged back down the steps and into the Jaguar, clicking the door locks the moment I was seated. I stared through the side window up at the house and debated with myself. Finally, I picked up my cell and hit speed dial. Red answered on the second ring.

"Hey, honey, where are you? We never got around to making any plans for—"

"Red, listen. I'm out at Pudge's place at Jordan Point, and something's wrong. I was here earlier today, and her car's out front but no one's answering the door. I'm back now, and same thing."

"She's probably with your other friend, the Scarlett woman."

"I thought that, too, but I don't have any numbers for her. At least not with me. And I called Pudge's cell while I was waiting, earlier today, and it rang inside the house. So I came back a few minutes ago and same deal. It doesn't make sense for her to leave her phone here if she's out with someone else. I'm worried."

"Want me to come over there?"

In the background I could hear the jingle of keys and the opening of the closet door in the foyer where we kept our jackets.

"Yes."

"Okay, honey, I'm on my way. How do I find this place? You know the Bronco doesn't have any GPS."

I gave him directions and promised to wait in the car for him. After hanging up, I let my head fall back against the soft leather of the seats and did my best to examine my actions. Or lack thereof. In the past I might have broken a window and climbed in to see what the hell was going on. Of course I would have gone in armed, but it would still have been a risky thing to try, especially on my own and with no one knowing where I was. Perhaps I'd been gaining a little wisdom as I slid inexorably into middle age. The idea made me smile into the darkness.

And of course I would have stayed there, safe in the cocoon of the Jaguar, if I hadn't caught the unmistakable sound of an outboard motor coming fast, only to be cut off abruptly.

And, a few moments later, a brief glint of wavering light playing across the back of the house.

Without thinking, I slid down in the seat, in the same movement pulling the gun from my pocket. I could feel my breath coming in short little gasps, and I forced myself to inhale deeply and relax. Well, as much as I could considering the situation.

Which is what, exactly? I asked myself, straining to hear any telltale noise that might let me know who had decided to pay a call on Pudge in such a clandestine manner.

The word brought a sharp memory of Devlin O'Hare, and I chased it out of my head.

The light did not reappear, and I'd begun to wonder if all this had been some trick of my imagination, perhaps engendered by my strange afternoon on South Forest Beach, when I caught the light again, this time reflected off one of the windows on the side of the house. I scrunched down a little farther, but that move completely cut off any view I had of what might be going on. Cautiously, a little at a time, I raised my head until I could just see over the edge of the door panel. But the windows had begun to steam up, fueled no doubt by my own rapid breathing and the cooling night air.

I felt blind.

Without taking even a second to think about it, I jerked upright, threw open the driver's door, and shouted.

"Hey! Who the hell is out there? I'm armed. Step out into the light and identify yourself."

I waited for what seemed like an hour, but no one replied. Still, the wavering glow, now that I was outside the car pretty easily identifiable as a flashlight beam, kept coming on.

I tried again, resting my hand on the roof of the car to steady my aim.

"I'm serious! Show yourself now!"

The damp air had made my hand on the gun a little clammy, but I couldn't stop to wipe it off. I gripped the handle of the pistol harder, thinking that stance would provide me some cover if whoever it was decided to shoot first and avoid any further discussion.

I caught movement, and I slowed my breath, just as Red had taught me the first time he'd taken me to the firing range. I could feel my finger sliding away from the guard and toward the trigger when a voice finally floated out from the darkness.

"Just what do you think you're doing?"

The words were spoken sharply, as one might address a child caught in some shameful act, but I recognized the voice immediately. I felt the breath rush out of me as I relaxed my grip on the gun and let my arm slide down to my side. A moment later, Mary Alice Stuart marched out into the glare of the porch lights, one arm up to shade her eyes.

"Scarlett, relax." I stepped out from behind the Jaguar and dropped the S&W into my pocket. "It's me. Bay."

"What on earth are you doing out here waving a gun around?"

I let out a long, slow breath, anger rising to replace the initial jolt of fear. "What the hell are *you* doing wandering around out here in the dark?"

We both turned at the sweep of headlights against the thick stand of trees.

The cavalry had arrived.

CHAPTER
TWENTY-FOUR

Red jumped from the Bronco, leaving it running, and I could tell by the way he gripped the pocket of his windbreaker that he'd come armed.

I spoke before he could misinterpret the situation. "It's all good. Scarlett—Mary Alice, that is—came by boat. We sort of startled each other."

I saw his glance slide to the bulge in the side of my blazer. "It's all good," I repeated.

"Fine." He cast a look at the house. "So your friend made it back?"

"Back from where?" Scarlett spoke sharply, her head pivoting toward the porch. "Are you saying Pudge isn't home?"

"Hasn't been, far as I can tell. I was here earlier, and her car was in the same place as it is now. And her cell phone is ringing inside the house. Red—"

"Who is this person?"

The Queen of Buckhead had returned. If I could have seen her clearly, I felt certain she would have been looking down her aristocratic nose at my husband.

"Sorry, I forgot you two don't know each other. Mary Alice Stuart, Red Tanner. My husband."

"The policeman," she said, and I could feel her leaning away, at least emotionally if not actually in any physical sense.

"Pleasure." Red had undoubtedly caught the vibe and didn't offer his hand.

"Yes, of course," Scarlett mumbled. She took a moment to gather herself, and a lot of the haughtiness seeped out of her voice. "So where's Pudge—I mean, Sylvia?"

"That's what I came to find out. Do you have a key?"

"What?"

"Well, you obviously came to see her, too. Are you staying

here? Do you have a key to the house?"

"No! I mean . . ." She made a concerted effort to pull herself together. "I was invited for dinner. I've been at my parents' in Beaufort." She shot a venomous look at Red. "They've taken the Lexus to do tests or something, and I . . . I can't stay on the yacht." She glared at my husband as if the search of the *Tiger Pause* had somehow been his fault. "They told me not to leave town. Sylvia invited me for dinner, and it seemed fastest to come by boat. My father . . ." She seemed to stumble over the words. "They keep a small outboard."

"So your friend is expecting you?" Red asked. He looked up at the dark windows reflecting only the few lights on the porch.

"Of course. Why else would I be here?"

Why else indeed, I thought. "It can't be easy being out on the water at night." I watched closely for her reaction. "I wasn't aware you were so comfortable with a small boat."

Out of the corner of my eye I could see Red raise an eyebrow, but he decided to keep quiet and let me run with it.

"It's not unusual. You of all people should know that you can't grow up around here and not be familiar with boats."

I hoped Red was catching the way her shoulders had tensed. "I never got the hang of it myself," I said in as non-confrontational a way as I could manage. "Never much interested me, to tell the truth."

"I can handle something like that if I have to," Scarlett said with a flash of anger, and I wondered if she realized she'd just moved herself up another notch on the list of possible suspects in her husband's disappearance.

Good thing for her we weren't the real cops.

"So what do you want to do?" Red asked, sliding closer to me. He laid a hand loosely on my shoulder. "I can get us in, if that's what you ladies want, or we can call the sheriff."

"No!" Scarlett's fingers clutched briefly at her throat before she added, "No, I don't think that's necessary. If she's simply sleeping or something, she'd be so embarrassed if we made a huge fuss of it." She had lowered her voice, and the old charm machine was cranking up. I remembered how quickly she could turn it on when teachers or her parents needed to be mollified. Or manipulated. She spoke directly to Red as if I had suddenly evaporated into the cool night air. "If you can get us inside, I'd be so grateful.

We'll just check to make sure she's all right. I'm beginning to be quite worried about her."

I resisted the urge to applaud her performance and barely managed to suppress an unladylike snort. "I agree. Let's get on with it. Red, do you have a credit card with you?"

I could see his smile in the glow from the porch lights. What seemed like a millennium ago, he had showed Rob and me how to use one to get back inside when we'd locked ourselves out of our place in Charleston. The experience had sent us scurrying out to the nearest hardware store for a more updated mechanism and a couple of deadbolts.

"Doesn't work much anymore, honey," he said. "Like everything else, door locks have gotten a lot more sophisticated." He turned to study the front of the house. "I may have to break out a window. If the place is alarmed, we could have company pretty quickly."

"Maybe that's the best way," I said. "I'm with Scarlett on this. Something's wrong in there, and I don't think we should waste any more time talking about it."

Without a word, Red bounded up the steps and leaned heavily on the doorbell. He followed that with his fist hard against the door. "Sylvia? Sylvia! This is Red, Bay's husband. If you can, get to the door right now. We're coming in, one way or another."

Next he rattled the knob, pushing without actually trying to force the door. After a moment with no response, he moved to the windows, cupping his hands around his face to try and see inside. He came back down the stairs two at a time.

"Let me have your flashlight, if you don't mind." He held out his hand to Mary Alice. "I'll see if there's any other easier way in. If not, we'll take out one of these windows."

"Hurry," Scarlett said, relinquishing the large silver flashlight.

We stood a few feet apart, neither of us speaking, following the progress of the bouncing beam of light as Red moved around the house. In a moment he trotted back in our direction.

"There's a window open a little on the kitchen side. I can lift one of you up and in, if you're willing."

Scarlett and I exchanged a glance. "I'll do it," she said, which made the most sense. For once my size gave me a decided disadvantage.

The whole process took little more than a couple of minutes.

Red hoisted. Scarlett pushed up the window and crawled through onto the counter. In a short time we were back at the front of the house, lights flashing on as we followed her progress from the back.

"She's not here." Scarlett looked flushed, whether from exertion or excitement I couldn't tell.

I pushed inside, my hand sliding into my pocket, Red right on my heels. Without prearrangement, we began checking the smaller rooms on the ground floor: bathrooms, closets, pantries. My only discovery was Pudge's cell phone on the table next to her favorite recliner. I clutched it in my hand as we met at the foot of the stairs.

Red flipped on a series of switches that illuminated the upper hallway. "Stay here."

I watched him move carefully up the steps, his Glock held down at his right side.

"Be careful," I said, jumping as Scarlett moved in to grip my arm.

We breathed heavily, almost in tandem, for what seemed like several hours before Red's anxious face appeared above us.

"Bay, call an ambulance. Mary Alice, take the flashlight and wait for them at the end of the drive."

"What is it? What's happened?" Scarlett's hand was again clutching her throat.

"She's hurt. Go!"

Red's shout sent both of us scurrying to obey. Scarlett dashed past me and out the door before I'd managed to get the three numbers punched into Pudge's phone. When I imparted the information to the 911 operator, I slid the cell into my pocket. Red had come down about halfway to make sure I had it handled.

"How bad?" I asked in a voice barely above a whisper.

"Someone beat the hell out of her. No telling how long she's been unconscious, but they really did a number on her face." His grimace told me it was more than just a couple of black eyes. "I don't think she'll be doing much modeling any time soon."

CHAPTER
TWENTY-FIVE

They wouldn't let any of us ride in the ambulance, so we took both cars and followed them around to the back of the hospital and the ER entrance. Scarlett sat stiffly beside me, not speaking for the few minutes it had taken us to make the short run.

Outside, all the other times I'd walked into this sterile environment crowded in on me, and I had to force myself to step through the automatic doors. The instinct to turn and flee into the night was so overwhelming I found myself nearly hyperventilating by the time Red joined us.

"No one's going to talk to us," I said as we huddled together just inside the door.

"They will have contacted the sheriff." Red patted my shoulder absently. "Hopefully they'll send Raleigh, since this probably has some connection to the guy that got—"

He cut himself off, his face reddening as he cast a quick glance at Scarlett.

"Sorry, ma'am," he mumbled and turned away.

She surprised me by laying a hand briefly on his arm. "It's okay, Red. I'm sure you're right." She sighed and let herself sink into one of the plastic chairs lined up just inside the emergency waiting room. "If this had anything to do with what happened to James, I'll never forgive myself." She dug in the pocket of her windbreaker and pulled out a crumpled tissue, which she used to dab at the end of her nose. "I don't understand," she murmured, more to herself than to either of us. "I don't understand."

I nudged my husband with my elbow, and we stepped away from where Scarlett sat, head bowed as if in prayer. Or maybe that was precisely what she was doing.

"You okay?" Red slid his arm around my shoulder.

"No. Tell me the truth, Red. How bad is it?"

"Bad. If she was unconscious when you were there this

morning, she's been out way longer than she should have been. I don't know that much about the medical part of it, but my experience with the department was that people who were in fights and got knocked out usually came around pretty quickly. Someone really whacked her." He pulled me closer. "I'm glad you didn't get a good look at her face."

"My God, Red, who would do something like this? You never met her, but Pudge is a stunningly beautiful woman, even at our age. If it was a robbery or something—"

"It wasn't. At least nothing I could spot in the short time I had while they were getting her stable and loaded up. No drawers open and rifled, lots of jewelry sitting around on the top of her dresser, plenty of computers and electronics undisturbed. The sheriff will go over it much more thoroughly, of course. We probably should have stuck around to talk to whoever they sent over to investigate."

We both looked toward the wide windows that spilled a soft glow out onto the parking area as a flash of red light caromed off the stand of trees behind it. A moment later another ambulance pulled in, the EMTs leaping out almost immediately to throw open the back doors. In a moment, they had the gurney out, wheels locked in place, and were pushing it into the ER. One of them held an IV bag as he trotted alongside.

"I hate this place," I said and let my head drop onto my husband's shoulder.

Of course it would be the odious Lisa Pedrovsky who finally stormed through the waiting room doors to plop unceremoniously onto one of the hard plastic seats.

"Oh, crap!" I muttered a moment before she wriggled out of her coat and smiled maliciously across at me.

Red had gone with Scarlett to try and contact Pudge's mother and/or sister. Hopefully they'd be able to get in touch with Carrie. If Mrs. Reynolds was indeed in some sort of care facility, she probably wouldn't be much help to her daughter. And, depending on her condition, it might be best not to inform her at all. No telling what kind of effect such shocking news might have on the poor woman.

No one had yet come out to give us any news about Pudge's

status, which didn't surprise me. Even if you were a blood relative, they tended to dole out information as if they were being charged for every word. At least that had been my experience, and I'd had way too much of it in the past few years.

"So you're up to your neck in another crime, eh, Tanner? Why am I not shocked?"

Pedrovsky had an annoying voice that perfectly matched her grating personality. Back when my late partner, Ben Wyler, had briefly worked homicide for the sheriff's office, he had apparently aroused the romantic interest of this horrible woman. Somewhere in her twisted psyche she'd decided that I had been responsible for dashing her hopes and dreams in that direction. But more than that she blamed me for Ben's death, an accusation I could never quite counter, even in my own mind. Guilt is an insidious thing, and one I was more familiar with than I wanted to be. Came with the territory, I told myself, but that whole situation with Ben had led to the whole situation with his daughter Stephanie which had caused my partner and dear friend Erik no end of grief . . . I wondered sometimes if the cycle would ever be completed.

In any case, despite what I had hoped might have been a thaw a couple of years back, it seemed apparent that any truce the detective and I might have enjoyed was about to be violated.

"You gonna talk to me, or are we gonna have to do the lawyer dance?"

Pedrovsky was overweight along with being overbearing, but she had what might have been a pretty face if she ever bothered to work at it. Not that I was one to talk. Makeup and I were virtual strangers, and I had no qualms about keeping it that way. Still, her studied aggressiveness wiped out any possibility that someone might label her attractive.

"Sylvie Reynaud is my client." I wasn't sure if that was still technically the case, but that was none of Pedrovsky's business. At least not at this point. "I went to meet with her this morning, found her car in the drive, and no one answered the door. When I tried her cell phone, it rang inside the house. I was concerned but not overly. I met with two other clients this afternoon, then de-cided to swing by Jordan Point again to try and connect with her. Once again I found the same situation. I called my husband to come out and help me decide what to do. In the interim, Mrs. Stuart arrived by boat to have dinner with Ms. Reynaud. The three of us became very worried and made several attempts to raise someone inside the house. As a last resort, we used a partially open window to gain entrance and found Ms. Reynaud badly beaten, and . . ."

I gulped and paused for breath, determined to get it all out at once.

"We called 911, and here we are. That's all I'm prepared to say at the moment unless you have specific questions about our actions in the past couple of hours."

Pedrovsky had been scribbling madly in a small notebook, the kind Mike Raleigh usually carried, and I hoped she'd been able to get it all down because I had no intention of repeating myself. I felt confident I'd given her everything she needed for the time being, and I was determined not to get into any discussion about the James Stuart disappearance or the relationship we all shared from thirty years ago. If she decided to go there, I'd be on the phone to Alexandra Finch so fast it would make her pudgy little head swim.

"What do you know about this client of yours? She married? Kids?" Pedrovsky looked up then from her note-taking. "Enemies?"

"To my knowledge she isn't married. I'm not sure she ever was. No kids. Again, that I'm aware of."

I hadn't given that much thought in my quick perusal of Pudge's background. Funny that she'd never married. Maybe the career thing occupied all her time and energy. Or maybe she'd just decided it wasn't for her. I hoped I'd have the opportunity to ask her about it one day.

"You skipped the good part."

"Excuse me?"

"Enemies, Bay. Someone who hated her enough to bash her head in."

"No! I mean, not that I know of." I swallowed hard and looked away.

"Huh. Well, you're just a fountain of information, aren't you? You say she's a client." The hefty detective wriggled around a little to settle herself more comfortably in the hard chair. "Why'd she hire you?"

"Confidential," I said, realizing almost immediately that response wouldn't satisfy Pedrovsky. "And nothing to do with this

. . . incident."

"And you know that how?"

"I . . . I just do." I hated how lame that sounded.

"Oh, and I'm just supposed to take your word for it. The great female Sherlock Holmes of Hilton Head has spoken."

That snapped me out of any faint intention I might have been harboring about sharing information with this odious woman.

"You really are a pain in the ass, you know that, Pedrovsky? Have you ever heard the old axiom about honey and vinegar? Do you really think this whole macho crap is going to induce me to cooperate with you?" My voice had risen along with my anger, and I glanced up to see the woman in the glassed-in reception area whip her head in my direction. "I'm done talking with you," I said more calmly as I stood. "If Mike Raleigh wants to speak with me, he can make an appointment. *You* can go to hell."

I whirled toward the automatic doors leading outside when I heard Red call my name, almost at the same moment Lisa Pedrovsky reached out to grab at my arm.

"You touch me, and I'll have you charged with assault," I said through clenched teeth, and she dropped her hand.

"Bay, what's going on? Oh," he added, suddenly realizing who was trying to heft herself out of the chair. "Detective. I think you'd better sit back down before you do something you'll regret."

They stared at each other for a long moment before she turned away. "Threaten me if it makes you feel any better, Tanner. Both of you. But I'll have your butts in an interrogation room in a New York minute if you try to interfere in my investigation." The smile she turned on me held nothing but contempt. "And then there's the little matter of breaking and entering. I don't think either one of you would fare too well in prison."

"Cut the bullshit, Lisa," Red replied in a totally reasonable voice.

"It's Detective Pedrovsky to you, civilian," she fired back.

"Whatever." Red turned to me. "Did you explain why we were there at the house?"

I nodded.

"Then we're done here. You know how to reach us if there's anything else."

"I'm not talking to her," I said. "The sheriff or Mike. Not her."

It sounded petty and childish, but I didn't care. I turned my back and moved a few feet away, and Red followed. "How is she?" I whispered.

"Don't know anything yet. Mary Alice called her mother and got contact information about the place where Mrs. Reynolds is staying. She didn't have anything on the other daughter, Carrie. She seems to have hit the road and not looked back a long time ago."

"We should go see Mrs. Reynolds. Where is this place?"

"In Bluffton, and there's no way we're going to get in this time of night. Besides, we don't have anything to tell her, at least not yet."

We both turned at the whir of the automatic doors and watched Lisa Pedrovsky stomp out into the night, her cell phone glued to her ear. I hoped someone on the other end was telling her to leave us the hell alone. I felt about ninety percent of the tension drain from my shoulders and neck.

"God, I hate that woman! Why isn't Mike Raleigh investigating? You'd think with the connection to the Stuart thing he'd be the one in charge."

"Maybe he is, but he wasn't available. Besides the lovely Lisa probably jumped at the chance to rattle your chain the second she heard you were involved."

"I'm not *involved*," I snapped, "no more than you are. We found her. We don't really know any more than that."

Red smiled and reached out to move a strand of hair away from my face. "Come on, honey, you know better than that. You don't seriously think this is just some bizarre coincidence, do you? No robbery, no forced entry? That open window was too high for anyone to make it up there without help, and we didn't find a ladder or anything they could have used to climb up. It was somebody she knew, someone she let in."

"So it could have had nothing to do with Scarlett or James. Speaking of whom, where is she? Scarlett, I mean?"

"She finally managed to bully her way into the ER." He smiled and shook his head. "She can be pretty forceful for a little bitty thing."

"She always was," I said and smiled back. "She may be small, but she can pack a lot of authority into that voice."

"So what do you want to do? We can hang out, but I have to

say I'll need some food sometime soon."

I'd completely forgotten we hadn't had dinner. As if on cue, my own stomach set up a low rumbling.

"Yeah, me, too. How about if we go grab something fast, then come back and wait for word. I don't feel right just going home and letting Scarlett handle all this, capable though she might be." I felt my throat constrict a little. "If . . . if Pudge doesn't make it, we need to take charge of letting her mother know. I don't want her to have to hear it from that hideous excuse for a police-woman."

"Sounds like a plan," my husband said and reached for my hand.

CHAPTER
TWENTY-SIX

In the end, we finally stumbled into bed around four AM, too tired and upset even to speak as we peeled off our clothes and collapsed. It was after ten before the insistent jangling of the phone dragged me struggling up into consciousness. Caller ID told me it was Sharese, and I felt a quick stab of guilt that we hadn't let her know where we were or what was going on.

"Everything's okay," I mumbled before clearing my throat. "I'm sorry we didn't call you, but it's been a hell of a night."

"I know," she said, her voice quavering a little. "Detective Raleigh is here, and he filled me in. He wants to know if he can come to the house." I heard her swallow. "He says it's important."

"Oh, God, did Pudge . . . I mean, is Ms. Reynaud doing okay?"

"I think so. At least, he didn't say . . ."

"Let me talk to him."

"Yes, ma'am."

I swung my legs out of bed and reached for my robe. I hadn't bothered with pajamas before crashing out, and I didn't feel like facing possible bad news completely naked. Beside me, Red stirred, and I reached out to shake his shoulder with one hand.

"Raleigh's at the office. He wants to talk to us."

He grumbled something and rolled over.

"Bay," I heard in my ear as I tucked the phone under my chin and finished belting the faded old chenille robe. "Sorry to bother you at home."

"Is Sylvia okay?"

"Far as I know. I mean, considering. I checked with the hospital a couple of hours ago."

I dropped back down onto the bed, and my husband sat up behind me. I turned to him and nodded.

"That's good. They told us last night it looked a lot worse

than it was. No bones broken, so she probably won't need surgery, but she had a nasty blow to the back of her head. She's going to be there for another couple of days."

"I know. They think she'll be able to talk to me this afternoon some time. That's why I want to get yours and Red's take on what went down. Can I come over and get a statement?"

"Sure, Mike, but I gave everything to Pedrovsky last night."

"What was Lisa doing there?"

"I thought she was handling the investigation."

He didn't reply for so long I thought maybe he'd hung up. "Mike?"

"Yeah, sorry, Bay. No, this is my case. The players overlap with the Stuart disappearance, so the sheriff wants to keep it all together. I was out on the holdup of a gas station over in Bluffton last night. Guy got shot. So maybe Lisa just decided to lend a hand." Again there was a long pause. "She give you any grief?"

"Nothing I couldn't handle," I said, forcing a lightness into my voice that I really didn't feel. "You know, the usual."

"Sorry about that. So, can I come over? I'd like to get going on this. We lifted a bunch of prints, and I need to get the names of the ladies who were there over the weekend for elimination. Not that it will probably mean anything, but I have to go through the motions. Everybody wears gloves these days. Too many crime shows on TV."

I could hear the weariness and resignation in his voice. "Sure. I'll put some coffee on. Give us about half an hour."

"Thanks, Bay. See ya."

I stretched and headed for the bathroom, giving Red a running commentary over my shoulder. He padded after me, rubbing a hand across his face.

"Another day in paradise," he mumbled as I cranked the shower up to just short of scalding.

We went over it all again, seated this time at the small table by the bay window in the kitchen. Caffeine and a couple of English muffins had revived my husband and me, and it took only a short time for us to relate our story. Again. I'd already handed over a list of the ladies who'd spent the night at Pudge's house, along with their contact information.

I carried Mike Raleigh's cup to the counter and refilled it. "What did Mary Alice Stuart have to say about it?" I asked, sliding the steaming coffee in front of him.

"She wasn't there. And I haven't been able to get in touch with her. That's one of the things I wanted to run by you. Got any idea where she might have gone?"

Red and I exchanged a look. According to him, Scarlett had bullied her way into the ER and set up camp for the duration, declaring she wasn't leaving Pudge's side.

"I don't know, unless it was back to her parents' in Beaufort." I stopped myself. "She came over to Jordan Point by boat last night, so she probably got a cab back to Pudge . . . Sylvia's. Was there a small outboard tied up at her dock?"

"Not sure. Let me check." He pulled out his phone while I scooped a dribble of peanut butter off my plate and licked my finger.

Red nudged me, then cocked his head to the side before rising. I followed him down the three steps and into the great room.

"What?"

"He's thinking it's too much to swallow that your pal Mary Alice has been at the scene of two crimes. You sure you want to help him find her?"

"Of course I do! If she's involved, she's involved. I don't owe her anything, and I'm certainly not covering her ass if she had anything to do with what happened to Pudge." I looked at his worried frown. "You think she did?"

He ran a hand through his hair. "No. Maybe. I don't know. But she was the main character in this little drama right from the get-go." He smiled then. "I've sort of come around to sharing your dislike of coincidences."

I smiled back. "Point taken. But Mike's going to catch up with her no matter what I say, and cooperating can buy us a certain amount of goodwill, right? I mean, you never know when we might need him to return the favor."

Red nodded. "Okay."

We walked back up to the kitchen just as Mike Raleigh hung up.

"No boat," he said, "so you're probably right. You have her folks' number?"

"Her maiden name was Pierce. Father is Edward . . . no, Edwin." I paused. "I'm not sure he's still alive. They used to live in The Point in Beaufort. Could be they're still there."

He looked up from his notebook. "Thanks. I'll get someone on it." He flipped the notebook closed and leaned back in his chair. "What do you think about all this, Bay? I mean, you've known these people a long time, right?"

"I'll repeat what I told you last time we talked. I'm *acquainted* with them. Except for Bitsy Elliott, I haven't laid eyes on most of them since high school. You want to know if I think Mary Alice is capable of killing her husband and disposing of his body. And of beating poor Pudge to a bloody pulp. All I can say is, based on my limited experience of her thirty years ago, the answer is no. But I can't claim to have any special insight into any of them at this point. And some of them I just met for the first time last week." I glanced over at Red. "People change. I can't believe they change that much, but . . ." I cut myself off with a shrug. "I'm afraid I can't tell you any more than that."

The detective stood. "Fair enough. Thanks for the coffee. I'll be in touch."

He looked tired, and his usually clean face showed more than a shadow of stubble.

I laid a hand on his shoulder before he could make his way out the front door. "Mike?"

He turned.

"What's Pedrovsky's role in all this? I don't want to have to run up against her again if I can help it, but at the same time I don't want to appear to be stonewalling your investigation. Any way you can keep her off my back?"

He shook his head. "Do my best. She's good at what she does, though, you know? The sheriff thinks very highly of her abilities."

"Well, she's got the people skills of a serial killer," I said, and he laughed.

"Understood. I'll try to keep her out of your hair." He sobered. "But this is a lot of mayhem for us to handle all at one time, you know? We pretty much need all hands on deck. She gets in your face again, give me a call. I'll do what I can."

"Thanks," I said and watched him walk wearily around toward the driveway.

The land line rang just as we stepped up into the kitchen. Red picked up as I began clearing the cups from the table.

"Bay."

I turned at the urgency in his voice.

"Sylvia."

I took the phone from his hand, a feeling of dread beginning to rise in the pit of my stomach.

"Pudge?"

"Bay, we have to talk."

"Where are you?"

"At the Westin. I checked myself out of the hospital and called a cab."

"Are you nuts? They said they were keeping you for at least a couple of days—"

"I don't have a concussion, and my face will heal. I need you."

"Pudge, listen to me. You have no business being on your own after the beating you took—"

"Just quit arguing and get your ass over here, okay? Room three seventeen. And bring my phone."

I stood for a long time, mouth agape, staring at the handset before placing it gently back in its charger.

The Westin is one of the two or three swankiest hotels on the island. Located just outside the gates of my own Port Royal Plantation, it sprawled along the beach, giving its visitors an unobstructed view of the Atlantic along with all the amenities of a world-class resort.

I parked the Jaguar in the outside lot and bypassed reception on my way to the elevators, followed the signs, and knocked on Pudge's door a scant fifteen minutes after her strange call.

Red was probably still stomping around the great room, fuming at my refusal to bring him along. Or to call Mike Raleigh. It had been like pulling teeth, but I'd finally been able to extract his promise to keep Pudge's whereabouts to himself unless he was specifically asked. I had no idea why she'd run from the hospital to a hotel—and not back to her own home. And I felt pretty certain she wasn't going to divulge those reasons to anyone but me.

I knocked again, leaning my ear against the door to try and

discern any sound or movement inside when it was unceremoniously jerked open.

"Thanks, Bay." Pudge stepped around me to give the hall a quick survey before urging me into the room. Suite, actually, I decided, drawn to the wide wall of windows facing the ocean.

I pulled myself away from the view. I'd expected to see her swathed in bandages, something that made her resemble a breathing mummy, but the only evidence she'd been in a hospital was a butterfly on a cut above her left eye and a square of gauze on the top of her head where they'd shaved away a patch of her glorious hair.

But her face! The bruises had begun to swell, the purplish hues mixed with some that were bordering on black. Her nose looked crooked, and I'd be surprised if it wasn't broken. The stunning former fashion model had been reduced to a . . . a . . . I groped in my mind for an appropriate word and came up empty.

"My God, Pudge!"

I reached instinctively to embrace her, and she jumped back.

"Please, Bay. Don't even think about touching me. I feel as if I've been run over by a very large bus."

I dropped onto one of the plush sofas in the wide sitting area, my legs refusing to hold me up any longer. "My God," I repeated.

"It'll heal," she said. "That's not important now."

"Not important? Someone did this . . . *this* to you, and you don't think it's anything to be concerned about?"

Slowly she moved to the chair opposite me and gingerly lowered herself into it. She reached for a glass of water sitting on the low table beside her and took a sip.

"God, that hurts! My lip is split, but I'm so damned thirsty I don't care."

I drew in a long, calming breath and leaned forward, my forearms resting on my knees. "Pudge, you have no business being out of the hospital. What on earth are you doing here?"

"Well, I couldn't exactly go home, could I? I'm pretty sure there are still cops crawling all over the place."

"How did you get a room? I mean, no one thought to bring your wallet or anything."

"Scarlett did. She knew I'd need my insurance stuff, so she pulled it out of my bag while they were loading me up. At least that's what she said. I called from the hospital and reserved the room so I didn't have to spend too much time hanging out in the lobby." She tried for a smile and winced at the pain. "Didn't want to terrorize the whole place or scare small children into nightmares." She settled back into the chair. "Did you bring my phone?"

I pulled it from the pocket of my jacket and handed it across to her.

"Thanks. I felt like someone had cut off my right hand without it," she said, immediately powering it up and stroking an index finger across the face.

"You really think this is a good time to check your email?" I asked.

"Don't get pissy on me, Bay. I need to see if Scarlett left me a message."

"About what?" When she didn't answer, I raised my voice. "Hey! You need to tell me what the hell's going on, and I mean right now. Do you know who did this to you?"

She kept her head bent over her phone, flicking that finger until I had an overwhelming desire to leap across the space between us and send it flying out of her hand. I restrained myself, but barely. A moment later she looked up.

"Okay." She tucked the phone beside her leg, and it seemed as if she relaxed a little.

"Okay what?"

"Scarlett is safe."

"Safe? Why wouldn't she be?"

She closed her eyes for a moment, as if gathering herself. When she finally looked up, I could see a range of emotions flicker across her battered face before she managed a lopsided smile.

"You're not going to believe it."

"Try me."

"I'm pretty sure I know who attacked me, although I didn't really get a good look at him."

When she hesitated, it came to me in a rush. "You can't be serious! How is that even remotely—?"

But she cut me off with the one name I'd half-expected and completely rejected as impossible.

She nodded once and said, very softly, "James."

CHAPTER
TWENTY-SEVEN

Pudge called room service for lunch. The moment she'd placed the order, she had retreated to the bathroom for a shower.

I wondered fleetingly if she'd been molested in some way, sexually, but Red hadn't said a thing about her being undressed or her clothes messed with, and Mike Raleigh had made no mention of it. Still, the thought refused to be banished, and I stored it away for future consideration.

As for her revelation that her attacker had been Scarlett's missing husband, I did my best to listen to her explanation with an open mind. It was tough. She'd gone down to the dock that morning to sit in the sun and just relax. She hadn't locked the door behind her. She never did, she told me, except when she was actually leaving the property. No one ever came back there—too hard to find, and it was almost impossible to tell there was even a house nestled among all that vegetation if you didn't know it was there.

I was doubtful about that, but I let it ride.

She came back in, did a couple of chores in the kitchen, and went upstairs to change. With Scarlett coming for dinner, she had shopping to do. Whoever it was had been waiting for her in the bedroom. He struck her on the back of the head the minute she stepped through the doorway, and that's all she knew. The beating had taken place while she was unconscious, and she didn't remember a thing about it. By the time she heard the doorbell—that had to have been my first visit to Jordan's Point that day—it was all over, her attacker long gone. She said she'd tried to get up, but she'd passed out again. Sometime after that, she'd come to once more, thought about the phone, but remembered vaguely it was downstairs. She tried to get to her feet, but lost consciousness after only a short crawl toward the door.

She didn't remember anything after that until she woke up in the ER.

I'd done my best to be gentle and supportive, but the question had to be asked.

"So if you never saw your attacker's face, why do you think it was James?"

She'd tried another lopsided smile. "I know how it sounds, Bay, believe me, I do. They found the dinghy with all the blood in it, and no one's heard from him since last Friday night. I know they're all thinking Scarlett murdered him, stuffed him in the boat, and dumped his body on Pinckney Island. Or in the water somewhere along the way."

She'd run her tongue over her lips at that point, and I could tell all the talking was causing her a great deal of discomfort.

"I know all that, Pudge. Just tell me why you think it was him."

"I saw his shoes. I mean, I didn't really *see* them, you know? But I must have caught just a glimpse, because it's the only clear memory I have of the whole thing. Those shoes stepping out from behind the bedroom door. Then it's all a blur."

"What kind of shoes?"

"Boat shoes. I don't know what they're called, Topsiders, maybe? Tan, with lighter laces and stitching. James always wore them when he was down here on the *Tiger*. Always."

I'd spoken softly. "Okay. But he's not the only guy on the planet with that kind of shoe, right? I mean, you see them everywhere on the island. It's almost part of the uniform, especially for boaters. And they have soft soles, so they're good for creeping around. If that's all you're basing this—"

"And his voice."

That stopped me. "What? He said something to you? You didn't mention that before."

Again she tried for a smile that turned into a wince of pain. "I just remembered."

"Come on, Pudge."

"I'm serious! He said, 'Bitch,' just before he hit me. It's not the first time I've heard that word out of the bastard's mouth. I'm telling you it was James."

I could see arguing with her wasn't going to get me anywhere, and I groped around for something to refute her outrageous claim. Before I could formulate anything remotely coherent,

Pudge cut me off.

"I'm starving," she'd announced, effectively derailing any chance for a logical discussion.

And she'd refused to pick up the conversation, retreating to the bathroom the moment she'd ordered lunch.

When I heard the rush of the water in the shower, I called Red.

"What's going on over there?" he asked the moment he picked up.

I gathered myself and launched into Pudge's narrative after warning him not to interrupt me with questions until I got it all out. It took a surprisingly short amount of time.

"So that's it," I concluded. "And you're probably about to tell me that knock on the head has scrambled her brain, but I don't think so. Her eyes are clear. She's coherent. Cracking wise about her injuries and the mess her face is in. It's a wild story, but I'm convinced she believes every word of it."

"James Stuart." He let out a long sigh. "If she's not gone completely off her rocker, what are the chances she's right? I mean, what are the chances that's not his blood in the bottom of that dinghy?"

"I don't know, Red. It makes absolutely no sense."

"What are you going to do?"

"I don't have a clue." I heard the water stop and rushed on. "I'm going to try to talk her into going home. Do you think they're done over there?"

"I can check. Malik should have the scoop. But maybe she's better off where she is." He paused. "In case, you know . . ."

I shuddered in the cool air of the expansive suite. "Yeah. In case. Listen, I have to go. I'll keep you posted on what's going on. Are you planning on heading in to the office?"

"Probably. Call me if you're on the move. And be careful."

There didn't seem to be an appropriate response to that, so I didn't offer one.

I had the phone back in my bag by the time Pudge emerged, wrapped in one of the hotel's luxurious robes.

"Lunch not here yet?" she asked.

I noticed that she hadn't gotten either her face or her hair wet. I tried not to stare at that remarkable bone structure, swollen and mottled with bruises, and the once luxurious fall of hair matted with sweat and hanging in long strings down her back.

"I know what I look like, Tanner, so spare me any phony reassurances, okay? One of the reasons I picked this place is they have a fabulous spa. I've used it a few times, and there's a girl here who can work miracles with makeup." She lowered herself into the chair opposite me. "She's making a house call in about an hour, so you'll need to be gone by then."

"I'm not going anywhere," I said, mimicking her nonchalance as I leaned back into the sofa. "And don't try any of Scarlett's highhandedness. Neither one of you intimidates me, okay?" I smiled. "Remember gym class? I've seen both of you naked."

That made her laugh, and I immediately regretted it when I saw her cringe in pain.

"Sorry. But we're not done here yet. The sheriff's people are looking for Scarlett, and they're going to have a fit when they find out you've bailed out of the hospital. I expect Detective Raleigh will be on my case the second he knows you're gone. And I'm not lying to him. So you'd better be prepared for—"

A knock followed by a call of "Room Service" interrupted me.

I went to the door and followed the young woman into the room.

"Just put it on the table," Pudge said, turning her face away. "Sign for it, will you, Bay? I'll be right back." She moved quickly into the bedroom as I did as she asked, adding a generous tip.

"Thanks," I said and closed the door behind the girl, then hollered, "All clear!"

I uncovered the steaming bowls of some sort of creamy soup, along with a basket of soft rolls, and a huge dish of applesauce. Not exactly a list of my favorite foods, but I had to admit it smelled wonderful. I arranged the napkins and silver on the dining table and poured Pudge another glass of water from the carafe on the bar.

"Hey, this is getting cold," I called a couple of minutes later.

When I got no response, I walked into the bedroom to find Pudge sprawled across the white duvet. My heart dropped into my feet in the few seconds it took me to scramble around to the opposite side where her head lay. Gently I touched her shoulder, relieved to find her breathing, evenly and slowly. It looked like sleep, something she probably desperately needed, but she could have been unconscious. Again. I hated doing it, but I had to be sure.

"Pudge," I said loudly, shaking her shoulder, "wake up. Your lunch is here."

She stirred, waving a hand limply as if to swat away an irksome insect, and I knew she was okay. At least for the time being.

Out in the living area, I stared for a moment at the meal laid out on the table, then cast a quick glance over my shoulder. No telling how long she'd be out, and the opportunity might not present itself again. Tiptoeing back into the bedroom, I moved as cautiously as I could. Pudge's cell phone lay a few inches from her outflung right hand. I held my breath and picked it up before backing out into the hallway. She never stirred. I pulled the door closed.

I sat down at the table, pushed the bowl of soup away, and reached for a roll. With another darted look toward where Pudge lay sleeping, I began systematically violating her privacy.

By the time she came shuffling in, I had finished both my lunch and my snooping. A neat list of phone numbers had been transferred to a notebook page now nestled safely in the bottom of my bag along with a transcript of Scarlett's text message that morning. I could have forwarded it all to my own phone, but I wasn't sure how much of a trail that would leave, and I didn't want to alert Pudge to what I'd done. A part of me knew I should feel bad, but another part knew it was necessary. I wasn't exactly sure why, not then, but the justification of keeping her safe slid easily into my conscience and rested comfortably there.

"Where's my phone?" she mumbled, moving gingerly to the table.

I pointed to the table next to the chair she'd been occupying an hour before. "I checked on you, and it was on the bed. Didn't want you rolling over on it."

She eyed me with more than a hint of suspicion before snatching it up. Her index finger flew again, and she appeared to be satisfied with whatever she'd been checking. She set the cell back on the table.

"This has gone cold," I said as I picked up the one full soup bowl. "Let me nuke it for you." I carried it to the microwave next to the small refrigerator adjacent to the bar without waiting for a response. "It's really wonderful."

I kept my back to her, apparently fascinated by the revolving turntable in front of me. "I can check and see if the sheriff is done with your place if you like. Wouldn't you be more comfortable in your own bed?"

"I'm not going back there. At least not for a while."

"I know it has to be traumatic," I said, turning, but she cut me off.

"I'm not scared, if that's what you're thinking. I wasn't kidding about the brown belt when those two morons tried to push us around on the dock. If James hadn't hit me from behind, he wouldn't have stood a chance." She paused. "And no, it wasn't one of them. I can see that light bulb clicking on in your head, Bay Rum, but it won't fly."

The microwave *dinged*, and I carried the steaming bowl back to the table.

"Why not? Hank Edison seemed like the kind of guy who might pull a stunt like this." I tried to keep my voice even and reasonable, but Pudge was right: I'd completely forgotten about James's two fishing buddies who had accosted us the morning I first saw the *Tiger Pause*. I set the soup in front of Pudge and took the seat across from her. "And, in case you've forgotten, they were both wearing boat shoes."

"Doesn't matter," she said before blowing across her spoon. "Umm, you were right." She swallowed carefully. "This is crazy good, but it hurts like hell." She downed some applesauce and seemed content to let the subject drop.

"Of course it matters. What if the one you punched in the gut decided to come back and teach you a lesson?"

Pudge spooned up more soup, wincing a little. "Get serious. That idiot couldn't find his butt with both hands. I'm not exactly listed in the Yellow Pages, you know."

"Get serious yourself. Google lives. Don't tell me some magazine hasn't done a story about the famous model who came back home to build a fabulous house on the water. Or some sleazy tabloid never speculated about Jordan Point or why you left New York."

I realized those were two questions I'd never asked her myself. Now that I'd verbalized them, I had to suppress an overwhelming desire to press her for answers.

She ate silently for a few minutes, ignoring me completely, and I left her to it. I let a scenario unravel in my mind, one in which Hank Edison—a much more likely candidate, I thought, than his pal Larry Ferrell—had somehow discovered Pudge's address and come creeping back to lie in wait for her. She had humiliated him in front of witnesses, and he'd been the one who had flung the insinuation of infidelity in Scarlett's face. Still, I had to agree, at least partially, with Pudge's assessment of the two men, that neither seemed to have the guts to pull it off, even if they'd felt the need. Besides, they were businessmen, not mob goons. At least as far as I knew. I remembered then that I'd never done the research I'd intended, either on the men themselves or their company, Stoney Brook Recreation and Management.

"I'm going to have Erik . . . I mean, Sharese check them out."

And that sent another thought careening around in my head—I hadn't heard from my partner in some time. I wondered if that augured good or ill for his mission in Arizona.

Pudge stood and crossed back to her comfortable chair. "Whatever. I'm telling you it was James. If you don't want to believe me, I can't help that."

I took my place on the sofa. "But *why?* Can you at least tell me that? Why would James Stuart want to hurt you?"

She shrugged. "Because he can. Because he likes it. And he's probably pissed off that I've been encouraging Mary Alice to leave him for about a decade."

"But if that's true, where is he? More to the point, where has he been? If he's still alive, you're suggesting that he staged this whole thing, blood and all." I thought a moment. "You know, Mike Raleigh, the lead detective, told me there was a lot of blood in the bottom of the dinghy. You think James killed somebody so he could use their blood to throw everyone off his trail?"

Saying it out loud made the whole thing seem ludicrous, a bad TV movie starring actors no one had ever heard of. Pudge echoed the sentiment a moment later.

"I know it sounds ridiculous, but what other explanation is there? I'm telling you it was James who worked me over, and nothing you can say is going to change that."

"So that's the story you're going to give Detective Raleigh?" I held up a hand when she started to interrupt. "Save it, Pudge. You may succeed in evading him for today, maybe even tomorrow, but he's going to track you down. Spin that yarn, and you'll be lucky they don't send you somewhere for a CAT scan to make sure your brain hasn't turned to scrambled eggs."

She laughed, and again I could tell it caused her more than a little discomfort.

"I swear you should have been a standup comic, Bay Rum. Isn't it funny how things—people, I mean—don't really change?" Her face sobered. "Well, of course we do, in a lot of ways. But not in the important things." Her eyes softened. "I always knew I could count on you. No matter what."

I cast a furtive glance toward where the purloined information from her cell phone lay in the bottom of my bag. I could feel my face warming, a flush of guilt that would have completely given me away if we hadn't been interrupted by a sharp rap on the door. Pudge clutched the lapels of her robe together and pushed herself up from the chair.

"I'll get it," I said as she made another hasty retreat into the bedroom.

The young woman was Asian and quite beautiful. "Good afternoon. I am Mai, from the spa. I have an appointment with Ms. Reynolds. May I come in?"

The makeup miracle-worker, I surmised and stepped aside. "I'll let her know you're here."

But Pudge had anticipated the identity of her visitor. "I'm in here," she called.

The woman smiled at me and carried her pack of equipment toward the hall. I followed until Pudge's stony face stopped me at the bedroom doorway.

"Thanks for everything, Bay. I'll talk to you later," she said, closing the door unceremoniously in my face.

CHAPTER
TWENTY-EIGHT

We sat huddled around my desk, Sharese with the ever-present iPad resting on her knees, her fingers flying as she took notes. Red slouched in the other client chair, his long legs splayed out in front of him. The scowl on his face hadn't softened in the half-hour we'd been discussing what our next move should be.

And I was fast losing control of my temper.

"Do you have anything positive to contribute, or are you just going to sit there looking pissed off?" I shot at him.

"What difference does it make what I think? You're going to do what you damn well please anyway."

Not for the first time during the meeting, I longed for Erik's steadying voice and innate ability to defuse things when Red and I found ourselves on opposite sides of an issue. Something that happened way too often, at least for my comfort.

"That's crap, and you know it. Sharese, have I or have I not invited comment—from both of you—about where we stand with this investigation?"

She studied the glowing screen of her tablet. "Well . . ."

"Don't put her on the spot, Bay. This is between you and me. Leave her out of it."

"She has just as much right to an opinion as either of us," I said.

"Of course she does. Did I say she didn't?"

The stern tone of her voice startled me. "Could you both please quit talking about me like I wasn't here?" Immediately she gulped and dropped her head. "I'm sorry! I shouldn't have—"

"Don't worry about it," Red and I said in unison, then found ourselves smiling weakly at each other.

"You make an excellent point. My apologies." Red reached over to pat her briefly on the shoulder. "But us sniping at each other is something you're going to have to get used to." He cast a glance at me. "We do it all the time."

That made me cringe, just a little. "He's right," I said. "But we don't mean anything by it. Sometimes you need someone to try and shoot down your theories, find the holes, so you can make sure you're on the right track."

I looked to my husband for confirmation, pleased to see his face had lost its unattractive scowl.

"Right," he said. "And, much as I hate to admit it, Bay is the boss. So, while you and Erik and I get a vote, she makes the final decisions." He softened it with a smile, one that didn't quite reach his eyes.

"That's bull— That's not exactly how it works, but let's leave all the angst for a while and get back to the matter at hand, shall we?" I leaned back in the Judge's swivel chair and steepled my hands under my chin. "Recap. Sylvia Reynolds hired us—" I glanced at my husband. "Okay, basically *me* to validate her suspicions about James Stuart's abuse of his wife. We did that, thanks in large part to Bitsy Elliott saving the emails Scarlett sent her. I'm not sure how well they'd hold up in court, but Erik would probably be able to authenticate them in some way." I paused. "When he gets back. The group and Pudge and I were all ready to confront Mary Alice, get her to press charges or else throw the bum out when he disappeared. While trying to figure out how he came to be missing from his yacht, we were accosted by two of his buddies, who were way more threatening than the situation warranted."

I opened my eyes and found Sharese staring at me. "You have the note about checking out those two and their company, right?"

"Yes, ma'am, I sure do."

"Good. Okay, then we go on hiatus, not sure whether or not we still have a client because Scarlett told me in no uncertain terms to butt out. Then Pudge doesn't come to her door, we go back and find her badly beaten, she skips out of the hospital, Scarlett goes on the run, and our victim claims it was James Stuart who attacked her. Based on some really questionable evidence, I might add." I looked at them both. "Anything I've missed?"

Sharese glanced down at her tablet, then back at me. "The boat and the blood," she said softly.

"Oh, right. Can't forget the evidence that Pudge's supposed

attacker is presumed dead, probably murdered. Maybe by his wife." I leaned way back in the chair and closed my eyes again. "God help us, this is a hot mess."

I could hear the undercurrent of humor in Red's voice.

"Just the way you like 'em, isn't it, honey?"

"Go to hell," I answered with not a trace of rancor. I jerked myself upright. "So here's the plan: Sharese, you check out Hank Edison and Larry Ferrell. You have the card, right?"

She nodded.

"Red, you and I are going to track down Scarlett."

"I still think we should give that information from her text to Mike Raleigh. She's still the prime suspect in her husband's disappearance, you know. It's not as if she's just some disinterested party. And weren't you the one lecturing me this morning about how cooperating with the cops might earn us some brownie points?"

"All that's true. But I want to talk to her first. She and I have never had a face-to-face the way we originally planned. If we have to, we can hold her and call Mike once I have a chance to try and get the truth out of her." I held up my hand. "Your objection is noted. If there's fallout, I'll take the hit."

"We'll all take the hit," my husband said, and I had to admit he had a point.

"I'm hoping to talk her into coming back with us. She has to know it makes her look even guiltier to be hiding out. As I've said before, she's not a stupid woman, Red. Let's give her a chance to do the right thing."

"Do you even know where this place is?"

"Sort of. We can head in that general direction and let the GPS get us close. Maybe I'll recognize it when I see it."

I began arranging the mess on my desk into neat piles.

"I thought you went there when you were kids." Red had risen and now stood hovering in the doorway.

"Once or twice. It's way out in the boondocks on some creek. It was her mother's family's fishing cabin. The Baldwins. And Scarlett wasn't allowed to go out there *unchaperoned*." I found myself grinning. "I swear Mrs. Pierce was a real throwback. The way she treated Scarlett you'd think they were living in the nineteenth century."

I slipped my bag onto my shoulder and slid past Red into the main office.

"So of course your gang had to defy her," he said, waving to Sharese.

"See you later," I said on my way out the door. "Call if you need us."

Outside, Red held the door of the Jaguar open for me.

"Of course we did," I said, picking up on his earlier comment. "It was almost a religion with us, defying the adults. Especially Camille Pierce. I swear she hovered over Scarlett as if she thought she might disappear in a cloud of dust right in front of her eyes."

My mind flashed back to my brief phone conversation with Neddie, about why women stayed with abusive husbands. *I wonder . . .*

"So where are we headed?" Red's question stopped that uncomfortable speculation in its tracks.

"Out toward Beaufort. Just get on 170, and I'll do my best to get us there. It's been a long time, you know."

"Oh, I know, believe me," he said with a grin, and I punched him in the arm.

"Just drive."

It took us a surprisingly short time, and I gave myself some bonus points for making us backtrack only once.

The narrow road was paved, which I didn't think it had been back in the day, and there'd been a lot of building in the intervening years. Sprawling Lowcountry homes set back and shaded by live oaks made it seem as if we might have stepped back in time more than a few decades. Most of them featured long wooden docks jutting out behind them, bridging the wide marsh until they ended at the meandering creek whose name still escaped me.

The proliferation of houses made it tough for me to get my bearings, but I finally spotted the incongruous little cabin nearly invisible between the rolling lawns of a couple of mammoth new homes. I wondered what the neighbors thought of the shanty nestled almost at the edge of the marsh and smack in their line of sight when they threw elaborate barbecues on their massive patios. It made me smile.

"That's it?" Red had slowed almost to a crawl while I was

craning my neck to find the cabin and now turned the Jag into what was probably referred to as the driveway but was in truth little more than some dirt ruts worn down over the years.

I laughed. "Yup. You have to hand it to the Baldwins. I bet this thing drives the neighbors bonkers!"

He smiled back. "Yeah, no doubt. I wonder why they haven't sold it. Based on what's around here, I'm guessing they could have made a fortune."

He brought the car to a stop when the tracks ended.

"I vaguely remember something about it not being able to be sold as long as there were direct heirs. Some restriction on the deed. Both her Baldwin grandparents are gone now, but Scarlett has grandchildren, so this place could be here into the next century."

We got out of the car into a soft breeze and the loud trilling of some birds high up in the pines that surrounded the house. It looked deserted and felt the same way.

"If she's here, where's her car?" Red asked.

"Good question." I led the way through ankle-high grass and weeds. "Someone must keep it maintained. This stuff would be up to our shoulders if it wasn't mowed occasionally."

My husband passed me and headed around to the left side of the frame cabin, which looked in remarkably good shape for its age. The roof appeared relatively new, and none of the paint around the small windows seemed to be peeling. I wondered why anyone bothered since it obviously didn't get much use, and I had to echo Red's observation about how valuable the land must be. It would have put a couple of kids through college, I thought, and that led me to another startling realization: through all this mess of James's disappearance and Scarlett's obvious suspect status, we hadn't heard a peep from her kids. Surely they must be aware of the situation. Why hadn't they come rushing to their mother's defense? Or at least got their butts down here to give her some moral support. Or maybe they had, and I just didn't know about it. But you'd think someone would have mentioned them—Pudge or even Scarlett herself. *Curious.*

I looked up from my musings when the screen door banged open. Both Red and I jumped, and I could see from the corner of my eye that his hand had gone automatically to where his holster would have been had he still been in uniform. Neither of us, though, had thought it necessary to come armed.

"What are you doing here?" the Queen of Buckhead demand-ed.

Red and I both relaxed our stances, and I covered the dis-tance to the house in a few short steps. "Looking for you, of course," I said in a matter-of-fact tone.

"Sylvia told you." It was an accusation tinged with the sur-prise of betrayal.

"No, she didn't. I'm a detective, remember?" It was a little disingenuous since I never would have thought of this place if I hadn't brazenly pilfered Pudge's phone records. "We just want to talk."

"I'm tired of talking," she said and turned, letting the screen slam shut behind her.

Red and I exchanged a look, then moved to the single con-crete step, onto the stoop, and into the little house behind her.

CHAPTER
TWENTY-NINE

"I don't get her at all."

I felt Red glance over at where I sat slumped in the passenger seat, my bare feet propped up on the padded dash, my head back, eyes closed.

"Hey, are you still with me?"

"Yes, I hear you."

"And?"

"And what? Let it rest for a minute, okay? I'm thinking."

Red stopped at the T-intersection with 462 and put the car into Park.

"What are you doing?" I let my feet slide to the floor mat and eased myself upright.

"Calling Mike Raleigh." His cell phone was already at his ear.

"Wait!"

"Why? She's the prime suspect in her husband's disappearance. You did your best to convince her to come back to town, or at least let Mike know how to reach her, but she wasn't having any part of that. She's hiding out, and we know where she is. It's our duty to let the sheriff's office know."

"Like hell! Put that thing down!"

I made a batting motion in his direction, although I knew full well I wouldn't be able to wrestle the cell away from him. Even if I'd thought that was a good idea, which I didn't.

He turned his right shoulder to me, and I punched it, none too gently.

"You want to start that crap right here in the car?" he said tersely.

"You think I can't?"

He held up his right forearm as a barrier, and I grabbed for it. The tussle lasted about three seconds before one of us—I'm not sure which—suddenly burst into laughter. A moment later we were both snorting and hiccupping, and an irate dispatcher was nearly shouting, "Beaufort County Sheriff's Office, how may I direct your call!"

Red managed to get himself enough under control to stutter, "Sorry, wrong number" before we once again set off on a round of uncontrollable hilarity. Only the sudden sound of a car horn right behind us cut us off. Red drew a deep breath, put the Jag in Drive, and burned a little rubber as he made the left back onto the highway.

I pulled a tissue from my bag and blew my nose. "We are a pair, aren't we?" I said a little breathlessly.

"Kung Fu fighting in the front seat of a Jaguar. Not many couples can claim that distinction," he said with a grin.

"Nor would they want to. I wonder what the guy behind us thought."

"Probably best not to know. We'll be lucky if he hasn't made his *own* call to the sheriff."

I wiped the last of the tears from my face and settled back down in my seat. "You know we don't have any obligation to rat Scarlett out. She's just a person of interest right now. She hasn't been charged with anything."

Red stared straight ahead. "And she's not our client."

I thought for a moment about that, and for some reason the kindly face of Devlin O'Hare popped into my head. I realized that, with all the chaos of the night before, I'd never given him— or Sharese—an update on that case. Or what turned out *not* to be a case.

"You're right. She's not. And if Mike Raleigh asks me if I know where she is, I'll tell him. But I don't see why we have to volunteer the information. At least not yet."

He didn't respond, his concentration apparently on his driving. But he didn't take his cell phone out again, either. I settled back down to think.

Our conversation with Mary Alice Stuart had been anything but productive. She didn't invite us to sit, but we did anyway. The inside of the cabin was surprisingly modern, and it struck me that she had to have updated it completely at some point in the past. I remembered a rustic, one-room setup with a tiny space partitioned off as a bathroom. There had been two sets of bunk beds along the far wall, a cook top of ancient vintage, and what I assumed had been the castoff furniture from the house in Beaufort, some of it looking decidedly out of place in the old fishing camp.

We'd come out once or maybe twice in that blast furnace summer between our junior and senior years to escape the heat of town and the strictures of our parents before somehow Camille found out and grounded Scarlett. I remembered that Scarlett had driven the ugly brown Chevy sedan her parents had decided was safe enough to trust with their only child. She'd been the first one of us to get a license, and we all chipped in for gas. The four of us—Scarlett, Pudge, Bitsy and I—had swum in the muddy creek, sunbathed on the dock, and eaten the food we packed in ice chests as we watched the sun go down until the no-see-ums and mosquitoes chased us indoors. We gossiped and smoked and played Monopoly until the wee hours, feeling very independent, very grown up.

I sighed, a little more loudly than I'd intended, and Red swung his gaze in my direction.

"What's the matter, honey?" When I didn't reply, he added, "You know I would have let you beat me up if it would have made you feel better."

That made me smile. "Just thinking about when we came out here as teenagers. It seems like a million years ago."

He reached over to pat my leg. "Not that long." He put his hand back on the steering wheel as we headed toward civilization and the madness that was Route 278 at five o'clock. "So what did you make of her story?"

I didn't know what to say. Scarlett had insisted that everything she'd told the girls and me last Saturday morning had been the whole truth. She didn't hear James leave, except for that one wakeful moment when she thought she'd heard a boat motor. She had no idea where he was or what had happened to him. I'd tried to get a read on her eyes, to see if I could catch any hint that she was lying, but I couldn't. She spoke quietly, calmly, and her gaze didn't waver. I had to believe she was telling the truth. At least as far as she knew it.

"I think she was being straight with us. Do I assume you don't?"

He paused before answering. "I don't know. She's a hard woman to read. You notice how she just completely ignored your questions about whether or not her husband abused her? I guess

I'd have to say there wasn't anything that set off alarm bells. If she sticks to her story and tells it just that way every time, I don't see how Mike can do anything but move on to some other theory of the crime."

"Assuming there was a crime."

"You're saying he just took off? What about the dinghy? And the blood?"

"Part of the staging. Do they even know for sure that it was human? The blood, I mean?"

His head whipped in my direction. "You think it's not?"

I shrugged. "I'm just hypothesizing here. I wouldn't think it would be too hard to get hold of something else, pig's blood, maybe. Isn't that supposed to be the closest to ours? Or no. Maybe it's the anatomy. I remember seeing something on *Law and Order*. Or *CSI*."

"You and your cop shows. And where would an Atlanta attorney get pig's blood?"

"I don't know. They probably sell it on the Internet. You can buy just about anything, or so I'm told."

He smiled. "Maybe we should Google it."

"I'm serious, Red. Until Mike Raleigh gets the results back from the forensics people, it's just an assumption. A good one," I added, forestalling the argument I could see coming. "But right now we don't know for sure. And, based on how long things like this have taken in the past, I'm guessing it won't be anytime soon."

"They searched Pinckney, you know." Apparently Red had decided not pursue my implied criticism.

"With dogs?" I knew they had a bloodhound to track fleeing suspects and to search for missing children and the occasional dementia sufferer who wandered off.

"Yes. No results."

"How about cadaver dogs?"

"I don't think so. Why?"

"Well, if the assumption is that Scarlett—or someone—did him in, James's body has to be somewhere."

"What about your friend's idea that he's the one who beat her up?"

I waved a hand in front of me. "I don't believe that for a second. Pudge was pretty convincing, but I think she's just confused.

Or lying through her teeth, although I can't for the life of me figure out why she would. I wonder what Mike will make of it."

Red didn't reply, and we lapsed into a comfortable silence. I felt myself slipping into a light doze, the kind where you're sort of asleep but also still sort of aware of your surroundings. I have no clue what made the idea pop into my head, but it jerked me wide awake.

"You know what? There's someone here on the island that runs cadaver dogs. I met her at one of those fundraisers Bitsy was always dragging me to." I fumbled in my memory for the name. "Susan—no, Suzanne something." I bent my concentration on the rest of the name, but it slithered away. "Damn! Anyway, Bitsy will know." I bent over and pulled my cell from my bag.

"What are you going to do?" Red didn't sound pleased.

"I'm going to get the name, and see if she's willing to take her dogs out to Pinckney."

"You can't do that."

"Why not?"

"Because it's a crime scene. Mike will have a fit."

I paused to consider that. "What if I ask him first?"

"Why would he want some civilians tromping around his crime scene?"

I could see we were on the verge of another argument, but this was one I didn't intend to lose.

"Get serious, Red. It's Pinckney Island. It's open to the public. I'd be willing to bet that a couple of hundred 'civilians' have already tramped through that whole area, at least the parts that are accessible. They didn't shut down the whole island, did they?"

Grudgingly, he said, "No. Just for a few hours, but then they didn't have any valid reason to keep it closed. They probably got some pressure from the town or the county bigwigs." He managed a smile. "Not good for the tourist trade to have one of its major attractions off limits because there might be a body stashed somewhere in the vicinity."

"Okay, then." I punched in Bitsy's number, still resident in my memory despite the fact it had been a number of months since I'd used it. "The agency will pick up the tab, and maybe we can settle it once and for all whether or not James Stuart is dead."

CHAPTER
THIRTY

"South Carolina Canine Emergency Response Team. Suzanne Greer. And she has a partner, Miranda Delahunt. And they spell it—canine, I mean—with just the letter and the number. You know, a *K* and a *9*. I can get her contact info if you like."

It was Bitsy at her most subdued, although I could sense the excitement hovering just beneath her matter-of-fact recitation of the names I hadn't been able to recall. We both were treading a little warily after our undeclared truce in Pudge's living room.

"Thanks, Bits. That would be helpful."

I stole a glance at Red's profile, but he seemed relaxed. Well, as relaxed as he could be in the endless stream of traffic heading for the island. I shuddered at the thought of what it would be like come July and August.

"Ready?"

"Shoot," I said, pen poised over my notepad, the phone tucked against my shoulder.

I copied the local number.

"Does this have anything to do with James?"

I thought I detected a slight tremor in her voice. "Why?"

"Oh, nothing, really, honey. Just curious."

"I don't want you talking about this to anyone, understood?" I thought about mentioning what had happened the last time she'd blabbed about one of my cases, but I was pretty sure she didn't need the reminder.

"Of course."

"Thanks for the information, Bits," I said, softening my tone. "I'll be in touch."

I hung up and had punched in only the first digit of the number when Red interrupted.

"You calling Mike?"

I shut down the phone and took a deep breath. "No. I'm still convinced it won't be a problem since it's public property. And I also remember these women said they work mostly for law enforcement, so they'll know how to handle themselves. I'll just get some information, and we can talk about it before I commit, okay?"

"I can tell you Mike isn't going to like it."

"Then I'm sorry about that, but it doesn't change anything. It's been five days since James went missing. If they were going to find anything themselves, they'd have done it by now, wouldn't they?"

"It's not something you can put a stopwatch on, Bay. You know that. What's the rush?"

I sighed. "I don't know. If it hadn't been for Pudge getting the tar beaten out of her, I maybe wouldn't feel so . . . Oh, hell, I can't put it into words. You know the feeling that things are coming to a head, that it's all about to spiral out of control if you don't get a handle on it right now?"

He reached across and gently patted my shoulder. "Yes, honey, I know that feeling. But in this case, I don't have it. Honest. I think it's too early to go running around as if the meter's about to expire." He smiled and put both hands back on the wheel. "But I also know that your instincts are pretty good. So go ahead and make your call. Just don't make any commitments until we talk about it some more, okay?"

It was reasonable, more reasonable than I had any right to expect, I supposed. Red had had a difficult time adjusting to being a civilian again. After his years in the Marines and many more with the sheriff's office, he was bound to struggle with split loyalties. I was sure he'd come down on my side, no matter what, but it wasn't always an easy choice for him.

I nodded, which, I told myself, wasn't the same as a verbal commitment. I smiled to myself and picked up my cell.

I had to be content with leaving a voice mail, so any further discussion on that subject had to be postponed. We called ahead to Mangiamo's and stopped to pick up a pizza, which I slid into the oven to heat up the moment we walked up the steps from the garage.

"You want me throw together a salad?" I asked as Red checked for messages on the land line.

"No thanks. Pizza and a beer will do me just fine." He paused. "There's a call here from your buddy Pudge."

I moved closer to the built-in desk in the kitchen as he pressed Play.

"Call me. I have a new cell." She rattled off the number before I had a chance to pick up a pen.

"Short, but to the point." Red handed me a pad of sticky notes. "Ready? I'll play it again."

I jotted down the number. "What's that all about?" I asked as the timer on the oven *dinged*. I set the pizza on a board and carried it to the table.

Conversation was temporarily suspended as we wolfed down all but one of the pepperoni and mushroom slices. I chugged the last of my Diet Coke and leaned back in my chair.

"See, this is what I mean. Something's going on with Pudge. Why would she need a new cell phone—or number? I mean, why now? Maybe—" I jumped up and retrieved my bag from where I'd dropped it in the hallway and fumbled around for the notepad.

Back at the table, I flipped back a page and handed it to Red.

"What's this?"

"While she was napping this afternoon, at the Westin, I copied a lot of contact info from her phone. I told you about Scarlett's text. That's how I knew where to look for her."

Red studied the names and numbers, then looked up. "You think she figured out you'd ransacked her phone?"

"I don't know. It's a possibility, don't you think? But she had dozens of contacts in there. I only copied down the ones I recognized or I thought might have something to do with this whole James business. Why would she want to lose all that information?"

"You don't lose it. You just synch the new phone with the old one, providing they're compatible, and it all goes over."

"Really?"

Red laughed. "You may have come a long way, baby, as the old cigarette commercial used to say, but you've still got a long way to go."

My cell jangled, saving us from another discussion of my inadequacies in the technology realm. "Bay Tanner."

"Yes, this is Suzanne Greer of the South Carolina Canine ERT. You left a message for us?"

She had a lovely French accent that reminded me immediately

of Alain Darnay, my former lover. The association made me shiver for a moment. "Yes. I'm a private investigator here on the island, and we're interested in retaining your services."

"If you have a missing person, we need to work through your local law enforcement."

"No, it's not a missing person. Well, technically, I suppose it is . . ." I knew I sounded like an idiot, but I didn't want to get into a lengthy explanation if this wasn't something these women could help with.

"Maybe you'd better give me some details."

I hesitated. "I'm not sure I'm prepared to do that at this point in time. Can you tell me about your fees?"

"If we're called in by law enforcement, there is no charge. And under our code of ethics, we can't work for individuals. But you said you were a private investigator. Are you licensed?"

"Absolutely. But hold on a second. You mean if, say my grandmother wandered off, I couldn't call you up and ask you to track her down?"

"No, ma'am. We're very careful not to interfere with anything that might involve a crime or become a crime scene."

So much for that, I thought. "So why did you ask about my license?"

"We can work for a legitimate investigator. In that case, there would be a charge. A lot depends on how far we have to go, whether or not it involves an overnight stay, and those kinds of factors."

"This would be local."

"The missing man from the yacht in Skull Creek Marina?"

She obviously kept up with the local crime beat. "Yes. I've been retained by an interested party, a friend of the family. They want to resolve the issue of whether or not Mr. Stuart is dead or alive, and they've become frustrated with the slow pace of the authorities."

The pause lasted a long time. "I'm not sure we should be involved in this. My understanding is that it's an ongoing criminal investigation."

"But they've released the scene on Pinckney Island, and it's public land. Surely that would make a difference."

Again she hesitated. "I'd need to consult with my partner. Would you have access to an article of clothing of the missing man? The tracking dog will need that to pick up a scent."

"Actually, I was thinking more of your cadaver dogs."

This time the pause lasted so long I thought she might have hung up on me.

"Ms. Greer?"

"When would you want us to perform the search?"

"As soon as possible."

"I'll get back to you by tomorrow morning," she said.

I thanked her and hung up.

Thursday morning found us huddled around my desk, trying to get back to the normal business of running the agency. The charity that inquired about our services had signed on, and Sharese had a whole stack of names to begin running backgrounds on. I'd given her a synopsis of the happenings of the day before, from Pudge's attack to our tracking down Mary Alice Stuart to my contacting of the K9 ERT.

"What happened with Mr. O'Hare?" Sharese looked up from her iPad. "When you didn't come back to the office on Tuesday, I sort of figured you might have been out with him."

"Who's Mr. O'Hare?" Red asked.

"My second appointment yesterday afternoon. After I thoroughly ticked off Isabel Tennyson, by the way. I think we've heard the last from her."

"Be grateful for small blessings," my husband said with a smile. "Anyway, O'Hare?"

I condensed my interaction with Devlin O'Hare into a few brief paragraphs, ending with his revelation that his wife was a retired spy who still had enemies lurking behind every shrub, and my decision to give it a pass.

"Is it true?" Sharese's voice held a note of awe. "About her being a spy?"

"I doubt it. He's a lovely man, but I'm not sure his elevator goes all the way to the top floor."

Sharese sighed. "He seemed really nice."

"He is. I just don't think he's operating in the same universe as the rest of us. I strongly advised him to contact the sheriff's office. Hopefully someone there will be able to deal with him, convince him he needs to seek some sort of help."

"I can't believe it," my husband said.

"What?"

"You're usually a sucker for a story like that, especially one that involves an elderly person."

I thought back to all the misery surrounding the Malcolm St. John business a few months before and bit off the stinging remark hovering just behind my lips. Red had a point.

"Well, I figured it was just the kind of thing you and Erik would have had a fit about, so I gave it a pass."

"Good girl," he said, and I shot him a look.

"Speaking of Erik," Sharese said, thankfully changing the subject, "he left a message for you yesterday."

"Did you talk to him?" I asked.

"No, it was after hours. He left a voice mail. I saved it as new so you could listen to it if you want. I also have a transcript."

She handed me a printout, but I wanted to hear firsthand what my partner had to say.

"How did he sound?"

"Normal, I guess. He said he'd try to reach you again this morning."

I checked my watch. Eight AM in Phoenix. "Put him through the minute he calls," I said, and she nodded.

"Yes, ma'am."

Red and Sharese headed off to their respective desks, and I sat back to listen to Erik's message.

Hey. Sorry I missed you. I didn't want to bother you on your cell or at home. I'll try to get in touch tomorrow morning. Nothing much to report from here. Stephanie's mom says she doesn't want to talk to me, that she's moving on with her life. I'd like to hear that from her, but I don't know if that's going to be possible. I've thought about approaching her when she comes out of work, but I don't think that would be too productive. I don't want her to think I'm stalking her or anything.

There was a pause.

Wouldn't that be ironic? Maybe this wasn't such a hot idea. I'm trying to decide if I should just give it up and come on home. I'll keep you posted. Anyway, talk to you tomorrow. Take care.

"Well, damn," I said softly.

I'd been afraid right from the moment Erik announced his plans that it would turn out like this. In a way, I thought, you had to admire Stephanie Wyler. She'd made a decision, and she was sticking to it. It would have been much more cruel to give Erik a hint of hope if she really had no intention of resuming their relationship. While I understood Erik's need to hear it directly from her, I could also sympathize with her unwillingness to see him again.

I shook my head. Here I was defending the woman who had terrorized me for several weeks, all the while smiling and pretending to be my friend and loyal employee. I felt certain her expressions of remorse had been genuine. Whether or not I would have ultimately forgiven her was a question I didn't really have to answer since she'd revealed her duplicity in a letter, left behind as she fled nearly three thousand miles away. Maybe that said more about her than anything else. She couldn't face me. And now she couldn't face Erik. The word *cowardly* popped into my head, and maybe that was the one I should stick with. One thing I knew for certain: I would never be able to trust her again, and I would bet, in his heart, Erik felt the same.

I eagerly awaited his call, and I would do my best to convince him to come back to where there were people who genuinely cared about him. To come home.

I looked up to find Sharese standing in the doorway.

"Am I interrupting?"

"No, just thinking. What's up?"

"I have that report you asked for. The two men who were going fishing with James Stuart. And their company."

I'd almost forgotten I'd asked for it. "Thanks."

She set it on my desk and returned to her own.

I skimmed through the few pages of printout. The company, Stoney Brook Recreation and Management was a sports conglomerate that managed facilities—tennis courts, golf courses, ballparks —and also represented athletes, primarily college kids looking to make it into the pros in a number of sports. Sharese had appended a partial list of their clients, and I didn't recognize a single name. So no Heisman Trophy winners or first round draft choices, at least as far as I could tell.

The background on Larry Ferrell and Henry—Hank—Edison proved more interesting. I'd been right about their having been jocks in their distant youth. Both offensive linemen, both playing for Auburn, which explained the connection with James Stuart. Hank had had a cup of coffee in the pros, but injury had cut short any dreams he might have harbored in that direction. Larry hadn't made it even that far.

I was just about to slip the report in the burgeoning Stuart file when something on the last page caught my eye. Sharese had run a criminal check on both men. Larry had come up squeaky clean. But not Hank.

Henry Jonah Edison had been arrested.

Twice.

Once for a drunken brawl in a college bar. Lots of guys run in, nobody formally charged, but he'd spent the night in the drunk tank along with several of his teammates. They'd been close to being kicked off the team until they managed to prove it had been townies who had initiated the fight.

But the second arrest was what caught my attention. Hank had pled no contest to beating his girlfriend nearly senseless the year after he got dropped by his NFL team. He'd paid a fine and done a hundred hours of community service because the girl backed out at the last minute.

Hank Edison was no stranger to abusing women.

I dropped the report on my desk, pulled out the note with Pudge's new cell number, and picked up the phone.

CHAPTER
THIRTY-ONE

"We need to talk. Now."

I didn't want to give Pudge any opportunity to get her temper cranked up, but she immediately balked.

"Now's not a good time."

"I don't care. I'm coming over. Are you still at the Westin?"

She waited a long time to answer. "No. I came home this morning. And I've already been grilled by your Detective Raleigh, and I'm not in the mood for any more of it. Give me a call tomorrow."

"Pudge, this can't wait. I wish I'd gotten to you before you talked to Mike."

"Isn't it sweet how you and the homicide detective investigating Scarlett are on a first-name basis? So cozy."

"Don't try that diversionary crap on me. Did you know Hank Edison was arrested for beating up his girlfriend?"

"And I should care about this why?"

"For God's sake, Pudge, because it isn't even the smallest stretch to think he was the one who attacked you!"

"I already told you—"

"Oh, cut the bullshit, Pudge! There's no way it was James. If he's not dead, he's long gone for whatever twisted reason. Why in hell would he hang around here? If he staged that whole blood in the boat thing, he did it for a reason, and the only one that makes any sense is that he planned to disappear. Why would he go to all that trouble and then jeopardize his whole scheme by sticking around for five days just to beat you up?"

I stopped to catch my breath and heard the unmistakable *click* when Pudge hung up in my ear.

"Damn you!" I said out loud, and that brought Sharese scrambling to my doorway.

"Is everything okay, Mrs. Tanner?"

"No!" I drew in a deep breath. "Yes. It's fine, Sharese. Sorry if I startled you."

"Is there anything I can do?"

"No thanks. It's all good." I wiped my hands across my face. "Just people."

"They can be a trial, no doubt about it."

That made me smile. "No doubt. Listen, I have to go out. Is it possible to route Erik's call to my cell phone? Or maybe, if he calls here, have him try the cell directly. This can't wait."

As if on cue, the phone rang on my desk. I snatched it up. "Bay Tanner."

A momentary pause, and then, "Is this a bad time, honey?"

Lavinia. I nodded at Sharese and sat back down in my chair. "No, it's fine. How's everything there?"

"Oh, about the same. You know. One day's pretty much like the last."

She sounded tired. No, *defeated* was the better word. I settled back and told myself to take it slowly.

"You sound a little down. Have you been working too hard again? You know, the garden doesn't have to get done in a single week."

"Oh, that's not . . . I mean to say, we've been making good progress out there, a little at a time. Julia is a big help."

"That's good. How is she? And Rasputin? Any more trouble with him?"

I wanted to let her know I was prepared to buy her story about how she got injured, even though a part of me still blamed my half sister. With everything else that had been going on in my life the past week or so, I had to admit I'd put the problems of Presqu'isle on my mental back burner, and I chided myself for letting it slip. Nothing should be as important as family. Nothing. And Lavinia was all I had left, Julia's DNA be damned.

"Things are just fine, honey. I miss seeing you is all." Her voice turned wistful. "Any chance you can stop in for a visit sometime soon? You just name the day, and I'll whip up something special for you and Redmond."

That made me smile. Lavinia was the only one who used Red's full name.

It was already Thursday, and the kids would be invading for the weekend. It would almost have to be Friday or late on Sunday, and I still hadn't heard from Suzanne Greer about the dogs. So much going on . . .

"Bay?"

"I'm sorry. Of course we'd love to come to dinner. Let me check with Red and get back to you, okay?"

"That's fine, honey. I know you're both busy."

I hated how sad she sounded. "We'll do it before the weekend is out, I promise. I'll let you know."

"You do that. And take care of yourself, hear?"

"You, too," I said a moment before hanging up.

I sat for some time staring into space. Things were changing. My *life* was changing. I thought back to the months after Rob's death when I had huddled in the beach house with only Dolores Santiago to keep me company. I'd literally dropped out, except for an occasional foray to St. Helena, mostly to keep my father off my back. Gradually, I'd eased myself back into living, bearing the physical and emotional scars of my husband's murder, wearing them, if I was honest, almost like a badge of courage. This venture, the inquiry agency, had given me focus, a way to channel the anger I'd felt at being cheated of my life with Rob. So much had happened in those years since, so much that had shaped the woman I'd become. Sometimes I felt proud of that; at others I wished I'd just taken the money and run away to some deserted island where there were no people with troubles, no pain of loss, no heartache.

I smiled and shook my head. That was ridiculous, of course. But every time I made myself acknowledge that Lavinia would eventually age and die, that every last vestige of my family ties would ultimately be severed, the sadness nearly overwhelmed me. Everyone went through it, I often reminded myself. At least I had no children to tear my heart out with worry. Just Red. And Erik. And maybe, eventually, Sharese. A family of sorts, one that would endure, at least for a couple more decades, if the gods smiled.

I stood abruptly, determined to shake off this sudden attack of gloom and doom. I had my bag slung over my shoulder when the phone rang. I waited for Sharese to pick up just in case it was Erik. A moment later she buzzed me.

"It's a Suzanne Greer for you. She says you're expecting her call."

"I'll take it." I dropped my bag back into the lower desk

drawer then stepped around to slide my office door closed. The less Red knew about this the better, I thought, at least for the time being. "This is Bay Tanner."

"Yes, Suzanne Greer. I've discussed your proposition with my partner, and we'd be willing to help you out, with a couple of conditions."

"That's great."

"Well, we'd need a retainer up front, since we haven't done business with you before. I hope you don't find that insulting, but it seems the prudent thing to do."

"Absolutely. That's precisely how the agency here operates. Just give me a figure."

She did, and it sounded more than reasonable to me. We arranged that I would bring the check with me when I met her out on Pinckney.

"That's the other issue. We'd like to do this late in the day when it's more likely there won't be a lot of people around. Not that the dogs would have a problem with that. It's just we don't want to attract a crowd or advertise what we're doing. It can be unsettling for some of them to know we're searching for a body."

"That makes perfect sense. When did you have in mind?"

"Do you want—or need—to be present?"

"I'd like to be. Unless it's a problem for you."

"No, I think it would be best if you *are* there. Just in case anyone tries to hassle us."

I substituted *the sheriff* for *anyone* and got her point. "Are you familiar with where the dinghy was found? I think that should be our starting point."

"There was a small inset map in the paper the day they found it, so I have a pretty good idea."

"I'm assuming, if there is a burial or dump site, it couldn't be too far from there. I have no personal experience, but I'm guessing it isn't an easy thing to haul a dead weight too far."

"That's been our observation as well."

I reminded myself that these two women had seen more of this kind of thing than I ever would. I felt as if the job was in excellent hands. We agreed to meet at the parking area of Pinckney Island at three thirty. The weather promised to hold, and there would be a slight breeze, something Suzanne told me could be helpful to the dogs.

After I hung up, I told Sharese to make out the check for my signature and reminded her to have Erik call my cell. I fidgeted a little, bouncing from foot to foot, but the door to Red's tiny office remained closed. I could barely hear his voice occasionally, obviously speaking on the phone, and I wanted to be out of there before he had a chance to quiz me about where I was going. Sometimes it was better to ask for forgiveness than permission. And besides, I hadn't actually *promised* not to make arrangements with the dog handlers. Not in so many words.

Check in hand, I made my escape.

"Tell Red I'm going out to Jordan Point. I'll be in touch."

Feeling much better about things than I had in quite a few days, I set off to duke it out—metaphorically speaking, of course —with Pudge.

I cursed long and hard when I pulled into the driveway to find Bebe Bedford's Audi parked out front, just behind the Range Rover.

Pudge must be rallying the troops, I thought as I slid out of the Jaguar. I couldn't see a boat tied up at the dock out back, but that didn't mean Scarlett might not be in attendance as well. Or maybe the sheriff had returned her car. Red and I had speculated about that out at the Baldwin fish camp, but had seen no evidence of it. And now that I thought about it, we never did ascertain how she'd made it out there. Maybe her mother had dropped her off. At any rate, all I needed was for the whole damn bunch of them to have reassembled, and I'd turn around and march right back out again.

I stomped up the steps and leaned on the bell much harder than I needed to. Still, it was almost a full minute before the door was grudgingly yanked open, and Pudge glared out at me. I gasped in surprise at the transformation.

"Yes, I know," she said, turning her back on me.

I followed her into the great room where, thankfully, only Bebe perched on the edge of her usual chair.

"Oh, Bay, isn't it just awful? Our own Pudge, the poor thing!"

I resisted the urge to make a gagging motion and neatly side-stepped Bebe's attempts to throw her arms around me. I patted her shoulder in passing and pulled my attention back to Pudge.

The transformation had indeed been miraculous. If I ever needed to look like a million bucks in a short period of time, I'd remember the lovely Mai at the Westin. There hadn't been much she could do about the swelling, but a lot of that had begun to dissipate. The bruises might never have occurred, so skillfully had they been camouflaged. Even the bandage, while still there, had been covered by a rearrangement of the hair around Sylvia's face. Apparently she hadn't been as successful with the patch they'd shaved on the top of her head. She sported a pink baseball cap studded with what I assumed were rhinestones.

"It is unbelievable," I said, shaking my head.

"I have all the special goodies she used, so I'll be able to keep it up myself. I'm not exactly a stranger to making up my face, as you might imagine."

"Well, I'm amazed. You look . . . well, your usual gorgeous self."

"Doesn't she?" Bebe twittered. "They could do a photo shoot right now, and no one would ever know—" She cut herself off. "Oh, but she's still in so much pain, aren't you, honey?"

"Quite fussing, Beebs, for God's sake! Bay, I know you aren't drinking." She waved a glass in Bebe's direction. "Another mimosa?"

"Oh, I shouldn't!" she said while extending her empty glass.

I put my bag on the floor and dropped into the chair next to her. "How did you know about Pudge's . . . misfortune?" It was a lame word, but I didn't know how much Bebe had been told.

"Scarlett called me. I always knew that James was a mean s.o.b. He was like that even in high school."

So she was buying Pudge's story. "Why do you think he did it?" I asked after a hasty glance in the direction of the kitchen.

"Because that's just the kind of man he is. Don't you remember? He bullied that poor Randolph boy until his mother had to take him out of school. Melvin, I mean."

"That's not true. It was just gossip."

"No, Bay, they covered it up. James's parents, I mean. They always did think the sun shone out of his butt."

If I had been drinking anything, I would have spewed it out. Apparently it didn't take much more than a couple of jolts of champagne in orange juice for Bebe to revert to a much cruder version of herself than I ever remembered from high school.

"Nicely put, Beebs." Pudge handed her a delicate crystal glass.

"Thank you. But I'm sure that's what happened. You don't forget things like that."

"Well, I think it's a crock," I said, modifying my own tendency toward less than acceptable language.

"You always were a sucker for him, Bay Rum. Don't think we didn't all notice how quiet you got whenever he was around. Scarlett always thought you had the hots for him yourself, just didn't have the nerve to make a move."

"Oh, now, Pudge, that's not fair." Bebe, ever the peacemaker.

"You're full of it, my friend, on this as on so many other issues lately," I fired back. "In the first place, Melvin Randolph had medical problems, and his parents hired a private tutor. That's what I heard from my mother, and she and Mrs. Randolph were tight."

"We all heard that story, but you're the only one who believed it. James made him strip in the boys' locker room and then threw his clothes out the window. Then he blamed it on Tony Rozzario, and everyone else was too scared to rat him out."

At that point, I would cheerfully have added a few bruises to the ones Mai had so painstakingly concealed. "And *that* was also a crock because Tony admitted it, if you recall. And besides, it was almost a full year after that that Melvin left school." I shook my heads. "Such gossips you two are. At least if you're going to spread rumors, get the facts straight." I forced myself to speak rationally. "And in the second place, I couldn't stand James Madison Stuart the Third. The reason I didn't have much to say around him was for Scarlett's sake. My gut instinct was to slap him upside the head just on general principles."

"Whatever." Pudge had suddenly lost her desire to fight and lowered herself gently into the leather recliner that seemed to be her chair of choice.

"Do you need aspirin or shall I get one of those painkillers the doctor prescribed?"

Bebe had leaped up, nearly sending her full glass of mimosa flying.

"No, just for God's sake leave me alone! Please, Beebs," she added in a softer tone, and Bebe subsided back into her chair.

"We need to talk," I said, glancing at Bebe. I was surprised when Pudge apparently got the message.

"You know what I'd really like?"

"What, honey?" Bebe stood, this time more decorously. "What can I do?"

"Some Ben & Jerry's *Cherry Garcia*. A couple of pints. I know Publix carries it. You know where that is, don't you? Would you mind?"

Bebe looked a little crestfallen, as if she were a child being sent from the room so the grownups could talk about sex and other forbidden topics. Which was pretty much the plan, as far as I was concerned.

"Well, of course, if that's what you'd like. Just let me get my purse."

We waited, Pudge sipping on her drink, which was probably a bad idea if she was popping pain pills, but I was pretty certain she wouldn't pay a damn bit of attention if I called her on it. In a flurry of Chanel No. 5, Bebe finally pulled the front door closed behind her, and we were alone.

Although I'd been hell-bent on forcing this one-on-one with Pudge, I found myself unable to get the conversation rolling. My client had allowed her head to fall back against the soft leather of the recliner, and, when I glanced over, her eyes had gone closed. I reminded myself that she'd been through a hell of an ordeal in the past couple of days, but a part of me remembered how well she'd been able to stonewall any attempt to get her to talk about things she didn't want to. Then and now. I groped for an opener that wouldn't send the possibility for rational discussion careening into an argument.

"How's your mom doing?" I asked, leaning back in my chair and draping one leg over the arm.

It took her a long time to answer, and I was almost convinced that she'd dropped off to sleep when she finally responded, although her eyelashes still rested lightly against her cheeks.

"Why?"

Not much, but a start, I thought.

"I wondered if she knows about your . . . injuries. Red and I thought about contacting her that night, but we didn't want to worry her until we knew for sure how badly you were hurt."

One eye fluttered open, and she turned it in my direction. "I'm glad you didn't do that."

"Why?" I echoed her.

"Because she's not well, and I won't have anyone bothering her." She spoke softly but with a hint of anger gliding just below the surface.

"Is it physical?" I asked. Memories of poor Malcolm St. John didn't seem to be far from my mind, even after several months. I wondered if they'd ever completely fade.

"What do you mean?"

"Oh, come on, Pudge. You know perfectly well what I mean. Alzheimer's is almost an epidemic these days."

She eased herself up and turned her head to look directly at me. "I don't see that it's any business of yours, one way or the other."

I sighed. "You can be a real bitch, you know that? I don't know why I forgot that over the past thirty years."

Strangely enough, she smiled. "I know. I've worked really hard at cultivating it. I guess it's something I learned after about a day and a half in New York City. That place can grind you down, especially if you're in my business. If you don't hold the bastards at bay somehow, they'll run you right into the ground."

"You know the Judge died."

I don't know why that popped suddenly out of my mouth.

"Yes. I sent you a card when I heard about it."

"Of course. I remember now." I fought the tears pooling behind my eyes. "It's just that sometimes I can't believe I'm technically an orphan." I forced a smile. "Even if your mother isn't altogether with it, you're lucky to still have her." I paused. "What about your dad?"

"What about him?"

I surrendered. "Okay, never mind. I'm just trying to make conversation here. But if you don't want to talk about your family, that's fine. Let's get down to business before Bebe gets back."

My intention had been to tell her about my afternoon plans, but she forestalled me.

"I wish Carrie was around."

Her sister, the one Red told me had taken off for parts unknown a lot of years before.

"You know where she is?"

Again her eyes fluttered closed. "No. I . . . *we* haven't heard from her in so long I sometimes forget I even had a sister."

"I'm sorry." It seemed grossly inadequate, but what else was there to say?"Is your dad still alive?"

"Yeah, and going strong, the son of a bitch. He exercised all my mom's powers of attorney and dumped her in that place without missing a beat."

"Are you in touch?"

"When I can find him. He shut up the house on The Point and hit the road. I get a postcard once in awhile—Europe, South America." She laughed, a bitter sound that made my stomach clench. "Maybe he's hooked up with Carrie again, and they're seeing the world together while Mom rots away in that . . . place."

Again? My heart rate kicked up a little higher as one possible implication of her words hit me, but there was no delicate way to probe for more information. Perhaps, I thought, that was a dog I shouldn't try to kick awake.

"At least you have them," I said somewhat lamely. "No matter how much of a pain in the ass they might be."

Silence once again descended, and I decided a change of subject was definitely in order.

"So how did Mike Raleigh take the news that you think it was James who beat you up?"

The footrest of the recliner snapped down, and suddenly Pudge was glaring directly into my face."How do you think any of this will help Scarlett?"

I gave her question the serious thought it deserved. "I don't know."

I realized this would be the time to tell her about the emergency response team and the dogs, but something held me back. Her insistence that James was alive, that he had attacked her in her own home, made me wonder just how strenuously she'd object to what I was about to set in motion. I didn't know why, but I was suddenly certain she wouldn't approve.

"But isn't that what I hired you to do—help Scarlett?"

She had a point. If James Madison Stuart the Third turned up dead . . .

"I'm sorry, Pudge. But I have this crazy notion that things will work out best if we know the truth."

I ignored her snort of disgust.

"Okay, scoff if you want. But we're not thirteen and sneaking a smoke in the restroom and lying about it to our parents. We're dealing with serious life-and-death stuff here. We don't have the luxury of playing games."

"I never thought of you as naïve before, Bay. We pretty much left that to Bebe."

That made me smile. "I'm a realist, Pudge. Always have been. Sometimes it's damned inconvenient, but I'm too old to change now." I paused. "I think we need to know what happened to James, even if it turns out not to be good news for Scarlett. If it makes things easier for you, consider me fired. The meter stops running as of this moment. But just so we're clear, I'm not backing off until I find out exactly what happened. If I have to do it on my own dime, so be it."

I glanced at my watch and realized I needed to get on the road. I had stops to make before I met up with the women from the ERT out at Pinckney.

"Look, Pudge, here's the bottom line. If they arrest Scarlett, we'll all move heaven and earth to make sure the whole damn world knows what she had to endure all those years. Battered wife syndrome, the whole shot. My friend Alexandra Finch is a dynamite attorney on these issues. We have the emails. We have yours and all the others' observations. If Scarlett finally had enough and killed her husband, we'll get her off."

I waited for the expected outburst, but it never came. Instead, I watched as a solitary tear slid from her puffy eye and slithered down her carefully made-up cheek.

CHAPTER THIRTY-TWO

I pulled into the visitor's lot on Pinckney Island a little before three-thirty to find the women and the dogs had arrived before me. Besides their vehicles—an SUV and a pickup—there was only one other car in the lot.

Each of them wore a crisp uniform with their team logo and a nameplate. I approached Suzanne Greer, and we shook hands.

"This is my partner, Miranda." We exchanged smiles and nods. "And this is Lucas. He's friendly enough, but I'd appreciate it if you didn't try to pet him."

The German shepherd regarded me with huge, curious brown eyes as he sat at Suzanne's feet, a lead fastened to his collar. From a crate in the back of the pickup, a black Lab set up a sharp series of barks.

Miranda Delahunt laughed. "And that's Murphy. He gets a little upset when he's not the center of attention."

"Will you use both dogs?" I asked, and Suzanne shook her head.

"Not together. If Lucas alerts to anything, we'll note the location and come back in. Then we may let Murphy have a go at it. It all depends." Her gaze became serious. "We're not going to do any digging if we get a response."

"Then how will you know if it's . . ." I swallowed. "Human. I mean, it could be a dead animal, couldn't it?"

Miranda answered me. "No. These dogs can tell the difference."

It suddenly occurred to me exactly what I had set in motion, and the realization was sobering.

"So now what?"

"We'll walk Lucas to the approximate spot where the boat was found and start from there."

I nodded, not sure what else to say.

"I'm glad you dressed appropriately," Suzanne said, glancing at the boots and jeans I'd thrown on after grabbing a quick burger at Wendy's. I'd also opted for a long-sleeved T-shirt with the Salty Dog logo. "I'm guessing we'll be getting quite a ways off the beaten path."

I watched as Miranda placed a notebook and pen in one of the pockets of her navy blue pants that looked a lot like Army fatigues. She also tucked in her cell phone along with two bottles of water. Suzanne also carried water. She noticed my gaze.

"We have to make sure we have enough for Lucas," she said. "We don't let the dogs go more than twenty minutes without taking a water break."

"Our first duty is to them," Miranda added. "To their safety and wellbeing. That's one of the reasons we go out together. The handler concentrates on following the dog, and the other keeps track of our surroundings, always watching out for any danger." She turned her head toward the dirt road leading into the heart of the island. "Around here, that mostly means gators."

I shivered in the waning warmth of the March sun. "Hadn't we better get started?"

In answer, Suzanne led the way out of the parking lot, Lucas straining a little on his leash.

We trudged through the dust, settled somewhat by the recent rain, talking little. I noticed that Miranda had taken her cell phone out and was glancing at it periodically. She stopped occasionally to make a note on the pad, then trotted to catch us up.

"Making a record of our location," she said when she caught me watching her. "We don't need it yet, but it's always a good idea to keep track of how you got in." She smiled. "So you can find your way out. I'll also make a record of the elapsed time, the dog's behavior. Things like that."

We crossed an open expanse of marsh, and I figured we couldn't be too far from Jordan Point, at least as the crow flies. A lot of pluff mud and open water stood between us and Pudge's house, but I marveled at how intimately all of this was connected, these small islets and hummocks of marsh grass seeming so incongruous with the steady beat of traffic on the bridges to Hilton Head as background. It was no wonder so many people flocked to trudge through the no-see-ums and humidity for the joy of escaping, if only for an hour or so, the bustle of civilization.

I seemed to remember we were close to one of the ponds where the shore birds—herons, ibis, and the occasional wood stork—nested during this time of year. There were also the migrating birds, heading back north, that somehow knew there would be a refuge for them here, a welcome respite on their long journey. I was craning my neck in that direction when Miranda called a halt.

"These are the coordinates we figured for the discovery of the boat," she said, tilting her head toward the bank of the marsh, now hidden behind trees and foliage.

Suzanne nodded and ordered Lucas to sit. From the pocket of her uniform pants, she pulled a plastic bottle filled with something lavender.

"What's that?" I asked.

"Carpenter's chalk," she said with a smile. "Watch."

She squeezed the bottle, and a puff of chalk exploded into the air, about two feet off the ground. "Checking for wind direction," she said. "And I do it at the dog's level, since he's the one who'll be most affected. If we can, we try to begin by going into the wind."

I nodded as if I understood, but apparently she could tell I was completely lost. "Scent for these dogs is like a cone," she said, putting her fingers together then drawing her hands toward her chest in a widening pattern. "The cadaver is at the point, and the scent radiates outward. If the wind is blowing toward us, the scent will carry farther, giving the dog a better chance of picking it up more quickly."

"Got it," I said. Then something struck me. "You know, if James . . . if the cadaver is out there, wouldn't it be smelling pretty strongly by now? I mean, it's only been less than a week."

"It depends," Miranda said, moving up beside me. "If it's buried, not so much until it hits the air." She paused, eyeing me closely. "And remember what I said about alligators. It may not be an intact find."

"Got it," I said, feeling my stomach rising toward my throat.

"You can stay here if you like," Suzanne said, rightly interpreting my dismay.

"No, I'll go with you, if that's okay." I sucked in lungful of clean, cooling air. "How's the wind?"

"Favorable," she said, laying one hand on the dog's head.

Even from a distance, I could see him trembling, as if he fully understood what was at stake and was yearning to get on with it.

"Ready?" Suzanne asked, looking at Miranda.

"Whenever you are," her partner said, once again checking the readout on her phone. "Are you going to let him off the lead?"

"I don't think so. I'm concerned about gators. Keep your eyes open. I'll give him as much leeway as I can, but I'm not comfortable letting him roam free at this point."

I waited, feeling completely useless as these two stalwart women discussed dead bodies and carnivorous reptiles. Finally, Suzanne nodded once at me then turned her attention to the dog sitting nervously at her side.

"Lucas?" The shepherd looked up. "Lucas, work!"

The dog leaped forward, his nose level, scanning the air around him, then bounded ahead, weaving from side to side in a wide arc that stretched his leash to its limit. Suzanne and Miranda trotted after him, and I had to scurry to catch up. Surprisingly, the dog led us across the road, away from the spot where the dinghy had been beached. Then I realized that this made the most sense. If I were going to dispose of a body, I surely wouldn't do it right on top of where anyone might stumble across it on their jaunt into the nature areas.

In no time we were past the pond, populated by only a few white herons, who took flight immediately, squawking, retreating into the sky at the first hint of the dog. Lucas ignored them and continued to weave back and forth, running to the full extent of his lead, sometimes stopping to sniff the air, before circling back and resuming his pattern.

"He moves out until he leaves the scent cone, then comes back to pick it up again," Suzanne explained.

She called him, and the dog reluctantly returned to her side. She uncapped one of the water bottles and poured some into his mouth.

I was grateful for the respite, trying to hide the fact that I'd been huffing more than a little for the past few minutes. Despite the passing of afternoon toward evening, the heat was still holding, and only a breath of the breeze the chalk test had indicated had made its way into the thick stands of trees and underbrush. I took the opportunity to slake my own thirst from the bottle Miranda passed to me.

"So Lucas definitely has a scent?" I asked, wiping my mouth

with the back of my hand.

"Yes," Suzanne said tersely.

As the going got more difficult, the dog slowed his pace, and Suzanne was able to reel in some of the lead. We slogged on, the humans detouring around dead, fallen tree limbs and clumps of vegetation, although there seemed to be some faint hint of a path. Or at least evidence that someone else had walked this way recently. Occasionally, we could hear the chattering of squirrels and the faint rustling that indicated there were other creatures disturbed by our passing, but Lucas never wavered from the internal grid pattern he'd established.

I guessed we'd been on the trail a good half hour, although it was difficult to judge the sun's position among all the foliage when Suzanne came to a halt. I moved up beside her, Miranda right behind me.

Lucas had narrowed his search to a few feet either side of a direct line in front of us. A moment later he let out a little yelp, then sat down abruptly beside a pile of dead limbs and barked loudly. Suzanne and Miranda exchanged a look.

"What's the matter?" I asked. "Did he lose the scent?"

"On the contrary." Suzanne let out a long breath. "Do you have the coordinates?"

"Got it," Miranda answered, making a notation on her pad.

"Lucas, come." Suzanne knelt as the shepherd reluctantly left his post, prancing in his excitement at having completed his mission. "Good boy, good dog." She ruffled the hair on his head and neck and pulled him into a tight embrace. "Good Lucas."

And then it came to me, on a soft rustling of the wind in the tops of the trees that surrounded us. It wasn't an overpowering smell, not what I'd expected based on all the fictional accounts of decaying bodies I'd read and watched, but enough for me to know exactly what it was. I turned my head and took in air in shallow little gulps.

"Are you all right?" Suzanne's voice seemed to come from very far away.

I nodded and forced myself to look back, one hand covering my nose and mouth.

She stood and studied the spot where the dog had alerted. "Stay," she said, and her look told me that included the humans as well as the dog. She made a wide arc, coming around from the back and paused for a moment, staring down. I saw her nod once, briskly, then return on the same path she'd created.

I could tell by her face Lucas had done his job.

"Do you know what the missing man was wearing?" she asked in a soft voice.

"No, I don't. What is the . . . I mean, what did you see?"

"Something dark blue, a shirt or jacket. And light hair."

"James has . . . had light brown hair."

She nodded again and moved around me to pat the dog once again on his head, then picked up the lead.

"Where are you going?" I asked.

"Back. We found what we came for."

"You mean we're just going to walk away?"

"It's a cadaver. It's obviously been well hidden, so this isn't an accident or even a suicide. We need to mark the location and notify the sheriff's office."

"But—"

"I understand, Mrs. Tanner. You want to know for certain if it's *your* cadaver." Again Suzanne and Miranda exchanged a knowing glance. "Trust me, you don't want to look. Besides, we have a code of ethics by which we operate. If we had been called out by the authorities, there would be someone coordinating the search, a headquarters where we'd report what we've found. And we would immediately evacuate the area. Because this isn't some training exercise. It's a crime scene, and we've already compromised it. It's unavoidable, but we try to leave as small a footprint as possible. I hope you understand."

I had absolutely no desire to lift up that pile of dead leaves and bracken to see if the body belonged to James Stuart. Unless there had been a disappearance that didn't make the papers, who else could it be? But it seemed wrong to leave it—*him*—out there, although I had no earthly idea what else I thought we could do at that point. I nodded and watched Suzanne tie several strips of bright neon-yellow tape in a rough circle around the area where Lucas had alerted. She cast one more look over her shoulder, then we both fell into line behind Miranda as she plotted our way back out the way we had come. I realized how important her job had been because our surroundings had all begun to look the same to my untrained eye. As I skirted the brambles she held aside for me and tried to concentrate on not tripping over something and falling flat on my face, I marveled that such expertise and dedication had existed for who knew how many years just a few miles from my own doorstep.

These women—and their dogs—were amazing.

When we finally broke out into the clearing, I was stunned at how much time had passed. The air was still fairly warm, although the breeze held a distinct chill that presaged sunset. The birds had returned to their roosts around the pond, their numbers having increased considerably, at least to judge by the wave of screeches and squawks that greeted our appearance. One sharp bark from Lucas sent them rising in a multicolored cloud into the waning sunlight.

We paused again for water once we'd gained the main dirt road, and Suzanne let Lucas run a little after praising him lavishly. I glanced across into the trees along the bank of the marsh, shuddering at the thought that someone had landed the dinghy from the *Tiger Pause* just a few feet away and somehow managed to transport James's corpse far into the woods, leaving it to rot away among the dead leaves and decaying limbs. One thing I knew for certain: it hadn't been Mary Alice Stuart. No way.

"Ready?"

Suzanne's voice made me jump.

"Sure."

I fell into step beside them, the dog strangely subdued now that his mission had been completed. He stopped every so often to sniff the bracken on either side of the road, lifting his leg occasionally to mark his passing.

"We'll notify the sheriff, give him the coordinates," Suzanne said as we neared the parking area.

"Is that something you have to do? I mean, right now?"

She didn't answer me immediately. "I'm not quite sure I understand what you're asking, Mrs. Tanner. They have to be advised about what we've found," she said softly.

"Of course. It's just that I'd like to be the one to do it." I shook my head. "What I mean is, I have a good working relationship with the detective in charge of the disappearance, Mike Raleigh, and well . . ." I faltered. "The thing is, he may not be too happy about this. I don't want any of the fallout landing on you."

The two women exchanged a look.

"As you wish," Suzanne said finally. "We'll be happy to lead them back in or provide any other information they might want from us."

"That's great. Which reminds me." I reached into my back pocket and pulled out the check I'd stuffed in there after changing clothes. "I forgot to give you this earlier."

"Thank you." Suzanne tucked it into the breast pocket of her uniform. "I'll calculate our time and expenses and refund you any difference."

We trudged back to where our three vehicles sat, the black Lab, Murphy, setting up an excited barking the moment we appeared.

"Poor boy, you feel left out, don't you?" Miranda crooned, pulling some dog treats from a container in the bed of the pickup.

Suzanne was also rewarding Lucas again after boosting him up into his crate in the back of her SUV.

"Are you going to let Murphy have a chance at it?" I asked, remembering that Miranda had said they sometimes let the dogs search independently.

"Not this time." She reached into the crate to scratch the fidgeting Murphy behind the ears. "We decided to let Lucas take this one because he's older and moves a little slower." She smiled at her dog. "Murph here is fast. Makes it hard to stay with him sometimes, even for us, but he always waits for us to catch up."

I nodded and held out my hand. "Well, I don't know what's the proper thing to say under the circumstances. I sort of hoped it would be an exercise in futility."

Suzanne gave my hand a firm shake. "Understood. I'm glad we could help at least put your client's mind to rest about what happened to that poor man."

"That remains to be seen," I said, stepping back. "Thank you for agreeing to help. And for your professionalism." An idea struck. "You told me you do this on a volunteer basis when law enforcement calls you in. Does that mean you shoulder all the expenses yourselves?"

Miranda smiled. "We do it because we love the work, especially when it's to help find a missing child or an elderly person who's wandered off. We have another shepherd, Buddy, we use in those kinds of situations. Anyway, it's always a thrill to be a part of returning a loved one to their family. That's our compensation."

"Do you accept contributions?" I asked.

"Yes, although we don't go looking for them. Once in a while we try to do a fundraiser, let people meet the dogs."

"Well, be sure to let me know when the next one is. Put me on your mailing list."

"Happy to," Suzanne said, pulling open the door of her SUV.

"And you keep whatever overage there might turn out to be from that retainer." I held up a hand to forestall her protest. "Please. It's something I want to do."

Suzanne smiled. "Thank you." A becoming blush tinted her cheeks. "Miranda, you need to give Mrs. Tanner the coordinates."

Miranda ripped off a sheet from her small notebook. "Here you go."

I took the paper and watched the two women, waving until their trucks had turned onto the causeway that would take them back to the main highway. I collapsed into the Jaguar, pausing a moment to glance at the paper I'd tossed onto the seat beside me. In a neat hand, Miranda Delahunt had written:

32° 14' 44" LAT   80° 46' 0" LONG

Something stirred at the back of my brain, and I felt the hairs rise on my arms. Quickly I counted the digits and felt no surprise at their number: eleven.

Minus all the indicators that represented degrees, hours, and minutes of latitude and longitude, I was pretty sure these were the same numbers someone had copied onto a single sheet of paper and mailed to me at the office in an envelope marked *Personal.*

I wracked my brain to remember when it had arrived. At least a couple of days before, maybe more.

It didn't make the smallest amount of sense, but there was no denying it. Someone had known *exactly* where to find James Stuart's body. And *I* had known all along as well, but I'd been too stupid to figure it out.

I sat for a long time, staring at nothing, while the possibilities bounced around in my head.

Twice I grabbed my phone, and twice I tossed it back on the seat, unable to decide who to call. Finally, I gave it up, backed the Jag around, and headed back to civilization.

CHAPTER THIRTY-THREE

I found Red on the back deck, stretched out on his favorite chaise, a bottle of beer dangling from one hand. He looked up when I stepped through the French doors.

"Hey, honey, where've you been? I was just about to fix myself a snack if you didn't show up soon. We never talked—"

He halted abruptly when I sat down next to him on the cushion.

"What's the matter?"

Apparently the anxiety must have shown clearly on my face.

"I went out with the ERT women. We found James."

"What?"

In a few concise sentences, I told him about the dog, the trek into the woods of Pinckney, the pile of dead leaves and limbs. The light brown hair.

"Why in hell didn't you tell me you were going out there today? I would have gone with you."

"And done what?" I leaned away from the accusatory look on his face. "Besides, you were against this right from the beginning."

"Only because I didn't want to alienate Mike Raleigh. Did you talk to him first?"

I could feel the tension rising into my neck from my shoulders. "No, I didn't."

Red sensed I was ready for a fight, ran his hand lightly along my arm, and lowered his voice. "I wish you hadn't made yourself go through that, honey. How bad was it?"

I moved away from him and dropped onto the other chaise, stretching my legs out in front of me. I closed my eyes and let out a long breath. The shiver that ran down my spine was, I told myself, only a result of the rising wind off the ocean.

"Bay?"

"Not as bad as I thought it might be. I never actually saw the body, but Suzanne described it to me. Sort of. And it didn't smell. Well, it did, but not really awful, at any rate." I sighed. "I don't see how it could be anyone but James."

I shifted my weight and heard the crinkle of paper. I pulled the coordinates out and handed them over to Red. "This is where he . . . it is."

He glanced at the paper. "Wait a minute. Aren't these the—"

"Yes. The same numbers that came in the mail."

"How the hell did someone know that, unless—"

"Unless they came from the killer? And don't start up about Mary Alice, okay? Why on earth would she send that location to me if she actually killed James? Besides, if you could have seen how remote that place was where we found the body, you'd know there's no way she could have managed that."

"Without help."

"And who's on the top of your hit list for that job, huh? Give me some names. Besides the women who were in the house with me the whole night."

"Okay, I get what you're saying." Red swung his legs around so that he was sitting on the edge of the chaise, elbows on knees, the empty bottle of beer swinging from both hands. "You could be right. Maybe your gang of friends and this whole battered wife thing has just been a distraction. It could be that Mike will have to take the investigation in a completely different direction. Look for business enemies or an affair gone wrong. Or maybe it was something so out there that no one's thought of it yet."

"Thanks."

"For what?"

"For being willing to entertain the possibility that Scarlett didn't have anything to do with her husband's death."

"I'm not ready to go that far, at least not yet. But, if I was in charge, I'd be doing a lot more digging into this Stuart guy's life up in Atlanta. Just to cover all the bases." He paused to look back over his shoulder at the gathering twilight. "I wish Erik was here. He'd be the best one to put on the guy's trail."

I shivered again as the last rays of the sun bounced off the glittering, placid surface of the ocean and disappeared behind the trees over the mainland. Red would know, without my having to say it, that I agreed one hundred percent. I missed Erik, too.

"I'm cold," I said, pushing myself up.

"Yeah, me, too. Can't wait for this weekend and Daylight Saving Time." He reached for my hand and pulled me to my feet. "What do you want to do about dinner?"

My mind flashed back to the pile of dead things—including James Madison Stuart the Third—and I shuddered. "I'm not hungry."

"Why don't you go get a shower and hop into your pajamas? I'll rustle us up something—maybe eggs or pancakes—and we can eat in front of the TV. Should be some good college basketball on tonight. The conference championships are in full swing."

His attempt to lighten the atmosphere made me reach out and hug him.

"You're okay, Tanner," I said, surprised by the little catch in my voice.

"Yeah, I'm a prince," he said, hugging me back. Then he slapped me on the butt. "Turn me loose, woman, and let me get to the kitchen. I have housewifely duties to perform."

Hand in hand we walked back into the house. I paused in the middle of the great room and turned to face him.

"What about Mike? I should call and let him know what we found."

"Why don't you let me do that?" He held up the piece of notebook paper he still had clutched in one hand. "This is all he really needs, right?"

"He's going to be pissed at us—at me. You shouldn't have to take the brunt of that."

"Let me worry about it, okay?" He kissed me lightly on the cheek and trotted up the three steps into the kitchen. "You've only got about fifteen minutes, so I'd get cracking if I were you."

I smiled and snapped a brisk salute as I headed for the bedroom.

Over-easy eggs, cooked just a little too long, and crisp bacon greeted me when I shuffled back into the great room. Red had set everything up on the coffee table, including a steaming cup of Earl Grey and a plate of English muffins. I'd taken his advice about the pajamas, adding my disreputable robe and my floppy slippers. I hadn't even bothered to dry my hair.

"That smells wonderful," I said, surprised that my appetite

had miraculously returned.

"We aim to please," my husband said, handing me a paper napkin with a flourish. He sat down next to me on the sofa. "You want me to light the fire?"

"Eat first," I said, glancing up to see he'd already found his basketball game on ESPN.

We watched and ate in silence for a while, and I managed to keep the mental image of James Stuart's decaying body out of my head long enough to allow me to swallow without incident.

"Box out!" Red shouted, startling me. "Lord Almighty, guys, you can't let them keep getting every rebound all night!"

"Who's winning?" I asked, tucking my feet up under me and cradling the mug of tea in both hands.

"Duke. By about fifteen over Clemson. We're getting killed."

"I assume the 'we' is Clemson?"

He turned to grin at me. "Gotta support the home guys, although I have to admit to a grudging admiration for the Blue Devils. They always have a hell of a team."

I'd never been much of a fan of basketball, but I nodded as if I agreed. The Judge and I had bonded very early over baseball, especially the Braves. I thought fondly of those nights after dinner, curled up on his lap in front of the TV, while he explained the finer points of the game to me. I wondered what he'd make of this case. I smiled. He probably would have told me to run like hell in the other direction the moment Pudge walked into my office.

I should call her, I thought. *Or maybe not. Later.*

"Did you talk to Mike?" I'd purposely waited for one of the endless timeouts and its accompanying cascade of commercials.

"Yeah."

I waited, but he began fumbling with the dirty dishes. "That's it? *Yeah?*"

He shrugged and headed for the kitchen. In a flash I was right behind him.

"Tell me what he said."

"Some of it's not repeatable." He smiled as he set the dishes in the sink. "Let's just say you're not his favorite PI at the moment."

"But what are they going to do about it?"

"They'll wait 'til morning, then go get the body. What did you expect them to do?"

I leaned against the counter while he loaded the dishwasher. "I don't know. I thought he might want to come charging over here and beat me up. Verbally, that is."

"I talked him out of it. He'll see us in the office sometime tomorrow, hopefully after he's cooled off a little bit."

"That bad?"

"Not really. About what I expected." He turned to look me in the eyes. "He has a right, you know. You should have checked this out with him first."

"And if he'd been against it, we still wouldn't know what happened to James. And he'd still be looking at Scarlett. At least this way she has some closure."

Red didn't respond, simply took my hand and led me back down into the great room. I flopped onto the sofa while he knelt in front of the fireplace and set matches to the newspaper and kindling. In only a few moments, the fire was crackling away, easing the slight chill and chasing away some of the dampness. I snuggled down and pulled the comforter over my legs.

"It's better this way, you know it is. And so does Mike. Now he's not operating with two different possibilities, a disappearance or a death. He can concentrate on finding a murderer instead of a husband who decided to kick his life to the curb and start over."

"I don't think he ever seriously entertained that possibility. That Stuart staged the whole thing." He paused. "Although there are elements that look a little like staging."

"You mean the blood? I didn't see the body, but chances are it came from him. From James. Who else's could it be?"

Red turned to face me and laid a hand on my arm. "What if that boat was supposed to be found somewhere else, away from the island? What if it was supposed to sink? It's only rubber, you know."

"No, I didn't. I thought it was fiberglass or something like that."

He shook his head. "Nope. An inflatable. Malik told me."

"Then all the killer had to do was poke a few holes in it and let it sink. Why didn't he do that?"

Red smiled. "*He?*"

"Okay, or she. The boat goes to the bottom, along with the blood, no one has any reason to search Pinckney, no body, no murder. The assumption becomes that James just took off, and

Scarlett gets her life back. Why didn't he—or *she*—do that?"

"Who knows? Maybe that was the plan and something went wrong. The better thing would have been to weight both of them down and sink him along with the dinghy. That would really have been the easiest way to dispose of the body." He paused. "Although that would pose some logistical problems. If they sank the boat, how would they get back?"

"Good point." I stifled a yawn. "You going to stay up for this whole game? I'm ready for bed."

"Is that an invitation?" He did that Groucho Marx thing with his eyebrows, and I laughed.

"Interpret it however you like, buster." I stood and stretched.

"There's always another basketball game," he said and took my hand.

I put off calling Pudge until we'd made it to the office next morning. It wasn't a task I was looking forward to. And neither was the announcement from Sharese that Mike Raleigh would be in to interview me at ten o'clock sharp.

As she handed me the rest of the messages, it suddenly occurred to me that Erik hadn't called as promised the day before.

"No, ma'am," she said when I asked. "I would have told him to reach you on your cell, just like you asked."

"Thanks." I pulled out my cell and checked it for missed calls in case I hadn't had service while I was tramping around in the woods, but there was nothing. I wondered if that portended good news or bad.

I had just picked up the land line when it rang. I let Sharese answer. A moment later the intercom buzzed.

"It's Ms. Reynolds for you on one," she said.

"I'll take it. Thanks."

I gave myself a moment and the benefit of a long, slow breath before I lifted the receiver.

"Good morning, Pudge. How are you feeling?"

"Pissed off, Tanner, that's how I'm feeling!"

"At me?"

"Yes, damn it, at you! I forked over a lot of bucks to you, and I have to read it on the Internet? About James's body turning up?"

I sighed. "Okay, I know. I just had my hand on the phone to

call you when you beat me to it. I'm sorry I wasn't faster than the speed of light."

"What in bloody hell were you thinking?"

"What do you mean?"

"I never authorized you to go snooping around with a pack of dogs! You seem to have a hard time remembering who's paying the damn bills around here!"

That stopped me for a moment. I chose my next words carefully. "No, you didn't ask me to find James's body. But I did." Despite my good intentions, I could feel my own temper rising. "And don't worry, *Sylvie*, the expense won't be coming out of your pocket. In case you've forgotten, we agreed yesterday that I was off the clock, at least as far as you're concerned."

"That's not the point! Don't you realize what you've done?"

"Yes, I know precisely what I've done. I've proved that James is dead." I waited, but she didn't respond. "And, unfortunately for you, I've proved that he couldn't have been the one who beat you up." In a softer tone, I added, "But I'm sure you already knew that."

"You have no idea what . . . Oh, the hell with it! I knew it was a mistake to involve you. I told them, but—"

"Told who what?"

Suddenly she sounded more sad than angry. "They'll be all over Scarlett now. The cops."

"I think you're wrong, Pudge. Oh, they'll go through the motions, but if you could have seen how deep in the woods . . . Well, anyway, I think this is going to be good for Scarlett, honestly I do. They'll know she couldn't have engineered this whole scenario, and they'll go looking somewhere else. In Atlanta, maybe with his business. Who knows what kinds of trouble he could have gotten into up there over the years?" I paused, recalling the first time Pudge had come pirouetting into my office. "And she's safe now. That's what you all wanted right from the start, isn't it?"

Again, I got no reply.

"At least now she knows for sure what happened to him," I said quietly. "Believe me, that's better than spending the rest of your life wondering."

The silence lasted longer as both of us, no doubt, remembered that there'd never been any question about what had happened to my first husband.

"It's all just so sad," she finally said in a subdued tone. "I know I called him names and wanted in the worst way to beat the hell out of him myself, for what he did to Scarlett, but like it or not, James was part of our past, our history."

I couldn't argue with that. It was a facet of the whole sordid story I'd been trying to suppress ever since I'd stood in the stillness of Pinckney Island and looked at the mound of debris that covered his body.

I opened my mouth to agree with her, only to realize she'd already hung up.

I sat for a moment before replacing the receiver, then stood up and walked through the reception area to the tiny cubbyhole that had become Red's office.

"I'm going over to Pudge's this afternoon. After we talk to Mike, I think we can put this one in the loss column and move on."

"How do you figure it's a loss?"

I perched on the corner of his small, functional desk. "Well, Mary Alice doesn't have to worry about getting the crap beat out of her every other day, so I suppose that could technically be called a win. I just want to be done with it, once I explain about finding the body yesterday. To them and to Mike." I paused. "Lavinia wants us to come to dinner, either tonight or Sunday."

"That was a quick change of subject." He thought a minute. "How about we make it Sunday? After we drop the kids off, since we're already over that way."

"You don't mind?"

"Why should I mind? Has Lavinia ever cooked anything that wasn't completely out of this world?"

I smiled, as I knew he'd intended. "Are you insinuating that my culinary skills aren't up to your rigid standards?"

"Nothing of the kind," he said with a grin. "But we all have our own areas of expertise."

I heard the phone ring, and a moment later Sharese stood in the doorway.

"It's Erik for you," she said, her smile as wide as I've ever seen it.

I scrambled off the desk and strode into my office. "Erik! Sorry I missed your call the other day. How are things going?"

"Good."

I felt my heart turn over. He and Stephanie had reconnected. They'd reconciled. They were going ahead with the wedding plans. He was never coming back.

"Bay? You still there?"

"Yes, sorry. So give me the scoop." I leaned back in my chair, ordering my blood to quit racing.

"Well, I finally had a chance to talk to Steph. Her mother actually arranged it, believe it or not. I think she got the message that I wasn't going away until that happened."

"And?"

"So we met for a drink last night. That's why I didn't call you during the day. I wanted to wait and see if I had anything to report."

I waited, but he didn't continue. "So do I have to come out there and shake it out of you?"

I sensed his smile. "No, you don't have to go that far." Then his voice sobered. "We had a really good conversation, very frank, about everything that happened last year. She feels really terrible about what she put you through. She doesn't have even a mediocre explanation for why she behaved the way she did. Delayed shock, her shrink told her, over her father's death, and maybe that's what it was. Anyway, she asked me to tell you again how sorry she is."

"That was thoughtful," I said, knowing I was unsuccessful in keeping the sarcasm out of my voice.

Erik paused. "Anyway, bottom line is that she won't come back to Hilton Head. Ever. She was very clear about that."

I held my breath, then let it out slowly. "And what about you?"

He kept me in suspense for only a moment. "I was wondering if you could pick me up at the airport around seven tomorrow morning?"

CHAPTER
THIRTY-FOUR

The news of Erik's imminent return buoyed me through the sometimes tense interview with Mike Raleigh.

He was angry and disappointed that I hadn't had the courtesy to let him know what I was up to. For once, I kept my temper in check and let him have his say. He grudgingly admitted that finding the body—and yes, it appeared to be that of James Stuart —had been a help to his investigation, not to mention a relief of sorts to his widow. He said a formal identification might prove difficult. Although he didn't elaborate on the reasons, I could pretty much figure them out for myself. I only hoped it had been because of the length of time the corpse had been out there and not because Suzanne's mention of gators kept running around in my head. DNA testing would take weeks, if not longer, and they still didn't have any results from the blood they'd found in the boat. However, it seemed a safe assumption that it belonged to James.

It could have been a lot worse, I thought. I'd insisted that Red sit in, and maybe his presence had held the detective a little in check.

"Still friends?" I'd asked just before Mike rose from his chair.

He'd studied me for a moment before allowing me a curt nod.

"One down and one to go," I said to my husband as I watched Mike Raleigh close the outer door behind him.

"The ladies?"

I nodded. Much as I told myself I wanted to put this whole case behind me, there was still a tingling in the back of my head that wanted to solve it. To find James's murderer and serve him up on a silver platter to Mike.

Hubris, I thought. I had no idea where to begin to look for suspects, if, as Red had suggested, the reasons traced back to

James's life in Atlanta. If the solitude of the *Tiger Pause*, the relative emptiness of the island this time of year, had given someone from up there the opportunity to bump him off, I didn't see that we—I—would have a snowball's chance in hell of figuring it out.

"Let's go out tonight, somewhere special." Red's voice cut across my gloomy thoughts.

"What are we celebrating?"

"Erik's on his way back, this case is over, and we can get back to normal. Besides, it's been a long time since we've been to one of the swankier places. Pick something really expensive."

"My, we are feeling our oats," I said, smiling back. "I'll think about it. Right now, I need to get over to Jordan Point. That's the last door that needs slamming on this thing."

Red laughed. "You do have a way with words, honey."

"Pudge said I should have been a standup comic."

"I wouldn't go that far." He stood. "I'm going to take the afternoon off. I called my buddy Dave, and he's going to take me out in the Calibogue for some serious fishing and beer drinking. That okay with you?"

"Knock yourself out. Just don't bring the catch home. I'm not up for cleaning fish."

"Deal. Call if you need me." He waved, stopping to speak to Sharese before disappearing out the door.

There were no extra cars in the drive when I pulled in behind Bebe's Audi, and I breathed a sigh of relief as I stepped out into the sunshine.

Which lasted precisely as long as it took me to mount the steps up onto the porch. Before I had even lifted my finger to the bell, the door burst open.

"What are you doing here?"

Pudge stood at rigid attention, as if she were a guardian at the gate.

"We need to talk," I said, craning my neck to see around her into the house.

She shifted her weight to block my view.

"I don't think so. I think we've said all we have to say to each other."

She wore platform sandals and those, coupled with her being

one step higher than I was, put us pretty much at eye level. I was determined not to be the first one to blink.

"So where's the rest of the *sisterhood*?" I said with more than a hint of sarcasm. "Are you all gathering for some sort of secret rites?"

I watched her face cloud over. "No one's here. You just can't leave anything alone, can you, Bay Rum? I should have remembered that."

"Yeah, you probably should have." I continued to stare into her eyes, and it suddenly occurred to me that she looked more scared than angry. "Listen, Pudge, all I want to do is say my piece, and then we can all go about our business."

"Let her in," I heard a voice behind her say, and suddenly Bebe's face appeared at the corner of the doorway.

"It's not necessary," Pudge answered, turning her head only slightly.

"Do it." The hard edge in Bebe's voice startled me, and I took a step back.

There was something in Pudge's eyes . . . I felt as if she was trying to tell me something, but I couldn't decipher what it was. Then I saw her jerk, as if she'd been poked in the back, and she moved aside, Bebe still hanging behind her. I had a sudden urge to turn and run in the other direction. To this day I don't know why I didn't. Instead, I took advantage of the opening and walked willingly into a nightmare.

CHAPTER
THIRTY-FIVE

I wasn't familiar with the model of pistol Bebe held steady with both hands, but I could tell immediately that it wasn't a toy.

"Sorry," Pudge said, backing awkwardly toward the living area with the gun still pointed directly at her back. "But you never could take a hint."

Bebe edged along with her.

"What in the hell are you doing?" I finally managed to ask. "What's going on?"

"Sit down, Bay, and shut up." She said it matter-of-factly, all of her usual simpering apparently cast aside. "You, too, Pudge. Over there." She jerked her head toward the sofa. "I want both of you where I can see you."

Pudge and I exchanged a look.

"And don't even think about trying anything." She glanced down at the gun in her hand. "Daddy taught me well. I know how to use it."

"No problem," I said.

I perched on the edge of the cushion, and Pudge did the same. I kept my bag pressed tightly against my side, although I knew it was pointless. The Smith & Wesson still rested out of reach in the glove box of the Jaguar, and my little Seecamp was gathering dust in the safe in the floor of my bedroom closet. I vowed that, if I made it out of there in one piece, I would never allow myself to go unarmed again.

"And now what, Bebe?" Pudge had kept her feet firmly planted on the heart pine floor, and I could sense the tension in her muscles. I wanted to communicate to her that it didn't matter a whit how good she was at tae kwon do or whatever it was she held a brown belt in. There was probably no human still alive after trying to prove he was faster than a bullet.

"I don't know," she said, again in that maddening tone of

someone discussing the weather or sharing a recipe. "I have to think."

I let my hand drop to the strap of my bag. There was a lot of stuff in there. Maybe I'd have a chance to use it in some way. I flexed my fingers and tried to appear as relaxed as Bebe sounded.

"Where's the rest of the gang?" I asked, looking around the room, using the opportunity to scan our immediate surroundings for anything else I might be able to use as a weapon. Nothing jumped out.

"We don't need them. We never did. Besides, I'm sick of the whole *sisterhood* thing. Especially Annie. God, I hate that woman!" Her voice rose with every word until she was nearly shouting. "Condescending bitch! She's nothing but a wannabe who slept her way into money. It didn't take me fifteen minutes in the same room with her to figure out she has absolutely no background. No class. Zero. Not like us. It's so damned unfair!"

I was beginning to get an inkling of where this was heading. My mind flashed back to the early reports Erik had assembled on the women who congregated in this sprawling Lowcountry home on Jordan Point. The downsizing. The loss of the house on Tradd Street. Pudge's remarks about Bebe's life being a hot mess. In less than a few seconds, the whole thing clicked into place.

"What happened, Beebs?" I hoped my use of our pet name for her might engender some remnant of the feelings we'd all shared so many years ago. The loyalty. The friendship. "Let us help you."

"It's too late for that," she said, a lot of the fight seeming to drain out of her.

I watched her walk around the recliner and lower herself into it. I tensed, looking for an opening, but the gun never wavered. She was right. Her daddy had taught her well.

"Maybe not," I said softly, shifting my weight farther forward. I put every ounce of sincerity I could muster into those two words. "Tell us what happened. It was an accident, wasn't it?"

She jerked, and her hand shot forward, the gun catching a glint of sunlight through the windows looking out over the tangle of trees and underbrush that sloped down to the water.

"What do you mean?"

Although the probable sequence of events tumbled like a freight train through my head, I forced myself to speak calmly.

"James. It was an accident."

"It wasn't my fault!" Her voice had gone shrill again in the still afternoon air.

"Was it Ralph?" Pudge had picked up on my intentions, and she, too, nearly crooned the words.

"Yes! It was all his idea! I didn't want to. I told him, but he wouldn't listen."

"I know, honey. We all know you aren't to blame."

I wondered if Pudge actually knew something or if, like me, she was just playing Bebe along, waiting for some kind of opening.

"He needed the money. He probably just meant to hold James for ransom, but things got out of hand, didn't they?" I leaned a little closer to the edge of the sofa.

"You don't know anything!" Bebe waved the gun to within a few inches of my face. "Get back! I swear I don't have anything left to lose!"

Pudge and I both jerked away from the yawning barrel of the pistol.

"Okay, Beebs, relax."

"Quit calling me that!" she shouted at Pudge. "I hate that name!"

"Fine," I said, holding up one hand, "fine. Beatrice. It really is a lovely name. I can't think why we ever stopped using it."

"I hate that, too. And quite trying to humor me, Bay. You can be a condescending bitch, too, you know. Always thought you were better than the rest of us, didn't you? And your mother! So proud of herself, and nothing but a common drunk."

There seemed to be no way to placate her, to restore some sense of reason. I was very afraid that she'd gone completely around the bend, and there was no pulling her back. Maybe we'd just have to make a move, take the chance that one of us would be able to overpower her before she pulled the trigger. Twice. I wished there was some way to communicate all this to Pudge. I could only hope that somehow she had reached the same conclusion. I tensed my thighs and shifted my weight to my feet.

But Pudge apparently had decided on a different tack.

"Well, then, what would you like us to call you, huh? Mrs. Bedford? Come on, you know you don't want that. You never loved him, did you? He was just a way to get away from home. Away from your *daddy*."

"You shut up about my father!" Bebe leaped to her feet. "I don't want to talk about that!"

I shot a quick glance at Pudge, wondering what in the hell she was up to. If she didn't watch it, she was going to get both of us killed.

"Of course you don't. None of us ever did. Maybe that was the problem. Maybe that was why we were all scared to death about confronting Scarlett. We had our own secrets to protect, didn't we?"

"I don't know what you're talking about! You just shut the hell up, Pudge! I mean it. You shut up right now!"

For a moment, the pistol wavered, the barrel angled toward the floor.

I dragged in a lungful of air and launched myself, swinging my bag like a golf club aimed directly at her face.

The first explosion sounded as if it had come from inside my head.

The second made the world go black.

CHAPTER
THIRTY-SIX

I had no idea how long I'd been out when I finally managed to force my eyes open.

I was curled in a fetal position, and the first thing I saw was Pudge's feet, one elegant sandal kicked off to the side.

I tried to raise myself off the floor, but the dizziness forced me back down. Tentatively, I lifted my hand to my pounding forehead, astounded when it came away bloody.

"I didn't shoot *you*, honey. You'll be okay."

Bebe's voice came from the far end of a tunnel, and for a moment I had to force myself to concentrate on her words. I opened my mouth, but nothing came out. I swallowed the bile rising into my throat.

"Pudge?" I croaked.

"You shouldn't have done that," Bebe said, and I suddenly realized that she sounded like a little girl. I almost expected her to giggle.

I drew a couple of deep breaths and eased myself upright. I slumped against the side of the sofa, the effort almost more than I could bear. Everything wavered in front of me as if it were bathed in a mist, but I could make out Pudge's body sprawled across the pine boards.

She wasn't moving.

My mind told me to go to her, but my body failed to comply.

"What have you done?" I whispered, and this time Bebe actually laughed.

"I shot her. She tried to hurt me, but she won't do it again." They were the words of a child, angry and triumphant.

"We need to help her," I said.

"Why?"

I pushed myself up a little higher. "Because she's our friend."

"She isn't! She said she was, but she tried to hurt me!"

"Bebe . . ." I began, then paused. "Beatrice, I know you didn't mean to . . ."

"Yes, I did! They're all like that. Annie and Jenny and Gill. Bitsy is nice." She smiled. "And you. Sometimes. I'm sorry I hit you, but you scared me."

I could feel my mind beginning to clear, some of the grayness starting to recede. "I know. I'm sorry, too."

I focused on her then, sitting in the recliner, her feet barely touching the floor. Something in her eyes told me she had gone to a place from which she might never return. I had no idea how to reach her, how to get her to put down the gun she still gripped tightly in her right hand.

"I'm thirsty," I said, snatching at the first thought to pop into my head. "Could I have a glass of water?"

"In a minute," she said, smiling.

"Maybe Pudge would like one, too. Would that be okay?"

I watched in amazement as the veil of madness lifted, and the look in her eyes sent a shiver down my spine.

"I didn't want to kill her. But she just wouldn't leave it alone. She kept asking questions. Why would James beat her up? Maybe it wasn't him after all. Then who could it be? I knew she'd figure it out sooner or later. I told him it was a bad idea."

I tried to wrap my head around what she was saying. "Was it Ralph? Did he hurt Pudge?"

"He was afraid she was going to tell, and then it would all be for nothing."

"What happened to James?"

"He wouldn't give Ralph the money! It was so little compared to what they have. And we would have paid him back!" Suddenly she shot upright in the chair. "And you're no better, Miss High and Mighty Fashion Model!" Her foot slashed out, connecting with Pudge's bare leg.

She didn't flinch.

"She could have given it to us, too, but she said she'd already lost too much money from Ralph's schemes. Schemes! All I wanted was my house back. My lovely house! Was that too much to ask? Was it?"

I shook my head. "Of course not. They should have helped you." I would have agreed to anything to keep her talking. Somehow I had to get Pudge help. If she wasn't already beyond that point.

"So Ralph said we'd just take him off the boat over to that little island and keep him there for awhile. We weren't sure exactly when, but then everybody showed up here, and he thought it would be perfect timing." She nodded once, as if agreeing with herself. "Scarlett would have paid to have him back, you know, even if he did hit her a lot." She shrugged. "It's no big deal. Ralph hits me, too. Just like Daddy did. You get used to it."

My stomach turned over, and it was all I could do to keep from vomiting. I could feel my blood thundering in my ears, and I willed myself not to pass out again.

"Did Ralph kill James?"

She drew herself up and ran one finger of her left hand along the barrel of the gun, almost lovingly. "No, I did that. I didn't mean to, but he just wouldn't shut up! He kept hollering and threatening us. He said we'd go to jail, and he told us all the terrible things that could happen to us in prison." She paused as if reliving the scene in her mind. "Ralph hit him with the oar. In the head."

I watched the madness creep back into her eyes.

"He hit him a couple of times. There was a lot of blood. I don't like blood. But then he still wouldn't be quiet, so we made him walk into the woods, way far back. I was a little scared 'cause it was so dark, but Ralph said not to worry. And then James tried to hit Ralph, and I had to shoot him." She giggled, a chilling sound that made me wince. "James, I mean, not Ralph." Then her face clouded over. "I shot Ralph later. At home."

I gasped, and she centered the gun on my chest.

"I know it was a bad thing to do. But he said he'd tell everyone I did it, all by myself." She shrugged. "I had to. You can see that, can't you?"

I jumped at the touch of Pudge's foot against my leg, just the barest movement, but my heart leaped at it. And I knew we had a chance.

"Of course I do," I said, easing my back away from the sofa just a little. "Everyone will understand." When she didn't respond, I took a chance and pushed myself to standing. "Do you think I could have that glass of water now?"

The gun stayed zeroed in on my chest, and I could feel sweat running down my sides.

"Sure," Bebe said, waving the pistol toward the kitchen. "You go first."

I forced myself to stand, clutching the table to steady myself, and stepped over Pudge's body. Bebe had taken only two steps when Pudge's hand snaked out and grabbed her ankle. For a moment she teetered. I whirled and snatched for the gun just as she tumbled forward.

"Nooooo!" she screamed a moment before her head cracked against the heart pine boards, and she stopped moving.

For good.

CHAPTER
THIRTY-SEVEN

"So who sent you the coordinates of the guy's body?" Erik asked.

The four of us sat around my desk as if it were a regular Monday morning, Starbucks containers scattered in front of us. I sipped my chai tea latte and gingerly touched the knot underneath the bandage on my forehead. It had taken a few stitches to close the wound opened when Bebe backhanded me with the pistol. It still hurt like hell, but I had been more fortunate than Pudge. The first bullet had buried itself in the heart pine floor. The second skidded along the side of her face, perilously close to her left eye, and there was some concern that it might have been permanently affected. I didn't think even the clever Mai at the Westin would be able to repair the damage this time.

"Jenny Carson," I said. "She told me the numbers just came to her as she was getting on the plane to go home after James disappeared, and she had an overpowering feeling she should send them to me."

"You believe that?" Red asked.

I shrugged. "There's no evidence she had anything to do with what happened on Pinckney. I think Bebe told us exactly how that went down."

"But you're buying all that clairvoyance garbage?"

Sharese spoke for the first time. "My mother is a good Christian woman, but she still fears the power of the root. She's told us lots of stories about haints and plateyes." She smiled. "The front door of her house is painted blue."

I smiled back, remembering how deeply ingrained were the old slave beliefs, even in someone as down-to-earth as Lavinia. And apparently Sharese's mama.

"So give me a better explanation," I said, leaning back in the chair. The headache had abated somewhat, but the light still hurt my eyes.

"How about they were all in on it?"

"What, like *Murder on the Orient Express?* Come on, Red. Why would Bebe take the blame if she could have laid it off on the rest of them?"

"I don't know. Maybe because she was nuts? It just seems a little convenient that this Jenny person should know the exact location of the body."

"'There are more things in heaven and earth, Horatio, than are dreamt of in your philosophy.'"

"*Hamlet.* William Shakespeare." Erik grinned. "Do I get the two points?"

I smiled back. "They're all yours."

"I hear the Charleston police found Ralph's body after Mike Raleigh contacted them." Red shook his head. "She plugged him in their bed, a double-tap to the heart. He probably never knew what hit him."

"I have a hard time feeling too bad about it," I said. "What's Mike's theory about how the actual murder went down? I mean, of James."

"All he really has to go on is what you and your model friend told him about this Bebe's confession, although it seems as if the forensics are lining up with what she told you. You said you thought you heard a boat during the night, so it could have been them." Red downed the last of his coffee. "He takes James off the yacht at gunpoint, stops to pick up Bebe, and off they go. It jibes with everything you remember, right?"

"I guess. I must have slept right through it."

"Maybe that's why she put you up in that room, away from everyone else, so you wouldn't be able to hear them coming and going in the middle of the night."

I sat back up straight. "I'm not buying it, Red, no matter how appealing it seems to be to you. And since there won't be a trial, I suppose we'll never know for sure. I'm content with knowing that Scarlett is in the clear. And safe, finally, after all these years."

The shrill of the phone made us all jump, and Sharese leaned over to pick it up.

"Simpson and Tanner, Inquiry Agents. How may I help you?"

Her cheerful face clouded up. "Oh, I'm so sorry. Would you like to speak to Mrs. Tanner?" She listened for a moment. "Yes,

I'll see if she's available."

She pushed the Hold button. "It's that Mr. O'Hare. He says he has some bad news to report."

My fingers brushed the bandage on my forehead. "I really don't want to deal with him right now. See if you can take a message."

Sharese stood and returned to her desk. I ordered myself not to pay any attention to her end of the conversation.

"So I see there's a message from Alex Finch. I'm guessing she's got a case for us."

"You should be home in bed." My husband spoke sternly. "The doctor in the ER said you should take it easy for a few days."

"I'm fine. I have no intention of lolling around feeling sorry for myself. Besides, I want to get up to the hospital and check in on Pudge. And I promised her I'd drive out to Bluffton and explain things to her mother. She doesn't want one of the ladies deciding to share the headlines from the *Packet* with her. She asked the nursing staff to keep her away from newspapers for a couple of days."

"I can do all that. You should be getting some rest."

"I can check in with Alex and see what she wants," Erik offered. "Why don't both of you take the day and just relax? I've been sandbagging for the past week, and Sharese and I can handle it."

His earnest face made me smile.

"Uh, just one thing, though," he added.

"What's that?"

"Well, I need to leave a little early today."

"Hot date?"

"Actually, yes." He blushed. "Sandy. I met her on the flight from Phoenix to Charlotte. She's an attendant with U.S. Air. She has a short layover tonight, and I asked her out for a drink."

"Fabulous!" I said. "I'm so pleased."

He grinned. "I thought you would be. So you two take a hike, okay?"

Red stood. "Works for me. Maybe we can have that fancy dinner we had planned for Saturday before Annie Oakley here got herself banged up."

"Go to hell," I said with a smile.

"Sorry to interrupt." We all turned toward Sharese, who had paused in the doorway.

"Yes?"

"It's that Devlin O'Hare, the one you met with last Wednesday?"

"Another nutcase," I said for Erik's benefit. In spite of my best intentions, my curiosity got the better of me. "What's his bad news?"

"They found his wife's car abandoned on a back road in Jasper County. He wants to hire you to find her."

Red and I exchanged a look. I stood and held out my hand to him.

"You and Erik can handle it," I said as my husband locked his fingers around mine. "We're taking the day off."

Neither of us looked back before the door closed softly behind us.

EPILOGUE

Red and I excused ourselves as we sidled in front of the families already seated in the bleachers, squeezing ourselves into a space technically large enough for only one and a half normal sized people.

"I had no idea it would be this crowded," I said, smiling my thanks to the woman next to me, who had scooted over as far as she could.

"It's a big class. Quite a bit larger than Scotty's was."

A pimply young man had handed us programs at the foot of the concrete steps, and I used mine to fan away the no-see-ums that danced in front of my nose. I turned my face upward, but there was no breeze to catch. All the bodies packed inside the football stadium had driven the already steamy June temperature even higher as evening settled in.

"I wish Sharese and her family, and Erik and what's-her-name could have joined us. They're probably stuck somewhere down on the field. They won't even be able to see Elinor when she marches in."

Red chuckled. "It's Melissa."

"Who?"

"Erik's what's-her-name."

"Well, I'm sorry, but there've been so many of them I can't keep track."

"Don't be like that, Bay. Besides, I think this one just might be more serious than the others." Red ran a finger around his collar, the unaccustomed tie making him even more uncomfortable in the heat. "He's been dating her now for what, a couple of months?"

"About that, I guess. I don't see him as much as I'd like anymore."

"The agency has grown so much. And you know he doesn't like to delegate to his employees." He laughed. "Gee, I wonder who he learned that from?"

I ignored his gibe and craned my neck as a stirring began at the far end of the stadium. "I think they're coming."

The band down on the field snapped to attention as the director stepped up onto the podium. A moment later the familiar strains of *Pomp and Circumstance* floated across the still, humid air. Red took his tiny camera from his shirt pocket.

"Will you be able to catch her from this far away?" I asked.

"No problem. These new gadgets are amazing. They zoom without you even having to tell them to, almost as if they could read your mind."

Another technology breakthrough I didn't understand, I thought, my mind drifting back to my time at the agency when it seemed as if every other day Erik came up with some new advancement we needed to take advantage of. In that, as in so many other ways, it was a relief to be free of all the responsibility.

Although I hadn't felt that way at the time.

When Sarah finally lost her protracted battle with breast cancer, Red and I had become fulltime parents. For awhile we stayed in the house in Beaufort, primarily so that the kids could finish their schooling and graduate with their friends. I wasn't happy about it, but we had little choice. It seemed such a short time since we'd sat in these same bleachers and watched Scotty receive his diploma. And he would have been right next to us on his sister's big night if not for his decision to join the Marines halfway through his sophomore year at Clemson. I did my best to talk him out of it, but he was determined to follow in his father's footsteps. I smiled to myself. Red's objections had been less than convincing, and I knew he was secretly proud of Scotty's choice, in spite of the dangers. The world was never safe enough when you had someone you loved in the military.

So here we were, marking another milestone in our lives. Unlike her brother, Elinor reveled in learning and would be delivering the valedictory address. Her scholarship to USC had been well-deserved. She vacillated between medicine and teaching as career choices, but she had time to settle in to college life and make up her mind. We didn't worry about Elinor.

I checked my watch. I hoped the caterers would show up on schedule so that everything was ready by the time we got back. I'd spent a good bit of the afternoon cutting and arranging flowers. That made me smile. Mother would have been astounded. Elinor had invited about a hundred of her closest friends, and I knew there would be parents, neighbors, and acquaintances, as well as Erik and Sharese and her brood descending on us the moment we walked in the door of Presqu'isle.

"There she is!" Red jumped up and began snapping or whatever one did with the new camera gadget, then settled back down to await the handing out of the diplomas and his daughter's speech. She'd rehearsed it so often I almost felt as if I could deliver it myself. Her father was nearly beside himself with pride.

I sighed, remembering all those who weren't here to share this moment: the Judge and Emmaline. Sarah. Red's parents. And Rob. Julia would have loved the party, but she'd been gone from Presqu'isle for a long time. Neddie had finally come around to seeing things my way, especially after the incident that had left Lavinia with a broken wrist. In the end, she'd been forced to admit that life was probably not going to get any better for my half sister and certainly not for Lavinia. Julia's increasingly erratic behavior had obviously become dangerous—just as I'd been insisting for more years than I cared to remember. The home Neddie had found for her was clean, bright, and offered around the clock supervision and care. Julia seemed happy enough, although she'd begun not to recognize me when I made my quarterly visits, something Neddie had warned me was not entirely unexpected.

I wasn't sure Lavinia ever quite forgave me for it, but at least my dearest friend's last years had been peaceful ones. The void her passing had left in my heart would never be filled.

Red turned to me, the smile sliding from his face. "What's the matter?"

I shook my head, and he reached across and wiped away the single tear that had leaked from the corner of my eye.

"Honey?"

"Nothing."

He leaned close to whisper in my ear. "Happy tears, I hope. Or are you worrying about what we're going to do with ourselves now that the last bird has flown the nest?"

I squirmed as he brushed his lips against the side of my neck. "I'm sure we'll think of something."

"I love you, Bay Tanner," he murmured and turned his attention back to the field.

I smiled.

"I love you, too," I whispered, so low he might not have heard.

AUTHOR'S NOTE

Once again I find myself in the enviable position of having the opportunity to thank those who have been so much help to me in the creation of the Bay Tanner novels. As I've said before, writing is a solitary pursuit, but it doesn't take place in a vacuum.

Rod Hunter of Bella Rosa Books has been my friend and publisher for a number of years. He made possible the trade paperback editions of the hardcover books once they'd gone out of print. After my husband's death, when I was vacillating over whether or not I had the heart for another book, he offered me the chance to work at my own pace in creating *St. John's Folly*. With *Jordan Point* as with all our other joint projects, he has been unfailingly supportive, pleasant to deal with, and always ready to offer sound advice. Our conversations are invariably punctuated with a lot of laughter. Thank you, Rod, for making the process so enjoyable.

I also want to acknowledge two remarkable women: Sonia Geiss and Marie Dotson of the South Carolina K9 E.R.T. They gave so generously of their time and expertise in introducing me to the world of emergency response teams and how they operate. I had no idea such dedicated individuals and animals existed right here in the Lowcountry. And a shout-out as well to Lucas and Murphy, who astounded me with their performances in the field. Extra dog treats all around.

Thanks to my sister Lynne, the insatiable reader, who always has something to contribute along the way, and to Sandy B, whose annual gatherings with her friends was the spark for my creating the group Bay encounters in *Jordan Point*. They welcomed me in without a thought and made me feel one of the gang. But be assured, ladies, that *no one* in the following pages bears the slightest resemblance to any of you. Honest!

Again, special thanks to Barry. My life is sweeter and richer because you're in it. You make me smile every day.

And finally, I want to acknowledge all the readers who have supported my efforts over the past fifteen years. You've taken Bay Tanner into your lives in a way I never expected, and I'll never be able to convey adequately how grateful I am.

Thank you.

ABOUT THE AUTHOR

Kathryn R. Wall wrote her first story at the age of six, then decided to take a few decades off. She grew up in a small town in northeastern Ohio and attended college both there and in Pennsylvania. For twenty-five years she practiced her profession as an accountant in both public and private practice. In 1994, she and her husband, Norman, settled on Hilton Head Island.

Wall has been a mentor in the local schools and has served on the boards of Literacy Volunteers of the Lowcountry, Mystery Writers of America, and Sisters in Crime. She is also a founding member of the Island Writers Network on Hilton Head.

Wall is the author of the Bay Tanner mysteries:
IN FOR A PENNY
AND NOT A PENNY MORE
PERDITION HOUSE
JUDAS ISLAND
RESURRECTION ROAD
BISHOP'S REACH
SANCTUARY HILL
THE MERCY OAK
COVENANT HALL
CANAAN'S GATE
JERICHO CAY
ST. JOHN'S FOLLY
LIKE A BAD PENNY (short story)
JORDAN POINT

All the novels are set on Hilton Head Island and in the surrounding South Carolina Lowcountry.

visit Kathryn online at: www.kathrynwall.com

CPSIA information can be obtained at www.ICGtesting.com
Printed in the USA
LVOW11s1520220816

501364LV00001B/275/P